**By William Rubin**

*Forbidden Beginnings:*
*Jacqueline's Tragedy*

*Forbidden Birth*

*Forbidden Cure*

*Michelle's Captivity*

A CHRIS RAVELLO MEDICAL THRILLER

# FORBIDDEN CURE

## OMNIBUS EDITION

# WILLIAM RUBIN

Crystal Vision
Publishing

*"All a man's affairs become diseased when he wishes to cure evils by evils."*
*- Sophocles*

# FORBIDDEN CURE 1

## DUPLICITY

# Prologue

I barrel down the street, a blur racing through the crowd. Arms and legs pumping as fast as they can.

Can't be late—too much at stake.

Heart pounding. Gasping for breath. But no time to rest. Gotta get there before they do the unthinkable.

Before they kill him.

Out of nowhere they slam into me, knocking me to the ground. My head smashes into the pavement. Disoriented, I stumble to my feet and ready myself to fight.

But they're already gone.

Head is throbbing and bloody. Legs wobbly, vision doubled. I press on, hoping I get there in time to save him.

# ▷ Chapter 1 ◁

Manhattan, June 2015

Dr. Jerome Gorelick leers at the young Jamaican woman. "Join me in my office, Ms. St. James. We have a pressing matter to discuss."

Kerline St. James smiles nervously, trying to mask the sensation of her skin crawling, as the anger flares inside her. *Always de same; men dinking dey can take 'vantage a me.* Gorelick started out pleasant, even fatherly when she joined the practice a few months earlier. But compliments on her hair and sense of fashion quickly morphed into crude, inappropriate remarks about her breasts and her ass. *What will it be dis time?* she wonders. How can she stop his advances and still keep her job?

She follows him down the long hallway, a tightness growing in her chest, dread building as each step brings her closer to his office. He waves her across the threshold and quickly closes the door behind her. Smiling, he extends a hand toward a chair opposite his desk. As he walks past the other side of the desk, the hand disappears from view. A chill runs down her spine as her eyes shoot toward the sound of the door locking. Her heart pounds as he makes his way across the tightly woven, gray carpet, to a small bar in the corner where he pours them both a drink. His back shields her view. Is he slipping something into one of the drinks? Anger and dread turn to fear and revulsion as he comes up to her and leans his fat ass against his desk. He extends one of the drinks to her. She takes it hesitantly, her mind racing, desperate to find a way out.

He offers a toast. "To one of the most sexually captivating women in the world." As he rests a hand on her thigh, several inches above the hem of her skirt, a perverse smile fills his pockmarked, bearded face. He squeezes her thigh now. "Your future is as bright as you're willing to make it, Ms. St. James."

Kerline stares back at the vile creature before her. She wants to scream, to pull away, but she's paralyzed.

Gorelick's hand creeps farther up her thigh, the hideous smile twisting into a scowl. "Drink up, Ms. St. James. Your future depends on these next few minutes." He downs half a glass of wine then places it on the desk. Leaning forward, his alcohol-infused breath upon her, he moves in for a kiss as his hand slides farther up her thigh. His lips are almost upon her. It's now or never.

She chooses now.

She throws her wine in his face and with a swift kick to the groin, disables him, pushing him onto the floor as she races around the desk. Her hands grope for the button he must have used to lock them in. Her heart races as she sees him slowly rise from the floor. *Where de 'ell is it?* He marches over to her.

"Playing hard to get, I see." He slaps her across the face with the back of his hand, then grabs her by the throat. "Guess you know I like it rough." In an instant he's on top of her as they sprawl out on the floor. His right hand tightens around her throat as his left paws at the buttons on her blouse, tearing them open. *Won't be long now.* He looks into her eyes, her fear arousing him even more. He smiles as her eyes begin to close. *Just a few more seconds to go...*

Kerline feels light-headed as his grip tightens around her throat. She feels him groping at her chest. *Stop 'im somehow... so weak.* It's no use. Her eyes begin to close as her hands flutter under his grasp. In a moment it will be inevitable. Then a voice screams out from the deep, reptilian part of her brain. *Nooo!!!* Her arm flashes through the air, her nails drawing blood from his face. The scream is his now. His right hand lets go of her throat and jumps to his face, pawing at the blood as it streams through his fingers.

Kerline presses her advantage.

She batters and slashes at his face until it is the embodiment of a bloody battlefield. Gorelick shrieks in pain as she throws him off, his head slamming into the edge of the desk. She lands a barrage of kicks to his midsection and groin, inflicting pain on him, not just for her but for all women who have fallen prey to his kind. With time she comes to her senses, the reptilian brain receding, the onslaught coming to an end. She stands tall and looks down on him with disdain as she spits out, "Ruin me? I don't dink so, man! I ruin you but good." She smooths her skirt, finds the button to unlock the door, and leaves him a whimpering, cowardly mass.

# ⟩ Chapter 2 ⟨

Martha's Vineyard, December 9, 2015

Six tiny flames pierce the darkness, illuminating Christine's joyful face. Dad and I sing in tone-deaf unison, trying to make this happy moment last. "...Happy birthday, dear Christine. Happy birthday to you."

My heart, ravaged by immeasurable turmoil and loss, aches with joy at the beauty unfolding before me. A vague pain creeps into my chest and spreads through my arms as I say a silent prayer that peace, an old friend all but absent in our lives, will find us again.

Little James, swept up in the excitement, giggles and bangs his hands on the sturdy, wooden table as his head bobs. My hand reflexively darts to my chest. The pain is crushing now, like a vise, but I try to shake it off. "Time to make your wish and blow out the candles, sweetie," I say.

Christine, brow filled with furrows, exhales with all her might. Five of the candles, overcome by the gust, die out. Light-headed, I brace myself against the table as the last candle wavers in steadfast defiance while Christine struggles to sustain her assault.

*So weak. Can't hold on much longer.*

Finally, mercifully, the candle relents, plunging us into the only state my soul knows of late, utter and complete darkness. I tumble down, the side of my head banging against the edge of the table. My flailing arms send two plates flying. They shatter onto the floor as Dad yells, "Chris!" and lunges after me as my head slams into the floor. My eyes roll back in my head as I struggle to breathe.

Slivers of moonlight stream through the dining room window, offering me a glimpse of the last thing I remember before blacking out: Christine's tear-filled, crimson face and her cries of "Daddy! Daddy!"

§

My eyes flutter open as images and sounds assault my senses. Bright white lights blare at me from overhead. Nurses scramble before me, administering oxygen and pushing meds into my IV.

"He's awake, Doctor!"

"Excellent. Push the metoprolol. Got to get that

heart rate under control. Have we got his doctor on the line yet?"

The monitors' alarms scream as I lay here, weak and drenched in sweat.

A nurse thrusts a cell phone into the hands of the doctor hovering above me. "Doctor Jacobs for you."

"We've got a patient of yours, Chris Ravello, in the ER at Martha's Vineyard Hospital. Blood pressure and heart rate through the roof. Not sure what's causing it... or how to get it under control. Afraid he's going to stroke out."

Jacobs' voice is strained, intense. "He's got pheochromocytoma. Must be in adrenergic crisis. You need to stabilize him ASAP, then transfer him to me. Here's exactly what you need to do to pull him through, Doctor...."

# ❯ Chapter 3 ❮

**D**octor Jacobs leans back in his chair. Managing my disease from the get go, since he diagnosed me about six years ago, he's never seen me in such bad shape.

"You gave us quite a scare yesterday, Chris. How are you feeling?"

"Like shit. Can't keep living like this. The attacks are out of control." I sigh and rub my neck as Jacobs nods.

"Tell me what's been going on."

"I had to resign from the police force a couple of weeks ago because of the pheo and retreat to the Vineyard with my tail between my legs, hoping that would settle things down."

"Clearly it didn't," he says quietly.

I look to my left at Dad, seated a few feet away, then back to Jacobs. Annoyance slips out. "That's the understatement of the year."

"Chris, that's no way to talk to—"

Jacobs puts a hand up. "Don't worry about it, Mr. Ravello. I understand, Chris. It's frustrating."

My eyes widen. *Yeah, no kidding.* I stare back at him. "I couldn't even make it through Christine's birthday without collapsing. Isn't there something, anything, we can do?"

Jacobs twists his head side to side. His voice is laced with frustration. "Most cases of pheochromocytoma are amenable to surgery. But as you know—"

"—mine isn't," I say with intensity.

Jacobs nods his head. "And all the tried and true medical treatments have been ineffective. Beta blockers during an attack. Meditation and other stress reduction techniques to prevent attacks." He hesitates. "The attacks are clearly getting worse, Chris. We were fortunate to pull you through this last one." He looks at me with concern. "But I'm afraid there's not much else we can do."

I rock back and forth on the examining table. "But, there is *something* we can try?"

Jacobs removes his glasses, rubs the bridge of his nose, and exhales forcefully. "There's one other approach... it's promising, but risky."

Dad perks up. I lean forward. "Life pretty much sucks as is, so what is it? How risky?"

Jacobs replaces his glasses and crosses his arms. "It's an immunologic-based treatment."

"A what?" Dad pipes in.

Jacobs continues, "It makes use of antigens, antibodies, it..." Dad's blank stare stops Jacobs mid-sentence. "In Chris' case the treatment would target the tumors in his adrenal glands so he no longer has these episodes of excess adrenaline production."

Dad nods his head. "Makes sense. So what's the catch?"

My eyes dart nervously from Dad to Jacobs. *Remember me, guys, the patient? Over here....*

"There's little margin for error. Over-treat your son and he'll suffer from adrenal insufficiency: constant fatigue, nausea, dizziness, fainting, and so forth. Under-treat him and we may incite the tumors to grow, worsening his condition."

"Short of death, I can't get much worse," I half-heartedly reply.

"There's a comforting thought," Dad grumbles as he casts me a disapproving look.

Jacobs shifts in his chair, crosses and uncrosses his legs.

"Let's bottom line it, Doctor. What's your experience with these treatments?" I interject.

Jacobs nods. "I've worked with a scientist, a Doctor Harold Hyslop, in treating about a dozen patients. He's a bit odd, unconventional, but absolutely brilliant." Excitement creeps into Jacobs' voice. "His research is eloquent and staggering in its breadth and depth." Jacobs pauses, takes a deep breath. "He personally designs and formulates each treatment based on the specific patient's disease and physiology. It's labor intensive, proprietary, and thus shrouded in secrecy." A look of admiration gives way to concern. "Given enough time and resources, Doctor Hyslop's treatments will revolutionize medical care for hundreds of millions of people. But I caution you, Chris, the treatments are still in their infancy. Unpredictable outcomes are the norm."

"How unpredictable?"

"Death and disability in some; miraculous cures in others."

Dad puts out his hands and turns to me with a scared look. "Whoa, now let's slow down here. Death and disability?" He shakes his head no. "Chris, there's got to be another way. We just lost your mother and Michelle. We can't take any chances...."

Steely-eyed I return Dad's gaze, shaking my head in frustration as I try to reign in my emotions. My voice cracks. "What else can I do?" I look back to Jacobs and take a deep breath. "This is it, right? No other options?"

Jacobs averts his gaze and runs a hand through his salt-and-pepper-colored hair before making eye contact again. His reply is little more than a whisper. "I'm afraid so."

A year and a half ago my life was filled with promise and prosperity. Anything was possible. Disgusted it has come to this, to relying on an unproven, possibly deadly treatment, I nod my head. Then listlessly, "It's a lot to take in, Doctor. Thank you for being so forthright." Dad and I lock eyes. Our sparring on this issue has just begun. "Looks like we've got a lot to talk about."

# ⊳ Chapter 4 ⊲

The dreary, starless night and cold, steady rain made following the doctor here unusually easy. The figure, dressed entirely in black, lurks in the shadows, alert, confident. He is less than twelve feet away now. Two empty hospital rooms lay just ahead, catty-corner to where the doctor is seated. Either would provide an ideal vantage point. He freezes as footsteps echo off the hallway walls behind him. His eyes dart to the right. A nurse approaches, moving directly toward him. "What do you want?" she says. His muscles tense as he readies to grab her. A few steps away she vanishes into a patient's room. "Let's see what all the fuss is about," she continues. The figure exhales, then scans the hallway and ducks into the first of the empty rooms. Crouching just inside the entrance, he gazes at the scene that brought him here.

Harold Hyslop, tall, erudite, sits across from his

brother Phil. Slumped in his hospital bed, Phil's skin has an ashen hue, testament to his heart's losing battle to perfuse him with oxygen.

"Rough day at the lab, Har?" Phil's voice is tinged with concern and guilt over how hard his brother has worked these last few years.

"Huh? No, everything is fine," Harold says with a shake of his head. "How are you feeling?"

Phil, ensconced amid a dizzying array of tubes and monitors, casts him a skeptical look as he clears his throat. "I'm hanging in there, brother. Any word on the transplant?"

Harold closes his eyes and takes a breath. "I'm afraid not, Phil."

Phil turns away from his brother and stares out the window. The dreary, black sky and rain mirrors his dark mood. "That's what I figured. Better not get my hopes up till they find me a heart, huh?"

Harold, unsure what to say, opts for silence.

"Look, I don't wanna seem like a cry baby. When I landed here eight months ago, I thought I was a goner." Phil rubs his bulbous nose, then re-adjusts the nasal cannula to improve its delivery of oxygen. "But, geez, how much longer do they expect me to hold on for?"

A deep-seated, familiar, and motivating anger wells up in Doctor Hyslop. "How long, indeed?" The doctor rises from his chair. "Two and a half years on the transplant list and there are still a dozen recipients ahead of you." He shakes his head and spits out, "Politicians and philanthropists get the organs they need just fine." Doctor Hyslop's fist strikes at the air. "While people like you are told they haven't found a good match just yet." Hyslop clenches his teeth as his face and throat flush. "The system is rigged for the wealthy, and the science, well, it's still in the dark ages as far as I'm concerned."

"Hey, Har, uhh, don't get yourself all worked up again." Phil motions to Harold to slow things down. "It, it's fine. I'm gonna hang in there till they find me a heart. You'll see," he says with hope.

Harold peers at his brother and squeezes his hand as his anger abates. "I know you will, Phil." Harold's eyes narrow. "And soon my breakthroughs will revolutionize transplant medicine, bringing an end to the abuses of the wealthy and the well-connected."

# ▸ Chapter 5 ◂

Dad skulks about my tiny kitchen, frustrated and impatient. "Chris, you heard what Doctor Jacobs said. The treatment could kill you!" He's right of course. But with two young mouths to feed and a body too broken down to sustain steady employment, I'm desperate for a cure—and fast—before the next attack kills me.

I feel for Dad. In the past sixteen months he's lost Ma and my wife, Michelle, and now his son faces a terrible choice regarding his own rapidly deteriorating health. I pull out a chair next to me as a peace offering, hoping to ratchet down the tension. "Why don't we talk this through?" Déjà vu washes over me. Michelle sat here many a night and spoke those same words to me. Now she is gone, gunned down in front of me during an FBI sting operation gone terribly wrong. And no amount of self-loathing, guilt, or regret on my part can bring her back.

Like fingernails on a blackboard, the screech of Dad's chair jars me from my thoughts. Arms folded in front of him, Dad settles in the chair as his lecture continues. "Son, with all this family's been through, you can't just sign up to be Doctor Hyslop's next guinea pig, no matter how promising the treatment. We need to take a step back, consider our options."

I raise a weary hand, then rest it on his shoulder. "Dad, you heard Jacobs. There really aren't other treatment options." I bow my head and take a moment, then steady my eyes on my father. "I thought quitting the police force and heading up to the Vineyard would clear my head, buy me some time to get better. We both know how that worked out," I say with a derisive laugh.

He nods with resignation.

"I need something to believe in, some kinda hope to cling to." A faint smile emerges from my frown. "I'm going to call Jacobs now, tell him I'm moving forward with the treatment."

Dad starts to protest but reconsiders as the realization sinks in: united and hopeful may not be enough, but it's all we have right now.

# ⊳ Chapter 6 ⊲

Eight small test tubes filled with green-tinged fluid sit before the experimenter. Each solution is sequentially numbered and varies from its predecessor in small but meaningful ways. The researcher finishes taking notes and returns mouse number four to its cage, where it scampers about with seven of its companions.

Three times more the investigator extracts a mouse, injects it with the solution via a long, thin needle, and returns it to the cage unharmed. Three times more the worker makes entries in the notebook, outlining in detail the latest failed attempt.

The investigator reaches into the cage for the final rodent, mouse number eight. It slithers away several times before the hand snares it, then holds it steady for the injection. Two minutes go by, the mouse unaffected by the solution. The worker's lips edge downward into a frown.

Then it happens.

The mouse's body twitches uncontrollably for a few moments. It races around in a tight circle four times as if it can outrun its fate.

But it can't.

Over the next minute, the mouse's pace slows to a crawl as the chemical ravages its system.

At two minutes and forty-three seconds post injection, the mouse stumbles forward a few final steps and falls down.

Dead.

The experimenter dutifully makes a final entry in the notebook as the frown transforms into a smile.

# ⟩ Chapter 7 ⟨

The early morning sun peers over the horizon, its rays stretching across the icy East River and the tangled, undulating mass of vegetation that overruns North Brother Island. On the west side of the isle sits a lone, ramshackle structure. In it, seated at a small workbench in the corner of his lab, Doctor Hyslop pores over the data on his most recent patients. He shakes his head in disgust as he scans the pages. The results are wildly inconsistent. Almost three-fourths of the patients he treated in the last eighteen months have made a full recovery. But it's the other fourth that worries him. Three patients did not survive the second dose, and many who did saw their diseases run wild within hours of that treatment. *The second dose is critical. Anyone in good health after that was cured by the third dose.* Eyes glued to his work, he doesn't even notice senior technician Todd Zigler's entrance until the young man's high-pitched voice pierces the air. "Another early start, Doctor Hyslop? Or were you up late again keeping Phil company?"

Hyslop looks up, his red eyes and baggy lids speaking for him. Zigler waves an accusatory, effeminate finger at him. "Oh gosh, you look *terrible*, Doc. You are not taking care of yourself at all." He shakes his head with disapproval, then folds his arms lightly across his small chest. "Can I get you some coffee or something?"

Hyslop stares back impassively, nods, and returns to his work as Todd glides past him toward the break room. Along the way the lab technician runs his finely manicured fingers across the work bench, past a dizzying array of expensive, state-of-the-art equipment. Blood chemistry analyzers, interferometers, and spectrometers fill the bulk of the counter top. A venting hood, centrifuges, test tubes, and other sensitive, delicate instruments take up the remaining space.

A few minutes later Todd re-emerges, presenting a fresh cup of coffee to his boss. Hyslop masks his disdain over the young man's French-manicured nails, sighs, and accepts the offering. Eccentricities aside, Todd has proven his most valuable asset, recruiting, assisting, and supervising a first-rate team of lab technicians despite the many drawbacks of their God-forsaken location.

"Made any breakthroughs this morning, boss, in our quest to outdo Grayson Limerock and company?"

Hyslop senses movement on the edge of his field of vision. He turns and spots his secretary, Kiki Aloni, moving furtively through the lab toward the coffee room. His voice booms, "A bit early for you, Kiki?"

She straightens up, her long black hair spilling off her shoulders. "Uh, yes, Doctor," she replies self-consciously. "I caught a ride with Todd this morning."

Hyslop nods, taking a sip of his coffee, then spits it on the floor in front of him. "What is this swill, Todd? Kiki!" She jumps to attention. "Make yourself useful." He shakes his cup. "Fetch me a fresh cup right away, and then be gone." Condescending, with a snicker he continues, "Todd and I have pressing matters to discuss that are well above your pay grade."

Kiki nods her assent and scurries off to the coffee room.

Todd tries to get his point across in a playful manner, to avoid Hyslop's wrath himself. "Hey boss. Maybe ease up on the Draconian approach, huh? The ladies can be kind of sensitive with that, you know?"

Hyslop, amused, looks Todd over, paying close attention to the young man's nails. "Never thought of you as an expert when it comes to the ladies."

Kiki dashes over, hands Hyslop his coffee, then hurries away. Hyslop yells after her, "Come back in about two hours. I'll need you to deliver the treatment we've been working on to Doctor Gorelick."

Kiki offers a quick nod, then disappears from the lab.

Hyslop holds up the cup. "Seems I have things well under control. Now, where were we?" Scratching his head, "Ah, yes. No breakthroughs this morning, Todd." Hyslop rubs the bridge of his nose. "I can't detect any patterns for the treatment failures. Can you pass me the calibration and quality assessment logs? Perhaps they'll shed some light on our failings."

Todd pats his chest. "I check on those daily and everything is always up to snuff." Zigler arches his eyebrows and shakes his head. "I know you don't want to hear it again, boss, but the prob is obvious in my opinion...."

"Yes, Todd, I know," Hyslop replies wearily, "'too many station chefs for you to keep track of'."

"Exactly. Even the teensiest, tiniest error by any one of them and our formulations can be ruined."

Hyslop stares at the ceiling and nods his head, his patience all but spent. "That's why I personally trained each technician to be an expert in all areas of formulation and trained you to catch any rare errors along the way."

A disapproving look fills Zigler's face. "That was fine when I only had two techs to oversee. But seven, well, that's really asking for trouble now, don't you think?" Zigler's eyes implore Hyslop. "We all want to plow ahead as fast as we can, but sometimes a breather's not a bad thing."

Hyslop's death-stare says what no words ever could.

Zigler replies with a huff, "Okay, okay, I get it, boss. Keep our worker bees humming along and keep my opinions to myself."

Hyslop's stare morphs into a thin smile.

Todd stares back, intimidated and self-conscious. "Okay then... off to work." He takes two hesitant steps away before coming to a stop and turning back. "Did you see the phone message I left on your desk last night from Doctor Jacobs?"

Hyslop's brow arches. "No. What's it about?"

"Apparently Detective Chris Ravello is in dire need of our services."

"The same Ravello who just arrested that serial killer Durand?"

"One and the same. Ravello's got a pheochromocytoma he badly needs our help with."

He tries to contain it, but a smile spreads across Hyslop's face. Turning away, in a soft voice he mutters, "Excellent. Just the case I need to test out two new theories."

> **Chapter 8** <

Kiki winces in pain as she flexes and massages her right hand. *This is getting harder and harder to keep under wraps.* Leaning forward in bed, she shakes her hair off her shoulders and rummages through her purse, anxious to find the pills before Grayson emerges from the bathroom. She pushes her car keys, lipstick, and a small pack of tissues aside, taking care not to disturb the vial of medication Hyslop entrusted her to deliver to Doctor Gorelick. Finally, she finds them.

Introduced in the 1940s as an anti-malarial medication, the pills are Kiki's last line of defense against the crippling effects of her rheumatoid arthritis. But the treatment has been failing her of late, the side effects growing more frequent and severe. Intense bouts of nausea, diarrhea, and blisters on the inside of her mouth leave her feeling weak, isolated, and vulnerable, a poor combination for a middle-aged widow of limited financial means.

Enter Grayson Limerock, the Chief Medical Officer/CEO of Immunogenetics Offerings. A tall, well-built, and charming Irishman, he and Kiki met at an industry conference six months earlier and mid-day liaisons away from her boss and his wife's prying eyes have been the norm since. Kiki smiles inwardly. Soon one of the two, Hyslop or Grayson, will find out how to make her whole again. Until then, her relationship with Grayson must remain a delicate dance of stealth and ingenuity.

The shower stops. Kiki hears the curtain open and Grayson's feet hit the bathroom floor as she struggles to free the pills from their container. Stabbing pain shoots through her fingers as she pushes and twists the bottle top. *Damn it, why do they make these so hard?* The cap finally begins to give. *Come on, come on,* she implores it. Suddenly, it flies open all at once, scattering pills onto the sheets and floor. Kiki grabs for the glass on the nightstand, knocking it over. Rivulets of water form, one stream threatening to douse the hotel room phone and clock. She grabs at the bed sheets, using them as a towel. Grayson hums as he dries himself off. She hurriedly gathers the pills in her hands and dumps them and the open bottle in her purse. Kiki jabs her mouth at a lone pill stuck to her wet hand. She swallows it just as the bathroom door handle turns and Grayson appears, towel wrapped around his waist.

"All yours, baby. What time is that asshole boss of yours expecting you back?" he says with a warm smile.

"He's buried in the lab the rest of the day so I can get back when I please." She sighs as she saunters over to him. "With any luck I won't see the jerk again until morning." She rubs a hand against Grayson's hairy chest as she nibbles on his ear. "What do you have in the afternoon?"

Grayson's smile hardens. "A couple of meetings about our newest biologics." He takes her hand in his and brings it to his lips. "Two rheumatologics that promise to challenge Harold's best creations."

Kiki smiles at him, then brushes her lips against his cheek as she glides away. "Brilliant *and* sexy." She winks at him and bats her lashes as she walks toward the bathroom door. "Leaves a girl weak in the knees," she adds, blowing him a mischievous kiss. "Powerless to resist."

Grayson smiles back as he watches the door close and hears the hiss of the shower. Reaching into her purse, he grabs hold of the vial and removes it. As he turns it over and over in his hands, his smile broadens. *I'm counting on it, baby.*

# ⊳ Chapter 9 ⊲

"You have placed yourself in a very difficult situation, Doctor. My associates want to kill you, to set an example to others who are slow to pay." Dmitri Korsakov leans back in the chair and takes a puff of his Montecristo cigar. Rings of smoke emanate from his mouth, dissipating as they rise toward the ceiling.

Jerome Gorelick sits behind his desk, a white-knuckled grip on his chair. A small stream of sweat runs down the left side of his stout, bearded face.

"Dmitri, we have been doing business for many years. You know I am good for the money."

Korsakov shakes his head, his heavily accented voice a mixture of disappointment and disgust. "You have lost control, Jerome, and seventy-eight thousand dollars is a great deal of money." Gorelick winces as Korsakov grinds the tip of his cigar into the oak desk, leaving a burn mark in its wake. "I have no choice but to let my associates have their way." He rises and turns to go.

Gorelick springs from his chair and stretches a hand out. "Wait! There must be something I can do to clear my debt?"

A sinister smile spreads across Dmitri's face as he wags his forefinger. "There is one thing. But I am not sure you have the stomach for it."

"What is it?" the doctor asks with trepidation.

Korsakov's smile broadens as he waves Gorelick back to his seat and sits down himself. "There are those in my organization who grow concerned about Irina. Estranged from me, her husband dead, her career in ruins, they fear she has little to lose and may betray us. My associates seek a permanent solution to this problem."

The blood drains from Gorelick's face. "Your own sister, Dmitri?" Gorelick wrings his hands as he whispers, "What would you have me do?"

"Kill her."

The rheumatologist winces, then averts his eyes and traces the edge of the desk with his fingers. A long moment passes before his eyes find Dmitri's again. "And who better than you, Doctor? Nobody would suspect."

Gorelick slumps in his chair.

"My sister is desperate. She will undertake whatever

treatment you prescribe, and that is how you will kill her." Korsakov waves his hand through the air. "Do this and your debt is forgiven."

Staring at the floor, Gorelick hangs his head as Korsakov trudges to the door. He turns to the physician and shouts, "Look at me! Forty-eight hours to save yourself, Doctor—not one minute more." The door slams behind him. Gorelick flinches, the color draining from his face as he grapples with the ultimate lose-lose scenario; violate his sacred pledge to "do no harm" or face the mobster's deadly wrath?

Dmitri nods to the receptionist on his way out, stepping aside so a beautiful, Asian woman can enter before he exits the office.

The receptionist smiles warmly. "Oh, hello, Kiki. We've been expecting you. Here, come this way."

# ▷ Chapter 10 ◁

Irina Malekoviec can hardly believe her good fortune as her fingers fly along the Steinway baby grand piano, bringing "Rhapsody in Blue" to life. True, the Gershwin composition is far easier to play than the Rachmaninoff Piano Concertos that propelled her to fame as a concert pianist. But, it's progress. A long-time sufferer of a particularly aggressive form of rheumatoid arthritis, Irina's career as a concert pianist is a dim memory. Four years ago she stood at the pinnacle of her career, but extensive joint damage to all her fingers and failed treatment after failed treatment have left her earning a meager living as a piano teacher. That is, until this latest treatment. The second dose of the injection was administered just a few hours ago after much counseling by her doctor on the risks of the procedure and its unpredictable results. Nothing much happened after the first dose, or in the first hour after the latest treatment. But as the day progressed, Irina's miracle began to unfold.

Gone was the interminable pain in her fingers that dogged her waking hours. Indeed, her fingers look less swollen and are more mobile than they have been in years. Irina glances at the antique clock on her coffee table. A gift from her great-grandmother from the old country, it still keeps excellent time after all these years. Ten minutes until her next appointment. It's just enough time to enjoy the rest of 'Rhapsody.'

For the next nine minutes, Irina's spirit soars as she glides along the piano, speeding up, slowing down, infusing the piece with her long pent-up emotion as she drives the music toward its climactic finish.

Then it happens.

The moment her killer longed for arrives.

Hemorrhages erupt on her arms and legs. The pain in her fingers and hands roars back. By the time Irina clutches her temples with the worst headache of her life, numbness has spread throughout her left side. She glances at the antique clock and the salvation that lies next to it. If she can only slide across the piano bench, reach her phone, there's still hope.

But it is not to be. Irina's head comes crashing down on the piano keys, playing the last and most dissonant notes of her life.

⟩ **Chapter 11** ⟨

NYPD Detective Kevin Kennedy carefully surveys the scene. Reminiscent of an early twentieth century music parlor, the Brighton Beach apartment shows no signs of forced entry nor damage to any of the vic's possessions. Antique gas lamps, a couch, and a clock fill one side of the room, untouched. Built in shelves of classic Russian literature line the adjacent wall. An old phonograph and a few Tchaikovsky records sit undisturbed atop a dark, wooden table in front of the bookshelves.

Nothing calls out for him to be here. Nothing except the body that lies slumped on the Persian carpet in front of the piano. Ravaged in a way that leaves him speechless, dumbfounded, Irina Malekoviec's face is frozen in a perpetual state of shock and anguish. Large blotchy areas of hemorrhaging cover her arms, neck, and face, yet not a drop of blood is anywhere to be seen.

Kennedy kneels down for a closer look. The whites of her eyes are clear and despite all the hemorrhages, her windpipe intact. That rules out strangulation. His eyes run down Irina's body, cloaked in a classic burgundy dress few women wear today. No signs of an entrance or exit wound either. *What the hell could cause so much damage without her spilling a drop?* he wonders. Only a couple of weeks removed from losing his partner, Chris Ravello, Kennedy feels the loss acutely. This is the detective's first new case since his partner's resignation, and he intends to work it alone, no matter how bizarre the circumstances. The hemorrhages are what pulled the Division of Medical Crimes, DMC for short, onto this case. But ten plus years on the job do little to enlighten Detective Kennedy as to their cause.

Kennedy sighs. *Chris would know what to make of this, but that ship has sailed. He has his own problems to deal with right now.*

"First case you're Acting Chief, right?" a junior Crime Scene Unit officer asks with a nod. "What do you make of it?"

Kennedy continues his survey of the body, then lifts the vic's dress. The same damn blotchy bruising runs up and down both her legs. The burly detective looks around the living room, intent on finding the murder weapon.

"Not sure, Joe. How are you guys making out?"

"Just about done." He holds up a plastic bag with Irina's appointment book. "Just finished dusting this. Wanna look?"

Kennedy nods toward the CSU officer as he begins examining Irina's mangled fingers. Without so much as a glance toward the officer, Kennedy extends his hand in frustration. "What the hell, seems like as good a place to start as any."

<h1 style="text-align:center">▷ Chapter 12 ◁</h1>

Kev and I sit at a corner table at Peekskill Brewery. During spring and summer this place is teeming with patrons anxious for their fill. But with the start of winter just around the corner, the crowd is sparse, making it a good place for us to grab a quick meal and catch up. In between bites of a burger, I pick at my sweet potato fries while Kennedy makes short work of his spicy buffalo chicken wings.

"So, Chief, how's everything going at the DMC since my sudden and illustrious departure?" I say with a wry smile as I down a local brew.

Mouth stuffed with chicken meat, Kennedy spits the words out. "It's a fuckin' mess, Chris."

"How so?" I ask, surprised.

"For starters, Kelly never even mentioned you leaving the force." Kennedy finishes chewing and clears his throat. He raises a mammoth hand to his face and pours down the remnants of his beer. "Just waltzed in, anointed me Acting Chief, and took off. All the guys were looking at each other like 'What the fuck?'"

I let out an involuntary laugh and shake my head. "Wish I could say I'm surprised, but we both know communication skills were never the commissioner's strong suit."

"Damn straight on that," Kev grumbles. "Least he could have given me a heads up, so I didn't look like a clueless moron."

"Which, of course, you were at that point...." I say with a broad smile and a shrug of my shoulders.

Kev gives me a stone-cold, killer stare—then roars with laughter as he smacks my shoulder. "Why the hell should that day have been different than any other?"

"Why indeed?" I reply as I rub my shoulder and wonder if I'll ever regain feeling in that arm.

Kev and I spend the next few minutes busting on each other. Epithets such as McMoron and Guinea Bastard fly back and forth, giving testament to just how mature and racially sensitive two grown men bonding over beers can be. Eventually, we corral our sideshow and get back on topic.

"Seriously, though, Chris," Kennedy says with concern. "I'm in way over my head as chief." Weariness, then playful optimism washes over Kev. "We sure as hell could use a chief with some medical know-how. It is the Division of Medical Crimes for Christ's sake. Know anyone?"

An amused smile fills my face. "There is this one guy. Smart as a whip. But... not terribly reliable," I laugh. "First, he bailed on a cush job as an NYC trauma surgeon, then he washed out of the detective biz after solving exactly one case." I hold up my index finger. "One case! Pretty hopeless fuck-up, if you ask me."

"Hmmm, sounds like our kinda guy. He'd fit right in with the DMC."

I lean back and nod my head a few times, trying not to reflect on all that has gone wrong the last few weeks. "So... working any interesting cases these days?" I regret the words immediately.

Kev nods back as awkwardness fills the space between us. We're no longer partners, no longer professional confidantes. Discussing an active investigation with me defies all police protocol.

We were never much on protocol.

"As a matter of fact, just caught a strange one earlier today...."

Kev fills me in on the details of the middle-aged, Russian piano teacher's death. I nod as my mind churns through the details of the case. I would love to offer my friend guidance, but short of examining the body, it would be pointless speculation. "Sounds like you've got your hands full, but McGowan ought to point you in the right direction."

Kev nods his head. "As long as she waters it down," he replies with a sarcastic smile, "and doesn't go all doctorly on me." Kev's voice fills with caution and concern. "Say, what's going on with your situation?"

I shake my head. "Still a mess. Had a full-blown attack on Christine's birthday that scared the shit out of all of us, so back to Jacobs."

"What'd he say? Can he help?"

I sip my beer and stare out the window. An old, green Cadillac pulls into the parking lot across the street. A rueful smile fills my face as a middle-aged, African-American couple and their kids spill out, hurrying into Home Style bakery for some decadence. I take a quick, involuntary breath, letting it out slowly as I turn back to Kennedy.

"Guess I'll find out tomorrow; he's got an experimental treatment lined up for me."

Kennedy's face scrunches up like a Shar-Pei. "What? Wait... tomorrow? You're kidding, right?"

I wince, realizing I hurt him by not sharing sooner. "Uh, yeah. But it's no big deal, just—"

"Experimental is never 'no big deal,' bud." Kev takes on a pensive pose. "You should've told me soon—aw forget it. What time's the treatment? I wanna be there."

I start to object but Kennedy's dark, brooding eyes bore through me. Different eyes, same disapproving look. Michelle's look. I shake my head. Seeing her everywhere is both agonizing and comforting.

I smile back at my dear friend as I rise from my chair and throw thirty bucks on the table. "Ten a.m.

at Washington General in the minor procedure area. Jacob's office can fill you in on the details." Kennedy rises. We look at each other, then shake hands and exchange an awkward hug.

As I head out to the car, thoughts of Michelle and the kids swirl around in my head. Fate has been beyond cruel to all of us. Cold air gusts off the Hudson, stinging my face as I climb into the Firebird. Sitting in the car, I stare into the dark, gloomy night and face the sobering truth Kennedy and I left unspoken—tomorrow will either put my life back on track or finish me off for good.

> **Chapter 13** ‹

"Dat's real fine 'is first treatment was so good, Shanny dear. But dat don't give 'im a job or a college education for God's sake..." Kerline shakes her head in frustration as she stirs the solution in the flask before her. "Yes, I know 'e's trying *real* hard, lassie, but trying, it don't pay the bills. You got your whole life stretched 'head of you, don't be drowing it away on the likes of 'im." Todd casts a sympathetic look Kerline's way. She catches his eye, repeatedly firing a pretend gun at her pretty Jamaican head. "Look, sweetie, momma got to get back to work now. We talk it out over dinner. Just you and me, no Jamal. You 'ear me?"

Todd glides over to provide moral support as Kerline slides the phone into her purse. "Sounds like you've got your hands full, Kerline."

Exasperated, she shakes her head and wipes tears from the corners of her eyes. "Like watching a slow motion replay of de worse damn dings I ever done, 'cept Shanteel is playing me part."

Todd puts his hands on the sides of her shoulders and rests his head against hers. "It could always be worse. Hang in there, sister, it'll get better."

Kerline grunts dismissively, "Oh yay? You gonna get rid of dat boy for Kerline... 'fore me daughter finds out de 'ard way what being nineteen, wid child, and all alone is about?"

Todd scrunches his nose and stares straight ahead. *Guess they don't bother much with platitudes in Jamaica.* "Wait, I'm confused. Jamal? Same Jamal who's one dose into Doctor Hyslop's treatment protocol?"

Kerline dabs her eyes again. "Yes, and dat dere's on me. I wanted Shanteel to feel me love and support for dat stupid boy a 'ers." Kerline roars with laughter. "A girl 'er age; ain't no better reason to dump a boy dan 'er momma approving of 'im." Her face turns deadly serious. "Shanny don't need to know 'er momma'd love to kill dat boyfriend of 'ers with me own 'ands. You know what dat boy done?"

Now perplexed. "Uh, no, what?"

"'e been stepping out on poor Shanny." Kerline shakes her head. "Even got 'nother girl pregnant, den talked 'er into getting rid a de baby."

"Oh gosh, that's terrible. So if Shanny knows this why wouldn't she break it off with him?"

Kerline's voice booms. "'e got dat silly Shanteel

convinced, man, de diabetes was de only ding messing 'im up, 'olding 'is scrawny ass back." She scoffs, "Wasn't no diabetes dat made 'is momma a crackhead, 'is daddy a bum." Her voice grows louder. "No sir! Wasn't no diabetes told 'im to step out on me girl or dat digging ditches is better dan going to college." Her anger spills over, the last few words spit out with disgust and disdain. "Now 'e done got 'er believin' in 'im, and in us being one big, 'appy family."

"I see." Todd gives Kerline a big hug then pulls back and smiles at her. "You and I sure have been through it, huh girl?" He shakes his head as he reminisces, "I thought the worse was behind us when we brought you over from that pig Gorelick's practice." He rubs her upper arms encouragingly. "But I guess there's a little more to get through."

Kerline laughs. "Sorry to go all Island-crazy on you, man. You a doll for listenin' to me ranting, but don't you go worrying 'bout Kerline. Dat Jamal, 'e just a boy, and dat Gorelick, well 'e gonna get what coming to 'im real soon. Me sure of it." Kerline makes a shooting motion with her hands. "POW, POW!" A grim look of satisfaction fills her face as she blows imaginary smoke from the tip of her make-believe gun. "Den Shanny and me, we finally 'ave some peace again."

# ▸ Chapter 14 ◂

Coming home usually conjures up warm and fuzzy memories. Bygone days of innocence and ease. Reconnecting with loved ones in a familiar, comforting setting.

Not so for today's homecoming.

Clothed in a standard-issue hospital gown that leaves me vulnerable and exposed, I am lying out on a stretcher, staring at drab gray walls that insidiously suck away my life force. Decades-old fluorescent lights buzz ominously overhead like vultures circling carrion. I lie here in the belly of the beast, the institution that reared me, the place I watched my mother rally from a coma last fall only to succumb to her own miracle cure minutes later. Would Washington General be any kinder to me today? Was my treatment a panacea or would it be death by lethal injection?

"...So you sign right here, Chris, then we can get

started. Chris? Did you hear what I said?" Jacobs stands before me, trying to mask his annoyance, pen poised for me to sign my life away.

"Huh?" I look to Dad and Kennedy, huddled together like misbehaving school boys banished to the corner. Back to Jacobs. "Uh, sure. Sign right here?"

"Yes." Jacobs looks on as I sign and Dad serves as a witness. "I'll be back in a minute with the nurse. Sit tight." I nod. As if there's anything else to do.

Kennedy looks around the room at the monitors and instruments, at the IV emanating from my arm. His eyes and mine meet and before he looks away, I see a glimpse of the rarest of Kennedy's emotions—fear. Next to me are two small Mayo stands, the kind used in the operating room to hold instruments. The first Mayo is empty except for a solitary ten milliliter syringe holding a green-tinged solution and an alcohol pad. The second holds a half dozen other syringes, all dutifully labeled and organized, and filled with powerful medications to alter blood pressure and heart rate and treat seizures. I take a deep breath and exhale slowly, doing my best to quell a sense of foreboding.

"Looks like you're in good hands, Chris," Kennedy says with feigned conviction as I finally turn away from the syringes. "I'm sure you'll do great."

Dad's eyes dart from Kennedy to me. "What'd Jacobs say to expect?"

I swallow. "Could be a rough ride. Won't know

till he injects me." We nod our heads in communal resignation. Kennedy fidgets his fingers as Dad rubs the back of his neck. I sit up and stare at the door, wishing this was already over.

Jacobs and his nurse march into the room, startling us. "All right, let's get started." Jacobs tears open the alcohol pad and wipes down the area of my IV he will use to deliver the solution. His nurse stands by the other Mayo stand as Jacobs uncaps the syringe and taps it, driving out the air bubbles. I eye him warily as Jacobs glances at me before settling in on his nurse. "First treatments are unpredictable; let's be ready for anything." *Gee, thanks for the last minute pep talk. Ever thought about becoming a motivational speaker?*

Jacobs pierces the tubing with his needle, injecting the medicine bit by bit. One milliliter. Two. I brace for the worse, squeezing the metal railings. He stares at the monitors above me, his face impassive, even cold. Three milliliters, then four. Nothing. Absolutely no eff—SHIT!

The monitor's alarm screams. My heart pounds against my chest as if trying to burst free.

"His blood pressure is 200/120, Doctor."

"I can see that, Nurse. Labetalol, please. No one's stroking out on my watch."

Dad's face fills with horror as the color drains from Kennedy's.

"What the fu—?...can't breathe... chest killing me..."

46

Jacobs pulls the first syringe out of my IV and empties the second into it in one push.

Feeling light-headed, dizzy. Vision is fuzzy... fading. Searing pain in my right eye and face. Oh God! "Aaarrggh!"

My entire body is on fire, sweat pouring out of me as I hear Jacobs bark orders and push meds. It's no use... this is not going to end well.

Then it happens.

The pain eases. My sight returns.

"BP is 160/95 and dropping. Pulse is 120 and regular. O2 saturation is—"

"I can read the damn monitors myself, Nurse!" Jacobs' eyes bore through them as he brings me back from the edge. "That's it. Steady, steady. Shit! BP's bottoming out now... O2 levels are dropping. Quick, give me the Epi."

*Oh God, gonna be sick.* I try to hold it in, but to no avail, as the contents of my stomach splatter on Jacobs and me.

Twenty harrowing minutes later, empty syringes littering the trays, my gown soaked and reeking, Jacobs has finally done it. He's pulled me through.

Jacobs rubs his hands against his shirt and tie and straightens his soiled lab coat. "You had us worried, Chris." He calls Dad and Kennedy over and addresses the three of us. "Gentlemen, it may seem like the worst is over, but the next twenty-four hours are critical if we're to cure Chris." He clears his throat and gathers himself. "We'll be running Chris through a battery of tests to measure his response to the treatment, and Doctor Hyslop and I will confer so he can refine his formulation prior to Chris' next dose."

"No disrespect, Doc, but shouldn't we maybe hold off on a second dose?" Kennedy glances at me. "Seems like Chris had an awfully hard time pulling through. Maybe we shouldn't push our luck right now?"

Dad nods in agreement.

"I understand your concern, Detective, and the decision is of course entirely Chris' to make. But you must realize this: we're at a crossroads where there's no turning back. Due to its immunologic nature, the timing of treatments is critical."

Dad and Kennedy stare blankly back at Jacobs, prompting me to intervene.

"You wouldn't get a flu shot in the middle of the summer— its effect would be lost before flu season kicked in. It's the same idea here."

Dad chimes in, "Makes sense," as Kennedy nods in agreement.

"I would take your analogy a step further, Chris. This treatment imprints itself on the recipient's immune system in ways we don't even fully understand, so the spacing of treatments is absolutely critical for their success. Mistime a treatment by even a day or two, and we will likely lose the opportunity to cure you."

"You mean, like, forever?" Kennedy asks.

"Yes, forever."

My eyes dart from Kev's to Dad's. I am weary, spent, but resolved.

Dad starts to object but I wave him off. The time for heated discussion is over. This disease will neither control nor define me. The cure is my last and only hope for a normal life, a life in which I love, support, and enjoy Christine and James the way I am meant to. I'll accept whatever risks I need to take to be whole again. Bowing my head, I close my eyes for a moment, then turn to Jacobs. "Understood, Doctor. Let's press on."

# ⊳ Chapter 15 ⊲

Detective Kennedy leans his massive frame back in the ten-year-old, pockmarked, wooden swivel chair. Badly beaten up, with two wheels in need of repair, the relic serves to remind him how much damage the NYPD inflicts on those who serve it. Kennedy studies the sparsely populated suspect board in front of him, blocking out the cacophony of noise and motion on this typical afternoon at Manhattan's 17th precinct. Drug dealers, prostitutes, and other unsavory suspects litter the halls and fill the bulk of the interrogation rooms. Detectives bark orders at each other and their underlings as they weave threads of evidence and leads into cohesive stories.

As acting chief, Kennedy could have a room of his own, a place to collect his thoughts and run the DMC away from the chaotic fray. But Ravello never took on such airs, opting instead to work at a desk abutting his own. That desk sits vacant now next to his and will for as long as he can make it so. No one can fill Chris' shoes, so why bother trying?

Kennedy stares at the suspect board. Little is known about Irina Malekoviec beyond the basics. Fifty-three years old, Russian, a former concert pianist, her career was torn apart by an insufferable case of rheumatoid arthritis. She spent her days these last four years in relative isolation in her one-bedroom apartment in Brighton Beach, in an area affectionately known as Little Odessa due to its preponderance of Russian immigrants. Piano lessons dotted her calendar, providing just enough money and companionship to keep her moving forward. Calls to her students pegged her as competent, demanding, and aloof. The students knew little of her personal life and social circle and suspected she was a loner. Kennedy's earlier call to Malekoviec's rheumatologist, Doctor Jerome Gorelick, has yet to be returned. A visit to Gorelick's office will likely be needed to spur the investigation along.

"Hey Chief, you've got a call," Simmons yells from two desks over.

Kennedy replies with a knowing nod, "Doctor Gorelick?"

"'Fraid not. It's a guy claiming to be Durand."

"What! How the hell's a guy holed up at Rikers get access to a phone?... And why in God's name would I want to talk to that loon?" Kennedy shakes his head in disgust and turns his attention back to the board. "Tell him I'm busy."

Simmons shrugs as he relays the message.

His face turns ashen as he covers the receiver.

"You're gonna want to take this, Boss…. Durand says Michelle Ravello is alive and well—but not for long." Kennedy freezes in his chair, then turns slowly back toward Simmons. All eyes are glued on the detective as the room turns silent and still. Kennedy stares blankly at Simmons as his eyelids open and close several times.

Rising to his feet, he shifts his weight back and forth. He grumbles a few inaudible expletives, then quietly, "All right, transfer it to my line."

The phone rings three times, four, five as Kennedy stares at it, circling his hand around the receiver. He lifts it to his ear in silence. "Good afternoon, Detective Kennedy. I trust your recent promotion is proving satisfactory?" Insincerity and sarcasm hang in the air. "Such a shame dear Doctor-Detective Ravello could not continue on in the position. Some men just handle stress worse than others." A throaty laugh fills the line. Kennedy's anger spills over.

"What the fuck do you want, Durand?" Kennedy says through gritted teeth.

"What indeed, Detective?" Durand's voice fills with false indignation. "Such hostility… you should be thanking me as I am the only one who can help you catch your killer and recover your partner's wife."

"Been hitting the catnip too hard, Durand? We buried Michelle weeks ago, so what the hell are you talking about?"

Durand sighs with disappointment. "So many questions, such little understanding. Why do I even try?" Then pointedly, "Your Malekoviec case, of course—it holds the secret to finding Michelle."

A chill runs through Kennedy. *How the hell...?* He spits out a flustered reply, "What about it, Durand? One of your deranged buddies have a thing for piano teachers?"

"Such a simpleton, Detective... ah, but like the 'little engine that could,' do keep trying." Then condescending, as if speaking to a small child, "Someday you may outgrow your diapers and play with the big boys. But today is not that day, Detective."

Kennedy strangles the phone with white knuckles as he struggles to contain himself. "We've got important work to get back to, Durand. So if you've got something to say, just spill it."

"To Ravello."

"What?"

"I have no time for underlings, Detective, no matter how fancy their titles." Then icy cold, "Only Ravello. Bring him *to me* if you want answers."

"Hello? Hello? Shit!" The sound of the receiver slamming into its cradle reverberates. Men jump back to looking busy while Kennedy stares at the phone, wondering what to do next.

# ◊ Chapter 16 ◊

"Todd Zigler?" Limerock extends a hand. "Grayson Limerock, Immunogenetics Offerings." Grayson looks at the box of donuts hoisted upon Todd's arm and laughs. "Bit of a sweet-tooth, eh, Todd?"

Limbs filled with donuts and a tray of coffees, Todd tries to shake hands, but settles for a nod instead. "Oh, they're for the office." He eyes Grayson warily. "Say, have we met before?"

Grayson flashes a smile. "No. I enjoyed the paper you and Harold Hyslop presented last year at the Miami Conference of Immunology and Biochemistry." He looks at Todd's full hands. "Can I help?"

"Sure, Mr. Limerock. That'd be great."

Grayson takes the coffees as the two walk out of the donut store at the corner of 10th Street and Avenue A, just north of Tompkins Square Park. Despite the early hour, two artists in black overcoats and gray fingerless gloves paint the park's landscape while an unsavory man lurks off to the side, in search of his next fix. Grayson and Todd head west on 10th, a stiff, swirling wind lashing at them.

"Heading toward Union Square? I'll walk with you."

"Sure." Todd eyes Grayson with interest. "No offense, Mr. Limerock—"

"Grayson."

"Uh, sure, Grayson, but didn't think this was your kind of neighborhood. Pictured you more of an Upper East Side guy."

Grayson laughs. "Well, you've got me there, Todd. Big brownstone on 82nd between Park and Madison." He turns more serious. "Chalk it up to a bit of slumming in the name of recruiting top talent."

"Okay?"

As Grayson and Todd come to a stop at the corner, the 'Don't Walk' light flashing across the intersection, Limerock rests his hand on Todd's forearm.

"Todd, I've long admired your work at Doctor Hyslop's lab. But quite frankly, your talents have outgrown him, and I'm prepared to offer you a substantial raise to come work for me."

"Oh, wow. I'm really flattered, Mr. Lime—, Grayson, but I can't leave right now. We're sort of in the middle of some big things at the lab."

"Not to mention the fallout from the woman's death who you were treating."

Todd yanks his head back. "How'd you know? I thought it was hush-hush."

Grayson flashes a confident smile and a wink. "You don't become the CEO/CMO of a billion-dollar company, Todd, without knowing everything going on in the industry."

The 'Walk' signal beckons as the crowd pushes around them.

Grayson grabs Todd's arm, holding him in place. "I'm impressed by your loyalty, Todd, but realize it comes at a price. The stench of a death tied to your lab can have a profoundly negative effect on your career. And once the police are involved, well, there's no telling where things may lead."

Grayson stares intently at Todd, then hands him the tray of coffees. "Be careful, Todd, and keep all your options open. You can never be sure which path you'll suddenly need to pursue."

# FORBIDDEN CURE 2

## REVELATIONS

# ⊳ Chapter 1 ⊲

Last night's talk with Durand behind him, Kennedy bounds up the stairs toward Chris' hospital room, still undecided on how much to share with his friend. At the third floor landing, Kennedy exits the stairwell and plows straight ahead. His pulse quickens as a familiar tightness diffuses through his chest. Reared by a drunken, abusive father, visits to the hospital were a staple for Kennedy, his kid sister, and their mother. Ten years visiting these institutions as a homicide detective has done little to quell his discomfort.

Badge hanging from a lanyard around his neck, Kennedy nods at an orderly as he marches toward the nurses' station. A second nod acknowledges the floor clerk, a large African-American woman of ill-tempered disposition, and two nurses preoccupied with their last minute, early morning charting. A few steps later,

Kennedy raps his knuckles on the private room Chris has called home since yesterday afternoon.

"Hope I'm not interrupting anything. Looks like a real party around here," Kennedy says with a smirk.

Ravello, bored by inactivity, brightens at the sight of his friend. "Oh yeah, just sent the dancing girls home after a night of revelry," he replies with a laugh and a smile. "It's really been la vida loco around here." Ravello reaches for the clicker and silences the TV's incessant drone. "How's everything going at the 1-7?"

Kennedy pulls a chair over to Chris' bedside and flops onto it. He hoped to ease into this, to get his bearings before diving in, but what the hell, why wait?

"Funny you should ask. Our buddy Durand rang last night before I left."

Ravello's face hardens; his eyes narrow. "What the hell did he want?"

"You're not going to believe this shit...."

"Try me."

"He knew about the murder case I just picked up, said he could help find the killer."

Ravello's face morphs to frustrated astonishment as his hands clench the bedsheets. "How's that even possible? The murder happened two days ago. Think he's involved?"

"That's my guess, but of course, he denies it."

Ravello stares out the window at the early morning sun rising over the East River, his frustration mounting. "If he's not involved, why play snitch? What's in it for him?"

Kennedy shrugs his shoulders. "He didn't exactly say." He shifts in the cramped seat. *Shit, I'd rather be anywhere but here right now.* "Apparently, he's done sharing with me for now."

"So, what, that's it, he's just dropping it?" Ravello says with confusion. "Why even bother calling in the first place?"

Kennedy averts his gaze, staring at the ceiling for a moment, before coming back to Ravello. "Nah, he just wants to, uh, talk to somebody else now."

"Yeah? Wh—mother fucker! Me?" Ravello shakes his head violently in disbelief. "No way, I'm out! I've got no reason to talk with that psycho bastard again."

"Actually, buddy, you might."

§

"You sure about this, Chris?" Kennedy yells to me as I throw my balled-up gown at the shocked ward clerk and fly down the hall. Kennedy lumbers beside me now. "What about staying for testing? What about your cure?"

"That's just gonna have to wait," I say impatiently as we reach the stairwell.

"Didn't Jacobs say it can't wait? You're either all in or all out, no turning back?"

I throw the door open, slamming it against the cinder block wall as I charge ahead and race down the stairs.

Kennedy's words bounce off the dull, white walls as he trails behind. "Guess I'll call from the car, tell 'em to get Durand ready for us."

# › Chapter 2 ‹

I implore Kennedy, "Come on Kev, faster, push it!"

Kennedy turns to me, a quizzical look on his face, as we glide through light, early-morning traffic on the Grand Central Parkway heading east. "Uh, buddy, we're not in a car chase, ya know. And you heard what they said, it's gonna be like twenty minutes before they bring Durand out."

I stare out the window of Kennedy's ancient Honda as we make the turn onto the Francis Buono Memorial Bridge, the only point of access to the island which houses ten of NYC's fifteen prisons. "Sorry. Durand's just got my goat again—as usual. I'll try to bring it down a notch or two," I say with frustration.

"Or ten," Kennedy says with a smirk as I let out an involuntary laugh, and he in turn grows more serious. "I wanna pummel Durand just as much as you, but we've got to play it cool in there to get what we need from him, agreed?"

I nod in assent as Kennedy reaches the gate. A guard checks us in and gives us directions to the Otis Bantum Correctional Center where Durand is held. A chill runs through me as the gate lumbers open before us and Kennedy inches the car forward. Rikers has a well-earned reputation as the world's largest penal colony and a human cesspool where violence, abuse, and squalor run rampant. A fitting place for the depraved, serial-killing bastard we are about to see.

A few turns later, Kennedy and I slow down and park his car. We march along dreary corridor after dreary corridor, through a series of highly secured check points, to a small room where Durand is being held for us. I take a deep breath and nod at the guards stationed on each side of the door as we enter the room. My anger swells as I lay eyes on the tall, lithe man seated before us, a man who terrorized this city, and my family, with a series of horrific murders earlier this year until Kennedy and I took him down a few weeks ago.

I scowl at the shackled sadist as Kennedy and I sit down across from him. "You seem no worse for the wear, Durand—what a shame."

A thin smile emerges as he replies, "A pity I can't say the same for you, dear doctor-detective." Then quickly with a laugh, "Or should I just call you Christopher since your illness precludes you from carrying on in your chosen professions?"

Kennedy growls at him, "Watch your fuckin' mouth, Durand."

So much for restraint.

"Call me what you will, Durand, but at least I'm a free man."

He sneers back at me. "Ill health, unable to work, you and your family's lives torn asunder with tragedy. Is that what you call freedom, Christopher?" My face flush with anger, he continues with a dismissive wave of his hand. "Ah, but let's dispense with the juvenile banter and get to the real reason for your visit." He looks at Kennedy and me in rapid succession. "Solving your crime and reuniting you with your dear, sweet Michelle."

"Why should we believe a damn word you say, Durand?" Kennedy snaps. "For all we know you're involved with the Malekoviec murder, and as for Michelle, where's the proof she's alive?"

Durand ignores Kennedy as he addresses me. "I have a score to settle with those who took out the Russian. As for your dear wife, Christopher, you know in your heart of hearts the woman you spoke to in my lab was not your wife." Pouty faced, a hand raised to his face as if dabbing tears, his voice is laced with condescension. "But you ignored those feelings, boo hoo, fearing that would mean she was already dead."

I lunge across the table and grab his throat, knocking him back in his chair, the chains running from his shackles to the floor the only thing keeping us upright. "You fucking bastard."

Kennedy dives in. "Chris!" as the door flies open and two guards join the fray. One helps Kennedy pry my fingers from Durand's throat. The other slams me forcefully back in my chair and screams at me as Durand gasps for air.

"You fucking crazy? We're done here."

Kennedy: "Shit, shit! Please officer, just a minute more." He holds his hands up. "Won't happen again, promise."

"Damn right it won't." Then begrudgingly, "He shouldn't even be in here, Detective, he's just a civilian now."

"I know, I know. Just cut us some slack; we're almost done here."

The guard looks at Durand then back at Kennedy. "Anybody else but this piece of shit and you'd be out of here, but this fucking baby-killer has it coming." The guard plants his back against the wall and rests a hand on his gun. His counterpart does the same. "One minute."

Durand's breathing becomes more regular. His eyes, filled a moment ago with fear, regain their luster. "She was a striking replica, indeed, but not your Michelle. Your Michelle lives under my men's lock and key. But a power struggle has ensued and threatens to create an untenable situation. We must act quickly to save your beloved, Christopher." Durand eyes Kennedy and me. "Forty-eight hours on the outside with both of you will be time enough to help you apprehend your killer and reunite you with Michelle."

Kennedy: "Get you released under protective custody? Are you fuckin' nuts?" He shakes his head side to side as Durand looks back at us impassively. "Even if we believed you, no way the higher ups go for it."

I stare at Durand, trying to read him. He'd screwed us plenty before, including stealing a body out of Michelle's coffin. Was that hers? Another clone? No way to know for sure without playing along, seeing where it leads us.

My voice is raw, unsteady. "Where's the proof she's alive? And what's in it for you?"

He smiles. "All of my clones possess a unique genetic marker, my signature, if you will. It will prove the buried woman is not your Michelle." Durand's eyes dart between the two of us. "Eliminating the death sentence."

"Excuse me?" I say.

"That's the price for my cooperation—take it or leave it."

The guard nearest to me nods to his partner as he wraps a hand around his gun. "Time's up." They detach Durand's shackles from the floor and lead him away as Kennedy and I look on, dumbfounded. As he exits the room, Durand turns his head back toward me. "There's an even more tangible sign you missed, dear Christopher. It too will confirm my story." Durand laughs as they push him through the door, his final words echoing in the hallway. "Time is short. Don't delay."

# ▷ Chapter 3 ◁

"You believe anything he said?"

Kennedy shakes his head as we press on toward Manhattan. "Honestly? I don't know what the hell to make of it. Michelle alive after all the shit that's gone down, after we thought twice that he killed her? That just blows my mind."

"And what he knew about the Malekoviec case. Where the hell'd that come from? Is he involved, or is it like he said, he's just got an ax to grind with a competitor he's keeping tabs on?"

Kennedy bobs his head slowly. "Could be something else altogether?"

"What're you thinking?"

"We always figured Durand had a snitch in NYPD but couldn't pin it on anyone."

"So that's where all the Malekoviec info is coming from. The bit about Michelle, it's just a con, the icing on the cake. We spring him and bingo he torments me up close and personal again, maybe even escapes in the process." I bury my head in my hand. "Aw, Christ. I can't survive another round of this shit."

We sit in silence, me stewing, Kennedy unsure what to say. A mile ticks by. We cross the Robert F. Kennedy Bridge, make short work of Randall's Island.

Then Kev pipes up, "You want me to drop you back at the hospital? I gotta get over to the 1-7, start digging deeper on Malekoviec. I could circle back tonight when I know more?"

I stare out the window, head spinning, insides a mess. "Yeah, might as well. I got nothing better to do. Hell, with any luck Jacobs won't even know I've been gone."

# ◊ Chapter 4 ◊

"**T**his isn't the Waldorf Astoria. You can't just come and go as you please, Chris!" Never seen Jacobs this mad, but it's that kinda day. Hell, what's one more fire to put out?

"I'm so sorry, Doctor. Kennedy needed my help on something urgently. It was early…, I didn't think anyone would miss me."

Jacobs whips his glasses off. "What the hell kind of excuse is that? 'I didn't think I'd be missed.' Really? That why you threw your gown at the ward clerk; you were going for the clandestine approach?" Jacobs grinds his teeth. "You missed two hours of monitoring and blood draws crucial in reformulating your treatment." He shakes his head. "Best case scenario, the risk of death or disability with your second treatment has now gone up sixty percent—and that's a best-case scenario."

"I, I had no idea."

"Of course you didn't. You were too busy going off half-cocked to consider the risks." Jacobs shakes his glasses toward the window a foot away. "When you took off earlier, why did you bother with the stairs? You could have just repelled down the side of the building instead. That would have been less risky than the situation you're in now, and at least nobody here would have seen you leaving."

I smile awkwardly, then peer out the window at the street below. "Three floors is kinda a steep drop for a guy in my condition. Didn't want to take any chances."

Jacobs looks like he wants to strangle me. "So help me God, Chris. You pull anything else, I'll throw you out that window myself." He takes a calming breath. "Now get back into bed and behave before I have security escort you out for good."

I give him the thumbs up and hop onto the bed, still wearing my street clothes. "Sounds like a plan. Say, anyone see that gown of mine?"

# ▷ Chapter 5 ◁

Kennedy applies the last of the pins to his suspect board, leans back, and reviews his work. *Finally, some progress.*

A head shot of Irina's estranged brother, Dmitri, who lives only eight blocks away from the deceased, yet has scarcely seen her in over a year. Dmitri, a successful entrepreneur, had come late to the dry-cleaning business, but the last four years has seen his fleet of stores grow from one to six. All in Coney Island, all in neighborhoods run by the Russian mob. No crime in that, no cause for familial discord—unless his laundering services extended beyond textiles. Unless his sister knew things she shouldn't have. Like the fact that Dmitri served as one of the mob's main bookies for high-net-worth clients in Brooklyn, Queens, and Manhattan.

Vladimir was Irina's husband of twenty-two years until an early and unseemly demise sixteen months prior, purportedly at the hands of the Russian mob. Poor Vlad was found holed up in a dumpster on 47th Street near 6th Avenue, his face an ashen shade of blue. Seems Vladimir's sticky fingers and big mouth rubbed other diamond district merchants the wrong way. It didn't take a magnifying glass or loupes to determine cause of death or the message being sent. A small bag of diamond's tucked in Vlad's mouth where his tongue should have been, took care of that. Either relationship could have made her resentful of the mob, putting Irina in harm's way. But her bizarre manner of death, what was that all about?

Kennedy grabs his notebook off his desk and flips through it. Irina's rheumatologist, Doctor Gorelick, heads a large university-based practice flush with cash. Located on Manhattan's Upper East Side, the practice specializes in hard-to-treat patients using investigative therapies from a multitude of clinical trials. Irina came under Gorelick's care just over a year ago, shortly after her husband's death, after growing dissatisfied with a series of traditional treatments by a rheumatologist in her neighborhood.

Despite high hopes, Malekoviec washed out of two of Gorelick's more promising trials within six months. Insistent on entering a third, five months later she was accepted into a treatment protocol designed by Doctor

Harold Hyslop and administered by Gorelick. Office notes showed the first of the treatments took place six days before her death and produced no appreciable improvement in Irina's condition and no side effects. Little is known about the effects of the last dose since no response was observed in the office and Irina died later that day. Kennedy rests his hand on the notepad. *My money's on that medication.* He picks up the notepad, tapping it repeatedly against the desk as he shakes his head in frustration. *Hyslop, Hyslop. Where the hell have I heard that name before?* Kennedy mumbles to himself, "Gotta pay him a visit. Maybe figure it out then."

"Looks like it's really coming along, Chief," Simmons says as he takes a drag of his Marlboro and blows the smoke out of the corner of his mouth.

"Didn't you get the memo, like ten years ago, Simmons? No fumar in el precincto," Kennedy says with a laugh.

Simmons eyes the cancer stick appreciatively. "The job'll kill me way sooner than this will."

"Specially if the commish gets wind of this."

Simmons licks his thumb and forefinger, extinguishing the cigarette between them. Kennedy looks on with amusement. "What?" Simmons says. "One of the benefits of playing classical guitar all these years. See—nothing but callouses."

"Matches your personality. So what's up?"

"Just thought you could use some help on this, that's all. Kinda tough working it alone."

Kennedy's first impulse is "no." He has men on it and is more than capable of running the case himself, and Simmons is a strange guy with a knack for rubbing others the wrong way. He looks the detective third grade over. Tall, reed thin, crumbled old dress shirt, and yellow tinged fingertips. *This guy's pathetic. I'll throw him a bone and see where it takes us. Anything to keep him off the nicotine.*

Kennedy scans his desk, sorts through the clutter. "All right, here's the list of Malekoviec's students from the last five years and her piano instruction books. You know classical music, see what you can make of it."

Simmons smiles, his yellow enamel on full display. "Thanks Chief."

"Yeah, yeah. Now grab your coat. We've got some suspects we need to interview."

# ▷ Chapter 6 ◁

The thirty-second boat ride from East 149th Street in the Bronx complete, Kennedy and Simmons tie up to North Brother Island's tiny, new wooden dock. They stroll past four other rowboats, all equipped with outboard motors. Ahead of them lies a short stretch of beach, two hundred feet beyond that a patchwork building surrounded by overgrown trees, poison ivy, kudzu vines, and swaths of porcelain berry. Old lampposts and fire hydrants dot the landscape.

"Jesus, what is Hyslop thinking having a lab out here?" Kennedy says with disgust as a flock of black ravens surge out of a tree just ahead and fly menacingly close.

Simmons' eyes scan the area, blinking rapidly, as if they are cameras snapping rapid-fire photos. "Looks like a scene from one of the *Planet of the Apes* movies," he says with a mixture of fear and awe. He climbs over an old fire hydrant and dodges the remnants of a curb. "Wasn't this place a hospital at one point?" he asks.

"Yeah. Pretty sure they kept 'Typhoid Mary' and a bunch of TB patients here back in the thirties." Kennedy shakes his head as he looks at the structure ahead, a mishmash of the original reddish-brown brick held together by large swaths of new wood construction, most of which wasn't painted or even stained. "Sure hope the city council gave Hyslop a good deal on this place. Doesn't even look like it's up to code yet."

A sign above the doorway, its font an impressive calligraphy that belies the surroundings, reads 'Institute of Immunologic Breakthroughs.' Kennedy raps his knuckles on the front door and jabs at the doorbell. Silence. Simmons shrugs his shoulders. "Not exactly a hotbed of activity, huh, Chief?" Kennedy turns the doorknob and pushes, but the door refuses to budge. Leaning his shoulder into it, he tries again, this time falling forward a few feet as the door jerks open. He catches himself just before his face hits the worn, hardwood floor and straightens up to his full height as Simmons trails behind and closes the door.

The startled woman seated in front of Kennedy looks on curiously. "May I help you? We weren't expecting any visitors today."

Kennedy displays his shield for the receptionist, an exotic-looking, middle-aged woman with jet black hair pulled into a taut pony tail. He glances at the nameplate before her. "I'm Detective Kennedy from homicide, Ms. Aloni. This is Detective Simmons. We'd like a word with your boss."

Aloni regains her composure as she looks up at Kennedy, her eyes locking on his. Then friendly, with a hint of a flirt, "Let me check his schedule." Her fingers fly along the computer's keyboard. "Hmm, Doctor Hyslop is in the middle of a reformulation at the moment. He can't be disturbed now but should finish up in another hour or so. Is there something I can help you with in the meantime?"

Kennedy absently taps his badge on the desk. No choice but to wait. "Irina Malekoviec was a patient of Doctor Hyslop's who died hours after her last treatment. I'd like to speak to anyone involved in creating the compound used to treat her."

"Yes, of course. I'll see what I can do." Aloni flexes her fingers several times, then waves the detectives toward a stack of wooden folding chairs propped against the far wall. As she rises from her desk, she adds, "Please pardon our informality and make yourselves comfortable. Would you like anything to drink while you wait?"

Simmons interjects, a nervous laugh and yellow-stained teeth on full display. "Got any Red Bull?" He winks. "Rough one last night."

Kennedy rolls his eyes. Aloni, puzzled, smiles. She turns left at the rotunda behind her desk and a few steps later reaches a door to the lab. She raps on the door, waiting a few seconds before going in.

Kennedy drifts over to the rotunda and grumbles, "Red Bull. Really, Simmons? Next time you have something brilliant to say, don't."

Simmons joins Kennedy in the rotunda, sunshine streaming in from their right through floor-to-ceiling glass panes that afford an excellent view of the island. Simmons jerks his head away from the glass, toward where Aloni disappeared. "Notice anything unusual about her, Chief?"

Kennedy stares at Simmons, his annoyance unmistakable. "What'd I just say, Simmons?"

"Flexed her hands a few times after working the keyboard. Might have arthritis, like Malekoviec."

"Yeah, so? Lot of people have arthritis."

"Could make her a suspect." The words come faster now. "Like maybe she's desperate for a quick cure herself before it's too late." Simmons nods his head with excitement. "She coulda, I dunno know, had someone in the lab play around with the medicine they gave to Malekoviec, hoping to speed up a cure for herself."

Kennedy's face sours. *What the hell am I gonna do with this crackpot? No wonder nobody wants him as a partner.* With his best stab at diplomacy, Kennedy says, "It's a bit doubtful, Simmons, but I'll interview her, check into it. Any other breakthrough observations?"

"Naw, that's all I'm saying."

Kennedy laughs as he unbuttons his coat and admires the view of herons nesting about twenty feet away, high up in the trees. Then with more sarcasm than he intends, "Any chance I can get that pledge in writing, hotshot?"

Simmons laughs nervously and resumes the head bobbing as Aloni re-emerges, hands poised in front of her chest. She notices Kennedy examining a small defect in the window. "What's this?" he asks.

"Oh, that. Our senior lab technician, Todd Zigler, likes to shoot for fun sometimes. I guess that one got away from him." She smiles. "Would you like to speak with Mr. Zigler now? He should be able to answer any questions you have until Doctor Hyslop frees up."

"Sure, that would be great." Kennedy stands up, eyes her hands. "All that typing must be rough."

Aloni's face reddens as she averts her eyes and rubs one hand over the other. "Yes, and the RA doesn't help."

"RA?"

"Sorry. Rheumatoid arthritis. It was in remission for a long time, but about six months ago it came roaring back."

Kennedy looks over to Simmons, his eyes speaking for him—*keep quiet, I've got this.*

"Sorry to hear that. Any cure for it?" Kennedy asks expectantly.

Her face brightens. "Not yet, but Doctor Hyslop will

change that soon. He's absolutely brilliant." A moment passes. Then awkwardly, "I have a lot of reports to catch up on. Mind if I lead the way to Mr. Zigler now?"

"That'd be great. Thanks for your time." Kennedy catches Simmons' eye and jerks his head. "Let's go."

# ▷ Chapter 7 ◁

Harold Hyslop leans back from the maze of test tubes, pipettes, and reagents before him, stretching his back and working the kinks out of his neck. "I just don't understand it, Todd. I've tested and retested the compound we gave Jacobs to use on Ravello, and I'm still at a loss for why he had an adverse reaction to it."

Zigler shakes his head in frustration as he peers at the empty injector he's holding. "I don't know either, boss. In earlier treatments the silicon coating on the syringe's rubber stopper leached into our compounds over time, but there's no sign of that here."

"Whatever the cause, we must eliminate it with the reformulation or risk an even deadlier reaction next time."

A light tapping on the glass door to the lab draws their attention. Hyslop, annoyed at the intrusion, hesitates, then waves his receptionist in. "I'm so sorry to interrupt, Doctor Hyslop, but there are two NYPD detectives out front. They'd like to speak with you about the compound we made for Irina Malekoviec."

Hyslop stabs at a ream of papers on the workbench, shaking them at her. "I'm in the middle of the Ravello reformulation. I mustn't be disturbed right now."

Aloni pulls back, stammering. "Uh, sure, sorry to interrupt."

Zigler, wide-eyed, looks at Hyslop, shakes his head. *Guy doesn't have a clue how to treat people, especially women.* "I'll speak with them in my office." He silently returns the syringe to its holder and rises from his chair.

Hyslop bows his head in embarrassment as he smooths out the papers on the bench. "I'm so sorry, Kiki. Ms. Malekoviec's death has me terribly upset... and in poor control of my emotions, I'm afraid." He nods to her. "Please accept my apology and assure the detectives I will be with them shortly."

Kiki is startled by the mea culpa. "Yes, Doctor, I'll pass on the message."

Hyslop turns back to his work, shaking his head and mumbling as Aloni and Zigler file out. "So little time... need to set things *right*."

# ❯ Chapter 8 ❮

"So, Mr. Zigler, what can you tell us about your work in the lab?"

Zigler wrings his hands. He bobs forward and back in his chair as he makes tentative eye contact with the detective. "Well, um, I'm Doctor Hyslop's senior lab tech." His eyes dart from Kennedy, seated to his right, to his odd-looking partner, Simmons, straight ahead and just to his left.

Kennedy leans forward. "And?"

Zigler squeals, his voice more schoolgirl than a twenty-five-year-old man. "Oh, like what do I do exactly?" Zigler blushes. "Well, I was brought in just over a year ago," eyes darting between the detectives, "to straighten out some issues the FDA had with our lab."

"What kind of issues?" Kennedy asks.

Eyes darting again. "Uh, look, I don't want to make

any trouble for Doctor Hyslop. He cleaned everything up, so we're good now."

Kennedy stares right through Zigler. "I'll be the judge of that."

"Okay, okay." Hands wringing again. "A few patients died. The cops came in, found they were all accidental, no charges or anything. But the FDA didn't like how Doctor Hyslop was doing some things, so they forced him to make some changes."

"What kind of changes?"

"Bless his heart, Hyslop was doing it all: intaking patients, doing formulation, supervising a few techs, doing quality control, etc., etc., and so on. They had him hire me, take some of that off his plate." Speaking as if an FDA employee now, he continues, "Make sure intake, formulation, quality testing, and dispensing medications are all separated from each other. Improve record-keeping and reporting of adverse effects." Zigler lets out a nervous laugh. "Everything's all peachy now. Doctor Hyslop's got his areas and I've got mine."

"I'm going to need the names of the deceased, all their treatment records, FDA stuff, the whole works."

"Sure, Detective, no problem."

"Getting back to your duties..."

"Sure." Zigler swallows. "I've recruited all the techs we've added in the last year. I supervise them, making sure they're handling their portion of the formulation process correctly." He fans himself, his white-tipped nails beating rapidly back and forth. "Whew. A little warm for December, huh?"

The detectives stare back in silence.

Simmons interjects. "How many other techs? They all work on the same compound at the same time?"

"Actually, there're seven others and me. They split into three groups of two, Group A working on the compound first, then Group B, and so forth."

Kennedy stares at Simmons before re-engaging Zigler. "I see, so it's an assembly-line of sorts."

"Exactly. A little unusual for a lab, but that's the way, Har—uh, Doctor Hyslop, likes it."

Simmons wipes his nose with the back of his hand and rubs it on the fabric of his chair. Kennedy eyes him with disgust. "So, you've got three groups of two. That's only six. What about the other tech?"

"They perform the quality control testing with me."

"Okay, which tech helps you out?"

"It varies; they rotate every week so everyone is expert with each role. The less experienced techs, I look over their shoulders a lot. The more experienced ones, well, I pretty much leave them be, just check over things at the end."

Kennedy nods. "When we're done, I'd like to see the schedule of who worked where on the Malekoviec compound and a complete list of the patients you've treated."

Zigler nods back, smiling, his fear easing. "Sure, no problema."

"So'd everything check out when you tested the Malekoviec medicine?"

Zigler bites his lip and squirms in his chair. "Uh-huh. The mixture was well within specs."

Kennedy's eyes narrow. "You don't sound too convincing."

Zigler wipes sweat off his brow with his hand. "This next part may not make a lot of sense."

Skeptically now, Kennedy says, "Try me."

"Being within specs doesn't tell the whole story."

Kennedy's eyebrows arch. "Yeah, how so?"

"The treatments Doctor Hyslop designs are so complicated, with each matched to a particular patient's physiologic and immunologic characteristics." Zigler's eyes dart between Kennedy and Simmons. "Yes, we confirm there are no glaring irregularities in our compounds, but..."

Simmons cuts in, "You guys really don't know." He nods his head excitedly. "The testing, it's basically a crapshoot, stab in the dark, right?"

Todd nods his head repentantly, the words tumbling out. "The last few months we've been moving *soo* fast. Signing up as many patients as we can. Working hard to get FDA approvals before our biggest competitor, Grayson Limerock and his Immunogenetics Offerings, beats us to it. Trying to figure out techniques to help Doctor Hyslop's brother Phil." He shakes his head in frustration. "We're working so hard on development, our testing can't keep up."

Kennedy leans back in his chair, his pensive look morphing into frustration. "That's just great," he moans as he ticks the points off on his fingers. "We have to figure out if we're dealing with a homicide, an accidental bad reaction to a medication, or something else entirely." Kennedy shakes his head, spitting the words out. "Now you, the quality control guru, are telling me you can't even properly test the medications you're manufacturing?"

Zigler squirms again, then says with resignation, "In a nutshell, yes."

Simmons: "So, you guys paying off the FDA or what?"

Kennedy glares at Simmons, clenches and un-clenches his right hand.

Zigler interjects, his laugh high-pitched and grating. "No, detectives, nothing like that. We have an exemption, similar to a Class II 501(k), from the FDA. It cuts out a lot of the red tape, cost, and reporting requirements, so we can get the drugs to market faster."

"Yeah, well good luck with that exemption if your patients keep dropping dead," Simmons says with a snort.

"Tell me about it," Zigler says dejectedly. "I'm the guy who has to report bad complications to the FDA. Never a fun job."

Kennedy's eyes tear through Simmons flesh as he growls, "Why don't you stick to taking notes, and I'll do the talking?"

Simmons pulls back, then shrugs. "Sure, whatever you say, Chief."

"Tell me more about your competitor. Limerock, right?"

"He runs a billion-dollar company based in Manhattan and is our fiercest competition."

Kennedy looks around. "No offense, but this isn't exactly a high rent district. How are you guys in the same league as Limerock?"

"Mr. Limerock may be better financed, but we've got a slew of patents he'd love to get his hands on," Todd says with pride.

Simmons jumps in. "Want 'em badly enough to kill for?"

Zigler shrugs his shoulders. "Uh, I don't know, maybe?"

Kennedy scribbles in his notepad. "So, what's this about Hyslop's brother?"

"Phil. He's got a failing heart, been on the transplant list for like years, but he's slipping away." Todd shakes his head with grief. "Doctor Hyslop's being trying to develop a compound that tricks the body into accepting organ transplants from anyone so he can get Phil the heart he needs in time."

"What, you mean like no more matching donors and recipients?"

"Exactly. It would revolutionize the field and save Phil. But it, well, I'm not sure we'll figure it all out in time."

Simmons cuts in. "You think Hyslop would cut corners with the testing to try and speed up a cure?"

Todd's eyes dart to the left. "Well, I know he puts a lot of pressure on himself to save Phil.... But no he wouldn't consciously do anything that could put another patient at risk."

Kennedy nods his head. "No, of course, not consciously.... But, who would know if he did? No way to test the compounds for sure, right?"

Todd shrugs, then says weakly, "I guess."

Kennedy turns to Zigler. "Once you test the compounds, how soon till they're shipped out?"

"Well, that's up to Doctor Hyslop. Sometimes he tests things further; other times the compound goes right out to the treating physician."

"And on the Malekoviec case?"

Zigler contorts his face. "I'll have to confirm, but I'm pretty sure it went straight out."

"All your techs here today?"

"All except Kerline St. James—she took a personal day. Been under a lot of stress."

"What kind of stress? Too much pressure from Hyslop?" Kennedy asks.

"No, well... uh, sort of half personal, half work related. Her daughter's dating a guy we're treating." He waves his hand. "It's all messed up."

"Is that even allowed, dating a patient that's being studied?" Kennedy asks pointedly.

"Huh, what? No, it's not like that. Shanny, she was dating Jamal way before that." Now stammering, he says, "Wasn't till after Jamal got someone else pregnant that Kerline got him in the study."

Kennedy and Simmons look at each other, puzzled.

Todd's face flushes. "S-sorry, I'm rambling."

"No problem. Take your time, Todd. Now why would Kerline get her daughter's cheating boyfriend in one of your studies? I would think she'd want to kill the guy, not help him."

"Well, she did." Trying to inject some humor, he makes his hand into a gun. "POW, POW!"

Kennedy and Simmons are not amused.

"Aw, geez, hold on a minute." Zigler exhales forcefully. "Look, this is none of my business. I don't know why I even brought it up, except it's why she's not here today."

"So, she's not here today because she's out killing Jamal?" Kennedy asks.

Todd wrings his hands. "No! No, that's not it. She's got something else completely different going on today."

Kennedy leans forward.

"Kerline's real bright, probably understands what's going on in the lab as well as anyone, and I was lucky to steal her away from that toxic office she was working at."

Kennedy scratches his head as he tries to follow. "Which office was that?"

"A Doctor Gorelick. Brilliant guy, but what a handful! Owes some Russian bookie a mint. Pompous. Nasty to staff. Well, Kerline's got a sexual harassment claim against him. I think there's a deposition or something today that she had to be at."

"Same Gorelick who used your medication to treat Malekoviec?" Kennedy asks as he scribbles in his notepad.

"Yeah, why? Is that important?"

"Not sure. We're just trying to get the facts straight. Okay, so we'll have to double back for her another time. But you've been very helpful, Todd. Can you start sending the other techs in one-by-one? We'll finish up with Doctor Hyslop."

Simmons looks up from his notes, realizes time is running short. "How bad is Ms. Aloni's arthritis? Has she—"

Kennedy waves Simmons off. "We'll be back in touch if we have more questions." Kennedy flips his notepad closed and gives Simmons another ocular beat-down while he offers a card to Todd. "If you think of anything else."

Zigler looks at the detectives warily. "Uh, you're kinda in my office."

Kennedy, polite and deferential as he rises. "Right. Any place else we can use?"

"Sure, there's a conference room down the hall, third door on your right." He nods quickly. "I'll tell Doctor Hyslop to meet you there when he's done."

"That'd be great." Kennedy hesitates. "Just one other thing. What're you doing with a gun out here?"

Zigler turns beat red. "Oh, my .38? You're probably gonna think I'm weird or something...."

Kennedy shakes his head no.

"We work real long hours out here, all by ourselves. Sometimes I just set up some old cans to shoot at to give myself a break from everything."

"That how the glass by the rotunda got nicked up?" Kennedy asks.

Zigler is mortified. "Guilty as charged. That one ricocheted on me."

Kennedy nods. "Thanks for your time," he says, then pushes Simmons ahead and marches down the hall, lacing into him just as the conference room door closes. "What the hell was that back there, the fuckin' ADHD version of Interrogation For Dumbasses?" Kennedy flares his teeth, trying to contain himself as a dumbfounded Simmons looks on. The Chief waves his hand dismissively. "I'll take it from here." He takes a slow, calming breath, staring at the detective, wondering how he's lasted this long on the force. "Why don't you go up front and keep to yourself, Simmons, okay? No need to ruffle anyone else's feathers."

§

"So, Doc, Malekoviec was quite the mess when

we found her. Any idea what went wrong with your medicine?"

Hyslop bows his head and shakes it slowly. "I wish I knew what killed her, Detective. I've pored over the data; there was nothing wrong with the medication."

Kennedy, seated across the conference room table, nods in acknowledgment. "You sure, Doc? From what I've heard, your meds are quite the mystery themselves."

Hyslop's neck snaps back. "I'm not sure what you mean. Who told you that?"

Kennedy folds his massive arms over his chest. "How can you be sure your medication didn't kill her?"

"Manipulating the human immune system may seem like magic, my medicines like the indecipherable potions of a wizard," Hyslop waves his pointer finger, "but I can assure you, everything we do in this lab is grounded in scientific fact and has passed muster with the FDA." Hyslop leans back, his hands forming a triangle. "Ms. Malekoviec's death has shaken many of us quite deeply, Detective. If my medication was in any way responsible for her death, I would be the first to admit it."

"Malekoviec had rheumatoid arthritis, right?" Kennedy asks.

Hyslop nods. "Correct."

"Pretty tough disease, huh? How hard is it to treat compared to other problems?"

Hyslop chuckles. "Curing patients with endocrine

and auto-immune disorders is straightforward for me, and helps unlock the secrets that will lead to my greatest accomplishment, eradicating the need for transplant patients to be matched with donors." Hyslop arches his eyebrows and waves a hand as if panning over a landscape. "In just a few years, my discoveries will transform medicine. Waiting lists for transplants, and matching donors and recipients will seem like barbaric medical practices from The Middle Ages, like bloodletting with leeches."

Kennedy looks at him oddly. *Talk about delusions of grandeur.* "Sounds real impressive, Doc. So, you were the last one to handle the medication before Ms. Malekoviec's treating physician?"

"Yes, I was. I reviewed all the testing on it, found it within specs, and had Todd give it to Ms. Aloni to personally deliver it to the treating physician." Hyslop closes his eyes, taps his fingertips against each other. "Yesterday, when I heard what happened to Ms. Malekoviec, I even reached out to her rheumatologist, Doctor Jerome Gorelick, to see if there was any of the medication left for me to analyze."

"And?"

"Unfortunately, the entire dose was used for treatment."

"I see. And what time did Aloni leave the island with the medication?"

"Hmm, it was probably around 9:30 or so."

"And she returned when?"

"I'm not really sure, Detective. You'd have to ask her. I was holed up in the lab, working on a formulation and didn't see her again that day."

Kennedy nods. "How do you recruit patients for your studies?"

"That can be a challenge, Detective. Everyone wants a cure for what ails them, but few patients are willing to risk themselves with untested medications," Hyslop says with caution.

"So who oversees your recruitment efforts?"

"Well, Ms. Aloni sends letters out to all the appropriate practices in the area, informing them about the studies we are conducting. But it's really Todd who handles patient intake. He interviews candidates, tracks who referred them, reviews their medical records." Hyslop scratches his head. "I give him inclusion and exclusion criteria for each of our studies, then leave it up to him to select the correct patients."

"I see. Todd wears a lot of hats around here, huh, Doc? You're not concerned it's too much for one guy to handle?" Kennedy offers.

Hyslop, annoyed, says, "Todd's been a Godsend. With financing scarce in our field, I appreciate Todd's ability to work independently in so many areas. It frees me up to focus entirely on my formulations." Hyslop takes a deep breath, staring at Kennedy intently. "And I can assure you, Todd handles all of his duties exceptionally well."

Kennedy looks through his notepad, then taps it on the table. There are more questions to ask, but he has no intention of tipping his hand to Hyslop so early in the investigation. "That'll be all for now, Doctor. I'll leave my card with Ms. Aloni in case you or your staff recall anything else you'd like to add."

Hyslop extends a hand across the table, his reply perfunctory. "Thank you, Detective, and good luck."

# ▷ Chapter 9 ◁

"**S**immons, run a background on everyone at Hyslops' lab and start trailing Aloni as well. McCarthy?"

"Here, Chief."

"Hyslop's main competition is a guy named Grayson Limerock, CEO of Immunogenetics Offerings. They're right here in Manhattan. He'd have a lot to gain from Hyslop's lab being investigated."

"Want me to question him?"

"Not yet. Don't want to give him a heads up we're looking at him. Just tail him real carefully."

"Aye, Chief."

McCarthy takes off. Simmons stays behind. "This just came over the FAX for you, Chief."

"What is it?"

"Not sure; didn't have a chance to look at it."

Kennedy grabs the papers and settles in at his desk,

clearing a swath in the center of it to write up his notes and organize a plan of attack. His cell rings

"Hey buddy, what's going on?"

"Just finished testing me, so Jacobs cut me loose."

"What about your next treatment? When's that?"

"Tomorrow, maybe the next day. What's up on your end? Anything in the investigation seem connected to Durand?"

Kennedy lowers his voice, using his body to shield against being overheard, as he organizes the list of patients. "Nah. Hard to say at this point if it's even a homicide. Could just be an accident or bad reaction to a med. Were three other deaths about a year and a half ago. Haven't had time to look into those yet." His eyes scan the precinct warily. "Lemme call you back in a minute."

"Uh, sure, no problem."

§

Kennedy scours the police garage as he slips into his car and calls Chris back. "Sorry about that. No headway on whether we've still got a mole at the precinct, so I'm calling from my car."

Chris nods on his end. "Okay, what've you got?"

"We're still collecting background, but a few things stick out. For one, the head of the lab, a Doctor Hyslop, and his assistant, don't see eye to eye on some things."

"Did you say Hyslop, Harold Hyslop?"

"Yeah, why?"

"That's the doc Jacobs is getting the meds from to treat me," Chris says, his voice filled with surprise and concern.

"Can't be." Kennedy ruffles through the papers. "I got a list right here, and... shit!"

"What?"

"Yeah, you're on it. Second name from the bottom." Kennedy squirms in his seat. "Man, wasn't expecting that."

Silence.

"Chris, you still there?"

"Yeah, yeah I'm here. If it is a homicide, you like the doc for it?" he says as a chill runs through him.

"Couple of things stuck out when we interviewed him and his staff, but hard to say."

"Like what?"

"Hyslop's confident there was nothing wrong with his treatment, says the medication passed all their safety checks before he had his receptionist hand deliver it to the treating doc."

"Who has their girl running errands? Hasn't the guy heard of Fed Ex?"

"They don't pick up from North Brother Island."

"What, why's he got a lab out there? That place is an overgrown jungle."

"Tell me about it." Kennedy laughs nervously.

"Simmons thought it looked like a scene from *Planet of the Apes*, and I gotta say, he's not far off."

"Least not on that. Guy seems a bit out there."

"You got that right. Two minutes into talking with the receptionist and he's got her pegged as a suspect."

"What? How's that?"

"She's got rheumatoid arthritis, just like the vic, says that might've made her desperate for a cure, tampering with the medicine to speed things along."

"Well, she was the last one with it, right? But even so, how's a receptionist gonna know the first thing about that kind of stuff?" Chris shakes his head. "Sounds like a pretty wacked out theory."

"That's Simmons in a nutshell. Wanted to strangle the guy when we were interviewing the lead lab tech. Just kept cutting in with one off the wall comment after another."

"So, what's this about the tech and Hyslop not seeing eye to eye on some stuff?"

"Like I said, Hyslop's certain his med was clean. Zigler, that's the tech, not so much." Kennedy pauses. "He said Hyslop's formulations are so far beyond anything they've ever handled, they can't even really test the stuff right."

"Hmm, could just be a difference of opinion.... Hyslop, Zigler, or the girl have ties to Malekuviec?"

"Not sure. Simmons and I are checking on it. But another tech, she used to work in the practice that treated Malekoviec, can't stand her old boss. Got a sexual harassment suit against him."

"Think she'd have it out for him enough to kill a patient of his just to make him look bad?"

"No idea. Sounds like she's got some anger issues, so who knows? Wasn't in yesterday, so I gotta catch up with her, see for myself. What about on your end? Any thoughts on the whole Michelle thing?" Kennedy says warily.

"Nothing concrete, just a firestorm of conflicting emotions." Chris sighs. "I'd love to believe she's still alive, but what do I do, have them exhume the body on the recommendation of a sociopath?" He shakes his head. "Nah, I gotta come up with something solid before going down that road."

"Yeah, I hear ya. Look, what're you gonna do about your treatment with this guy's meds?"

Chris shakes his head in disgust as he paces the hallway. "I don't know, I need to think about it." He stops and rubs his face. "In the meantime, can you keep this under wraps at the precinct? I don't want anyone there knowing about my condition."

"Sure, no problem. You gonna tell your dad?"

"No way, he's giving me enough shit about the treatments already."

Kennedy sees two detectives walking his way and tries to hide his massive frame in the old Honda. "Uh, look, I gotta go before anyone lays eyes on me. I'll call you tomorrow after the autopsy results."

# ⊅ Chapter 10 ⊲

"Honey, you hardly ate your dinner. Is everything okay?"

Ben and Freida Zigler exchange worried looks as they sit on the sofa in their tiny, two-bedroom home in the Flushing section of Queens. A dank chill fills the air.

"I'm fine, mother, just a little tired," Todd says, a cascade of emotions filling him as he stares at the weathered, brown upright in the corner. Growing up destitute in this shoebox of a house, he clung to the hope the piano would bring him the notoriety and wealth he yearned for and deserved. He sighs. Not everyone's dreams come true.

"Do you want to play something for us, Son?" his Dad offers. "We haven't heard you in ages."

Todd wiggles his long, painted fingernails for them. "It's a little tough now with these."

His dad looks away. *Six months since he came out, still can't make peace with it.* "Anything new at the lab?"

"The police are investigating us," he says blandly.

His mother, a tall, stout woman, clutches her chest. "Oh my, whatever for?"

His father looks on in shock. "I thought everything was above board, going great. What happened?"

"You know how Doctor Hyslop's been anxious to drum up patients for his studies really quickly?"

They nod in agreement. Ben speaks first. "Is that Grayson guy still your stiffest competition?"

Todd nods. "Yeah, Limerock and his Immunogenetics Offerings are really turning up the heat of late. Even chased me down at the donut shop the other day, trying to steal me away." Now frowning, he continues, "What was I saying? Oh yeah, a few of us in the lab wanted to help Harold, so we recruited some people we know as patients."

Freida smiles at her son. "Yes, I remember. You were sweet enough to get your old piano teacher in a study after she had nowhere else to turn."

Ben grumbles, "Not that she would have done the same for you."

Freida says, "Now Ben, that's not fair."

"Isn't it? Nine years of lessons, of her telling Todd he'd have a promising career, and she just changes her mind." He snaps his fingers. "Pulls the plug on him like that. I wanted to kill the woman."

"No need for that now," Todd says with caution. "The police found her dead in her apartment. They think our lab had something to do with it."

Frieda gasps. "That's terrible."

Ben says, in a snide tone, "Serves the cold-hearted bitch right, she—"

"Ben!" Frieda rises to comfort Todd, burying his head in her ample chest as she wraps her arms around him. "Oh honey, you must be devastated." She sniffles, fighting back tears. "I know things with Irina didn't work out like we hoped." She casts Ben a disparaging look. "But she was a special lady."

Todd says flatly, "Yes, mother. I can't believe she's gone."

"I hope this doesn't hurt the lab. It can—" Ben says before being interrupted again.

"How can you be so heartless? A woman's dead... our son's grieving."

Todd peels himself off of her, offering a sad smile to his mother. Years of her drama have perfected his role as dutiful son. His voice is high but steady. "You're both right to be concerned. It's an unspeakable tragedy, but we have to be mindful of the lab's reputation too. If our medication killed her and word gets out... I don't know what we'd do."

"He's right, Freida. We've got to keep this under wraps, hope things blow over for Toddy's sake." Then sternly, "Not a word of this to anyone, you hear?"

She nods her head quickly, then scampers teary-eyed to the hall bathroom.

Ben looks at his son evenly. "Guess what comes around, goes around." He pats Todd on the arm. "Remember to watch out for number one. It's what Irina always did."

# ⊳ Chapter 11 ⊲

As Todd walks into the donut shop on 10th Street, he spots Limerock standing at the counter looking impressive in his handmade, Italian suit and dark overcoat. "Round two of 'slumming for recruits,' I see?"

"Afraid so, Todd." He smiles. "Some recruits play harder to get than others."

Todd nods at the girl behind the counter. "The usual." Then shaking his head at Grayson, "You were right about the police. Worked us all over the other day like common criminals."

"Let's hope they don't get a whiff of anything wrong. They'll never leave you alone."

"Speaking from experience?"

Grayson shakes his head. "No, but just look what they did to poor Martin Shkreli. And that was about money, not murder."

"Murder? Who said anything about murder?"

Grayson puts his hands up. "Police talking, not me."

Todd gathers his order and turns to go, but Grayson blocks his path.

"Todd, you're one of the rising stars in our industry, and no amount of tragedy in Doctor Hyslop's lab could convince me otherwise." Grayson nods his head. "That's why I'm sweetening my offer. I'll make you Director of R & D, tripling your current salary. You'll have a staff of forty-five reporting to you, and you can jump ship before any further disaster strikes down Hyslop's lab. What do you say?"

Zigler eyes him carefully. "Why do I get the feeling this is as much about me leaving Harold's lab as it is joining your company?"

"Survival of the fittest, Todd. If I can strengthen my company while weakening Harold's, all the better." He nods. "This is a very lucrative and prestigious position, Todd. Opportunities like this don't come by very often."

"I understand. But why go out of your way to put the full court press on me? From what you said the other day, Harold's lab is done for if the police implicate us in Irina Malekoviec's death."

"That's true, but let's hope it doesn't come to pass." Grayson shakes his head. "Publicity like that would be very damaging to our industry."

"What do you mean?"

Grayson motions him toward a table. "A patient

death from an immunologic-based treatment would create a public uproar. The liberal media would have a field day with it, painting us all as greedy, Frankenstein-like scientists." Grayson shakes his head, then bears his alabaster teeth. "In short order we'd have more government regulation and oversight, less grants for research, and the truly greedy ones, the insurance companies, would use this as an excuse to deny paying for our treatments by labeling them experimental and unsafe."

"Wow, you've really thought this through."

"I have, Todd, which is why I'd like you to join a council I'm creating. It will be composed of thought leaders from every branch of our industry: private sector, academics, regulatory groups, and so on. It's important we control the messaging about what we do, not those who oppose us." Grayson searches Todd's eyes. "I want you on the council regardless of whether you choose to work for me, understood?"

Todd looks down at his watch. "Look, I'm running real late and this is a lot to think about. Give me your card and I promise I'll give you a call after the dust clears at the lab."

Grayson smiles. "You certainly are a noble one, Todd, hanging in there when others would be fleeing for the nearest exit." He rises, hands Todd a business card, and shakes his hand. "Fair enough. Here, my cell's on the back."

Zigler gives a quick nod as he gets up. "Thanks. I'll be in touch." And he walks briskly away.

# ⊳ Chapter 12 ⊲

Her soft and sensual blue eyes fill me with warmth, hunger. Her smile radiates love and peace, awakening long dormant feelings.

My mind pulls back from the close-up. I see her naked body, her long, flowing, dark hair, her smooth and supple neck. The body I long for, the spirit I can't be without.

Then disaster strikes.

A small crack, a tiny fissure at first, forms around her navel, spreading like an earthquake in all directions. Terrifying fear fills her face, her mouth opening in a silent scream as the image shatters before me.

I lunge forward in bed, my body soaked in sweat, my heart racing.

Michelle.

Feeling empty and alone, I stare into the darkness,

wishing she was next to me. I lumber out of bed, check on the kids. Good, sleeping peacefully.

The stairs creak under my weight, the moonlight spilling in the front door, casting an eerie shadow on the floor below. I turn right into the dining room, then the kitchen. Grabbing a lone glass, I reach atop the cabinet for solace. I pour myself three fingers of Ballantine's Scotch, swirling it in the glass before me.

So real and yet so fleeting. The vision of her haunts me, clouding in my mind as my dream-state gives way to wakefulness. Something about her calls out to me, reassuring me she is still alive. But how, where? I shake my head in anger. *How can I trust anything after months of torment, after burying her twice already?*

# ⟩ Chapter 13 ⟨

"The cause of death was acute and complete kidney failure due to glomerulonephritis, Detective. This lead to widespread organ damage and a fatal heart attack."

"Globerulo..." Kennedy says with a shake of his head.

"Glomerulonephritis. The victim's kidneys were destroyed, obliterated by some toxin I have yet to identify." The ME, Doctor Audrey McGowan, looks down at the dissected kidney in her hands. "If you look here, Detective Kennedy, you can clearly see—"

Kennedy, his skin pasty and wan, begs off. "I'll take your word on that, Doctor McGowan." He swallows hard. "Any idea what caused all the bleeding in the skin?"

McGowan leans back, a hint of a smile on her face. *Poor Kennedy. I'll need a different approach.* She slides a thin, white drape over Irina's corpse. "I've sent samples of the kidneys and skin for what's called immunofluorescence microscopy. It's a special kind of staining. The results should be back soon."

Kennedy says, his color and strength returning, "Well, anything else you can tell me in the meantime?"

"Whatever did this attacked her with unprecedented speed and potency. Death overtook her in a matter of minutes."

Kennedy nods his head, reflexively swatting his notepad into his hand. "Okay then. Guess we'll wait on the tests you ordered."

"Slides, actually."

"Huh?"

"It was slides for the immuno-, aw, uh, never mind. Say where's Detective Simmons? I thought he was working this case with you?"

"I've got him chasing his tail at the precinct." Kennedy smirks. "It's the one thing he seems to be good at."

McGowan raises her eyebrows. "Well, we all have our limitations, Detective."

Kennedy, frustrated, looks down at the covered body and mumbles, "'Cept Chris. He'd be all over this shit."

"Pardon me?"

Heading toward the door, Kennedy pauses, turns his head back and offers a rueful smile. "Never mind, Doc. Thanks for your time."

# ⊳ Chapter 14 ⊲

"So, Ms. St. James, you worked for Doctor Gorelick?" Kennedy asks.

Kerline nods her head. "For 'bout sixteen months. Todd 'e brought me over during de summer."

"Tell me about Doctor Gorelick."

"Great doc, 'e refers a lot to Doctor Hyslop. Dat's 'ow I got to know Todd."

Kennedy nods. "I understand Gorelick is not well-liked by his staff."

Kerline looks down, smooths a skirt that doesn't need it. "Gorelick, 'e not a nice man. Nasty to staff. Gamblin' problem. Drinks too much." She peers at Kennedy. "Ya know what 'e done to me?"

Kennedy stares back. "Why don't you tell me?"

Anger flashes across Kerline's face. "'e start out nice, like 'e want ta be me friend, but before ya know it, de true 'im come out." She smooths the skirt again.

"Told me 'ow pretty I was, 'ow fine I be lookin' in me clothes. For I know it 'e's pressing up 'gainst me, kissin' and gropin' me." She shakes her head viciously. "Disgusting man, dat Gorelick." She makes a spitting motion. "Disgusting."

"So you filed charges against him for sexual harassment and assault?"

"Ya man. Ain't about no money, is about stoppin' 'im from doin' it again to somebody else."

"I understand. Have you had any contact with Doctor Gorelick or any of his staff since you left?"

"Just Sally. She be workin' de front desk for 'im, stayin' far way from 'im as she can." Kerline lets out a derisive laugh. "God bless! Dat Sally, she de only nice one dere."

"Did you ever see Doctor Gorelick drinking in the office or doing anything else inappropriate?"

"'Side from de sexual stuff wid me?"

Kennedy nods quickly. "Yes, aside from that."

"Well, sometime if you stop by 'is office and 'e on the phone, 'e hang up real quick like. And other times 'e 'ave dis mean looker come by named 'Mitri. Dey always 'ave de door closed, wid lots a yellin' when 'Mitri dere.'"

"Mitri or Gorelick?"

"D-Mitri. Gorelick, 'e just sit dere and take it me guess; not speak much."

Kennedy taps his notepad on the conference room

table. "How about a patient named Irina Malekoviec; do you remember her?"

Kerline nods in recognition. "Oh yay. Nice lady; kept to 'erself mostly, but nice. She a patient for 'bout six monds 'fore I left. Got no luck wid all dem studies Gorelick tried on 'er. 'Bout a mond 'fter I come 'ere, I seen we preppin' some medication for 'er."

Kennedy's eyes narrow. "Did that surprise you?"

Kerline waves her hand at the detective. "No way! Like I told you, no damn ding Gorelick tried be workin' on 'er. When dat 'appen, you be damn sure Gorelick send over 'ere for treatment, try and make 'er better dat way."

Kennedy stops writing, looks up from his pad. "Tell me about Jamal Richards."

Kerline laughs hard and winks at Kennedy. "You be really pushing me buttons wid dat one."

Kennedy says cautiously. "How so? Isn't he a patient of the lab's?"

"Yah, 'e is, cause a me."

Kennedy puts on a confused face.

She waves her hand at Kennedy again. "Might as well tell it like it be—you just gonna find out later, anyway. Jamal been dating me daughter Shanny, and stepping out on 'er de whole time." Shaking her head, she continues, "Got a girl wid child. Dank God it not me Shanny! Made 'er get rid of it. Dat boy bad, bad news."

"So why help him?"

A smug look overtakes Kerline's face. "I figure me try and 'elp Jamal. If it don't work out, maybe Shanny she lose interest, break it off."

"And?"

Kerline slaps her thigh, startling Kennedy. "Ain't 'ad no damn luck wid it. She still wid dat damn boy!"

Kennedy nods in acknowledgment, then looks through his notes. "Just about ready to wrap it up, Ms. St. James... Can you tell me what work you did on the medicine used to treat Irina Malekoviec?"

"I done de quality testing on de molecule." Then smiling, filled with pride, "Todd, 'e know 'ow good I am; 'e just look over what I done 'fore sending it on out."

"I see." Kennedy eyes her carefully. "What do you know about the three deaths that happened with Doctor Hyslop's patients about a year and a half ago?"

Kerline pulls back. "Year 'n a 'alf? Way 'fore I got 'ere." She stares at the floor, trying to remember. Thinking out loud, she says, "Hyslop don't tell nobody 'ere nodin' 'e don't have to. But, Toddy mention dem once or twice, said Hyslop was working too 'ard, wearing too many 'ats. Dey made 'im back off, slow down, 'ire Toddy to pick up the slack."

Kennedy reaches out, shakes Kerline's hand as he smiles. "We're all set for now, Ms. St. James. You're free to go. Here's my card in case you remember anything else."

"Dank you, Detective. I be sure to do dat."

# ▷ Chapter 15 ◁

Bing Crosby's lilting voice fills the room with Christmas cheer. A bowl of popcorn stands ready for stringing on our tree. This first holiday season without Michelle is excruciating for me, but I keep it light, festive, for the kids' sake. "Which one should we put on next, kiddo?"

"The big angel, Daddy, the big angel," Christine says with glee.

James nods with excitement. "Yeah, the angel."

"The angel it is. Hey Dad, can you pass me the step stool," I say with a grin. "I've got an angel to mount." Dad looks at me with amusement, a smirk stretching across his face as the kids open up a box of tinsel.

"Uh, yeah, that didn't come out quite right," I say with a laugh as I climb up.

Dad points to my backside. "Your pocket's ringing, Son."

"Huh?" I look toward my back pocket, catching myself as I almost slip. Back down I go. "Hello?"

"Chris, it's Doctor Jacobs, I have some good news. I've spoken to Doctor Hyslop. He's redesigned your formulation and is confident he's eliminated the problems from the first dose."

"That's great," I say with a painted-on smile. I nod to Dad and mouth "Jacobs" as I place the angel down. Covering my other ear, I walk out of the living room toward the front hallway.

"Yes, it's very promising." *So why do I detect hesitation?*

"Chris, a lot rides on this second treatment."

"I know. We went through it the other day, the timing and all," I say nonchalantly.

"Well, there's more to it than that." Jacobs clears his throat—*never a good sign.*

"Based on my experience with prior patients, the second dose will be decisive." His voice drips with foreboding.

"Yeah, how so?" *Is it gonna be the one Hyslop kills me with, just like the pianist?*

"Many patients had unpredictable, poor results the first time around, similar to what you went through."

*Why is he drawing this out? See spot. See spot run. Geez, I wish he'd just get to it so I can decide.*

"Those who were ultimately cured had two things in common: the second treatment improved them dramatically and their third treatment followed exactly five days after their second dose."

There's that damn pause again! "Uh-huh," I say distractedly, my head a jumbled mess.

"The third dose has to be timed precisely to 'lock in' the treatment. If it's given too late, the effect will likely be lost forever." Jacobs exhales forcefully. "A third dose given five days after the second confers a 94 percent chance of a cure. By day six that falls to 72 percent and by day seven to 14 percent."

I nod my head in agreement and hold up two fingers. "I get it, Doctor. Scout's honor. No disappearing anymore like the last time."

"That's right, Chris. Any delay would be irreparable."

"Say, what about the patients who didn't do so well with the second dose. How'd they end up?"

A moment of excruciating silence. *Shit, why'd I have to ask? More deaths tied to Hyslop that we don't know about?*

His voice becomes grave. "Three did not survive the second dose. Those who did became severely compromised within a few hours."

I look over my shoulder, smiling wistfully at the kids as they drape silver and gold tinsel on Grandpa's head. *So much at stake here, so much we don't know yet about Hyslop and his treatments.*

I rub the side of my face. Arresting Durand thrust me into the public eye, and my resignation was never announced. As far as Hyslop or anyone else in the public knows, I'm still Chief of the DMC. Would he be so brazen as to kill an NYPD division chief in the midst of his lab being investigated? Unlikely. But if Malekoviec's death was an accident like the other three, I could still be next. I shake my head. And if I stop now, what's there to look forward to? A life of disability, of being controlled by my disease?

Dad sticks his tongue out at the kids and grabs Christine playfully as she and James giggle. I take a deep breath as the realization settles in. *No way to give them the life they deserve without taking my chances.*

"Chris, are you there?"

"Yeah, I'm here. When can I get the next dose?"

"Tomorrow morning at nine would work. Is that good for you?"

"That'll work, Doctor. I'll see you then." I stare at the phone for a long moment, then slip it into my pocket and stride toward the living room, determined to reclaim the life I've left behind.

# FORBIDDEN CURE 3

## SORDID ASPIRATIONS

# ▷ Chapter 1 ◁

"**M**ore wine, darling?"

Grayson's voice reaches out to her from his large master bathroom. "By all means. Not every night we get to play at my house."

Kiki eyes the closed bathroom door as she slides the crushed sleeping pill in a baggie out of her purse and pours it into his drink. "I'm absolutely loving this, darling. Your place puts the Ritz-Carlton to shame," she replies as she stirs the drink to dissolve the powder. "You'll have to send your wife away more often."

Grayson pops out of the bathroom as she finishes mixing and joins her in bed. He leans over, kisses her passionately, and takes the offering.

"If only it were that easy." They click glasses. "To tonight," Grayson says, downing the entire drink while Kiki sips hers and smiles provocatively.

§

Kiki glances at the slumbering Grayson, her hands poised over the laptop. *Let's see what you've been up to, darling, what you know about Irina's death.*

Minutes fly by, coalescing into hours as Kiki searches Grayson's laptop, left open when he went to the bathroom earlier. At last, her diligence is rewarded, her anger sparked. *How could he have found all this out? Formulas, compounds we're working on.* She shakes her head. *So much for feeling bad about using him... he must have found a way to use me to access our computers. But how?*

Kiki skim reads pages upon pages of pilfered proprietary information, understanding little except for the extent of his espionage.

*Nothing on Irina yet. Wait, what's this... notes on us?*

"Wooing Todd Zigler is central to shuttering Hyslop's operations. Zigler is highly skilled and knowledgeable. His loss would devastate their operations. Assessment: competent, caring, loyal. Everyone's best friend. Weakness: grew up poor. Burning desire for wealth, recognition."

Kiki's eyes scroll down, finding notes on herself!

"Widow, financially precarious situation. Friendly, well kempt. Average intelligence at best. Joined Hyslop's staff nine months ago from one of his referring doctor's offices. Presumably motivated by the hope Hyslop will find a cure for her arthritis before the disease destroys her livelihood."

Kiki looks at the bed again. *Smart enough to knock you out cold, asshole.*

"Harold Hyslop: astute, creative scientist. True innovator. Poor people skills. Moody, condescending at times with staff, particularly Kiki Aloni. Will use that against him to turn her. Over-reliance on Todd Zigler is another weak point. Motivated by brother Phil's desperate need for a heart transplant. When Hyslop is at his most vulnerable, will recruit him with the promise of..."

Kiki's eyes grow wide as Grayson begins to stir. *Shit! Should have been out longer than this.*

She moves quickly, closing each file she accessed, then folding the screen down over the keyboard. She glides across the room and slips into bed as Grayson awakens. "Oh God, what happened? Head's killing me," he groans.

She rubs his temple. "Maybe it was the wine, darling. I've got a splitting headache too." Slipping out of the covers, she heads to the bathroom. "Have any Tylenol or Advil?"

Grayson sits up in bed. "Second drawer on the right, in the vanity. Bring me three Advil, will you?"

"Of course, darling."

Grayson slides over to the nightstand where Kiki put the two wine glasses, her jewelry, and two full glasses of water. His eyes scan the area as he downs the water. *Never felt like this after wine. Like I'm—what the!* He picks up the empty wine glass, noting a trace amount of white residue at the bottom. His eyes dart to the lipstick marks on the other glass, still two-thirds full, then the closed computer on his desk. Grinding his teeth, he curses under his breath as Kiki emerges from the bathroom.

He contorts his face into a wide grin. "Ah, my love. Always the cure for what ails me." He kisses her softly.

She offers him the Advils and a glass of water, speaking to him in the cute, little voice usually reserved for children. "Drink up, darling. Time to make you all better."

# ◊ Chapter 2 ◊

So here we are again. Same drab, bombshell-bunker style procedure-room at Washington General. Same cast of characters: Jacobs, Dad, Kennedy, and me. The tension is thick, the mood a trace of hopefulness, yet subdued—as if we're ready to call the funeral home but hoping we don't have to. Gotta lighten things up before I suffocate.

"Hey Kev, you know this doesn't count as our guys night out?"

He smirks and jabs a thumb toward Jacobs. "Oh no? So how come Doctor Jacobs said he's got the first round?"

Dad rolls his eyes and shakes his head.

Jacobs, surprised by our irreverence, almost cracks a smile. Almost. Back to deadly serious, he looks me in the eye. "Chris, this reformulation can help you tremendously, but it will take three minutes for its efficacy to kick in. Before that you may experience a roller coaster ride of adverse effects as your body adjusts to it." Jacobs pulls off his glasses, rubs his eyes and temples, and sighs. "No matter what happens, we need you to ride it out. If I intervene *at all* in the first three minutes, the medicine's positive effects will never be felt and we'll have lost our chance for a cure." He nods. "Do you understand?"

I swallow and nod back. *Time to find out if Hyslop has it out for me.*

Kennedy interjects. "How rough a ride we talking about, Doc?"

"Ever been on the Cyclone at Coney Island, Detective?"

"Shit," Kennedy says, under his breath.

Dad turns away, his face filled with worry.

Jacobs replaces his glasses and signals to his nurse, who stands poised over two trays filled with medications. "Ready?"

"Yes, Doctor."

"Make note of the time I begin the injection and update me every thirty seconds."

Jacobs pierces my IV tubing with the tip of his needle. "I want you to tell me everything you're feeling, Chris."

I hold on tight and nod my assent.

The green-tinged fluid fills my IV, then dissipates as it flows through my bloodstream.

"Thirty seconds, Doctor."

"So far, so good," I say. "A warm feeling. Definitely bet—"

My arms and legs go rigid. Waves of uncontrolled spasms ripple through my body as my eyes roll back in my head. Bodily fluids flow out of all of my orifices.

Jacobs: "Intubation tube, airway kit ready. He's seizing! Carnexiv STAT."

The nurse slaps a syringe of the antiepileptic in his palm. Jacobs' hand hovers near my IV as I bounce all over the stretcher.

"BP holding at 110/64, Doctor. Pulse is 130 and climbing." Concern seeps into her voice. "O2 sat is dropping: 90, now 86, 80 percent." She glances at her watch. "One minute, Doctor."

My lips turn blue.

Jacobs' eyes hold steady on the monitors. His hand creeps closer to the IV. Beads of sweat build on his brow and trickle down the sides of his face.

Kennedy, frantic, says, "Do something, Doc...."

Light-headed, dizzy. Struggling to hold on.

"One minute, thirty seconds, Doctor! O2 down to 74 percent, pulse 150 and irregular!"

Jacobs talks under his breath. "C'mon, damn it, just a little more time!"

The blue hue spreads out across my cheeks, a sea of oxygen deprivation washing over me. *Not sure I can hold on much longer.*

"Two minutes, Doctor."

Jacobs, frozen in place. His eyes break free of the monitors. They run quickly along my cold, clammy body, assessing my condition as I careen uncontrollably. Dad, terror in his eyes, implores him, "Please, don't lose him."

"Two and a half minutes, Doctor." Wringing her hands. "He's in a fib now! O2 sat plummeting."

Jacobs' eyes dart to the monitors, to me. Turning to the nurse, he drops his syringe on the tray. "Laryngoscope!" Jacobs lunges onto the stretcher, flailing his arms in a desperate effort to control me. Kennedy rushes over. "I got it, Doc." In one motion he brushes Jacobs aside, grabs my arms with his gigantic hands, and forces me to be still. "Do what ya gotta do, quick."

Jacobs is panic stricken. "His mouth." Kennedy release his grip and lunges forward, using his chest to pin my body down. He grabs my face in his meaty, oversized hands, straining against my jawbone. With a scream he pries my teeth open as Jacobs rams the laryngoscope's metal guide in. "Can't hold him long..." A plastic tube, then an attachment follows.

"Three minutes, Doctor."

"O2 at 15 liters!"

*Sweet Jesus, at last!* Oxygen pouring into me, filling my desperate, depleted lungs and starved blood.

The convulsing becomes less violent, then stops. I lay in the bed, feeling like I was just run over by an eighteen-wheeler.

The nurse's voice fills with hope. "Heart rate becoming regular, Doctor. O2 sat climbing."

Jacobs slumps forward, a disheveled, spent mess. "Thank God." He wipes his forehead with the back of his hand. "I'm going to extubate him now and drop the O2 down to four liters via a nasal cannula."

Kennedy pulls away, in disbelief I made it. He grabs Dad in a bear hug and yanks him off the ground like a rag doll, dancing around. "Fucking A, we did it, Bill!"

Dad gasps. "Kev... can't... breathe."

Kennedy, startled, releases his grip, gently sets Dad back down. "Sorry, Bill. You okay?"

Dad smiles broadly. "I'm fine." He makes his way to my bed as Jacobs finishes adjusting the cannula and steps aside. "You okay, Son?"

Weary, eyes half closed, relief washing over me in waves, I muster a smile. "Yeah... Anyone get the plate number on that semi?"

§

"How are you feeling, Chris?"

I smile back at Jacobs. "Surprisingly good, like someone lifted a huge weight off of me."

He nods, a hint of a smile. "All the blood work is normal, and your vitals have never been better." He toys with the stethoscope draped over his neck, the smile finally breaking through. "Safe to say, the worst is behind you."

I'm buoyed by a new sense of hope. "You really think so, Doctor?"

He nods affirmatively. "Doctor Hyslop's group is tightlipped with their results, but I'm very optimistic, Chris. Out of the dose-two survivors the only patients who had bad outcomes were those who deteriorated within five hours of the treatment." Jacobs looks at his gold Rolex, folds his arms over his chest. "Nine hours post treatment now. We should be in the clear."

"So what's next?"

"You head home now, and we give you the final treatment in five days to lock in the effect."

I shake my head in happy disbelief. "That's great! Any restrictions? Any concerns about dose three?"

"No, none. In fact, you'll probably feel better, stronger than you have in years without the drain of the pheo." He pauses. "I'll touch base with Hyslop today. In the meantime call my office, get the treatment scheduled." He turns serious. "Remember, it has to be five days from today. A day or two late and the chances of a cure drop precipitously."

Jacobs rolls his eyes as I salute him. "Ay, ay, sir, I'll get right on it."

With a shake of his head he's off as I reach for my cell to call Kennedy, then Dad. "Hey Kev, got a clean bill of health. Any chance you can spring me now?"

# ⊳ Chapter 3 ⊲



Just inside the Capital Beltway, due north of DC, two prominent members of the FDA's Office of Special Medical Programs discuss the latest data from Immunogenetics Offerings.

Director Frank Presby arches his eyebrows as he leans back in his chair. "I've got to say, Paul, this is impressive. When Limerock's Group gave us an update six months ago, I didn't think there was any way we'd be green-lighting them. But they've done a complete one-eighty."

Deputy Director Paul Wooden, seated on the opposite side of Frank's massive Mahogany desk, shakes his head in disbelief. "I know. At that point I thought Hyslop's treatments were more promising than

Limerock's. But this data, and some of the whispers I've heard, has me reconsidering."

"What kind of whispers?" Presby asks.

"That Hyslop's next round of reporting will contain at least one fatality," Wooden says with a knowing nod.

"What, another one? We're supposed to be notified within seven days of a treatment death."

Wooden cuts in. "Actually, they came off probation a few months ago, so they don't have to inform us until their next reporting date, which is the end of January."

Presby plants his elbows and forearms on his desk, leans forward, and surveys Wooden's face. "Check into your source's story. I don't want to get blindsided in a few weeks like they did to us last year."

Paul rises from his chair with satisfaction, smooths his sports-coat, and turns to go. "Will do. I'll get right on it."

"And Paul, be discrete. No one else in the know until we're certain what's going on."

Wooden gives a quick, confident nod then disappears down the hallway.

# ▷ Chapter 4 ◁

"**Y**ou oughta spend a few bucks and get the wheels on this hunk of junk aligned. Definitely pulls left," I say with a good-natured laugh as I slap Kennedy's right shoulder. The Titanic gave a smoother ride than Kev's ancient Honda does, but it's all good today as we ride north on the Deegan, toward Dad's house in Ossining, to meet him and the kids.

Kennedy nods and grins. "So after washing out as a surgeon and a police detective, you're an auto mechanic now?"

"Hey, a guy's gotta make a living somehow, right?"

"Bud, you never even changed windshield wiper blades growing up," he says with a booming laugh.

My face contorts. "You've got a point there, big guy. Guess it's back to the 'help wanted' section for me."

Kennedy jerks his head toward the direction we came from. "What a mess back there. You sure Jacobs knows what the hell he's doing with the experimental stuff?" He shakes his head. "I thought you were a goner at one point."

"Yeah, me too. Wouldn't have bothered with my nice skivvies if I knew what was gonna happen," I say sarcastically. "But seriously, I feel better than I have in years, and now we know Hyslop's not trying to kill me."

Kennedy nods. "Wasn't sure there for a while."

"Me neither." I intertwine my fingers and crack my knuckles. "Looking forward to sealing the deal in a few days with the last treatment."

"I hear you. What're you gonna do with yourself in the meantime?"

My face takes on a puzzled look. "With all the crazy shit that's gone down, I didn't really think that far ahead." I exhale and shake my head. "One thing's for sure, I'm going to bear hug the kids. They have no idea how wrong this all could have gone, but I do."

Kennedy pats his chest where two of Durand's bullets tore through him back in July, one clipping his aorta. "Yeah, man, we've got enough scars to last a lifetime. Time to move on to better days."

I nod in acknowledgment, Kennedy's words ringing true, yet also unsettling me. Staring out the window as we drive past the Cross County Shopping Center and a maze of interconnecting Parkways, I realize how long the road to recovery is that stretches out before me. In a few days I'll have my health back, but then what? How do I support myself and the kids? Do I try to get my job at Washington General back? Or plunge headlong again into the life of depravity of an NYPD detective? Maybe I have other marketable skills and talents that can set me on a different path?

Kennedy lets up on the gas as we head through the toll plaza's E-ZPass lane. Far up on the hill sits Stew Leonard's and Costco, both bustling with holiday activity. In front of us a long, crowded stretch of the New York State Thruway. There are lots of questions to answer, for sure. But they all pale in comparison to the unspoken one, to the question I've barely had time to consider since we met with Durand. *Are you out there somewhere, baby, or have I really lost you for good?*

# ⟩ Chapter 5 ⟨

The shimmering glass building stands sixty-four stories high on Manhattan's Upper East Side. Finance, asset management, building management, and accounting firms fill the lower fifty-eight floors. The upper six are home to Immunogenetics Offerings, a multi-billion-dollar company at the forefront of design and development of biologics, proteins genetically engineered to command and control the human immune system. Grayson Limerock's office occupies the entire east side of the sixty-fourth floor. Limerock smiles as he looks at the meaningless dots scurrying along the street far below. Adjusting his gaze, he stares at the chilled waters of the East River, at the tangled mess that blights his otherwise pristine view. He shakes his head. *North Brother Island. What a God-forsaken, fitting place for him.*

Grayson continues conversing with his chief of information technology and security as he makes his way to the wet bar, gliding past an eclectic collection of paintings, including Picasso's Nude, *Green Leaves and Bust*, and Van Gogh's *Vase with Fifteen Sunflowers*.

"Are you *sure* we have no vulnerabilities? We can't afford to lose even a nanobyte of our proprietary technology."

Jack laughs as he folds his hands over crossed legs, resting them on his finely pressed pants. "Our firewalls have firewalls, sir, so nothing is getting in, or out, without my permission." Jack picks a strand of hair off his pants and tosses it to the floor with disdain. "You and I are the only two with unfettered access to the system."

"As it should be." Grayson raises an empty tumbler and nods.

"No thank you, sir. Bit early for me."

Grayson offers a wry smile. Then pressing him, he goes on, "With the ability to revolutionize treatments in the fields of rheumatology, endocrinology, and transplant medicine, there are hundreds of billions, if not trillions, at stake. We can't afford to become the next Target, Equifax, or Uber."

"I understand your concerns, sir. But rest assured, we employ the most sophisticated, corrupt hackers in the world to attack our systems daily, searching for inadequacies."

Grayson offers a begrudging nod. "Fair enough. How about our other project?"

Jack treads lightly. "The monitoring technology you embedded continues to yield invaluable information, and there are no signs the recipient has detected us. Has it met your expectations?"

Grayson eyes him carefully as he sips his Scotch. "Yes, very much so."

Jack nods. "If there's nothing else, sir..."

Grayson circles in front of his laptop and powers it up. Eyes glued to the screen, he waves his hand dismissively. "Keep me appraised, Jack."

Limerock settles in at his desk as the door to his office closes. He depresses the intercom. "Hold all my calls for the next hour," he says, releasing it before there is time for a reply. A crooked smile curls across his face as he slips into the server again, undetected. "Let's see what gifts you have for me this morning, darling. And rest assured last night's little stunt won't go unpunished."

# ⊳ Chapter 6 ⊲

Kev grips the steering wheel with white knuckles as he navigates the steep, serpentine descent along Dad's driveway. A steady stream of expletives erupt as the Honda lurches over patches of ice. Unrelenting, icy winds from the Hudson River below lash the car. Kev's curses peak in intensity as the car skids around the final hairpin turn, a wheel sliding off the asphalt, dangerously close to the precipice overlooking the river below. As we enter a brief straightaway that leads to the house, a relieved Kennedy exclaims, "Love the privacy and views and all, but geez, your dad ever heard of rock salt?"

Kev loosens his grip on the wheel as he pulls under the carport, and Dad emerges from the front door of his brown-shingled contemporary. The kids trail just behind, excitedly yelling, "Daddy!" I collect heartfelt hugs from everyone and wipe tears of joy from my eyes as Kennedy and I work our way back to the kitchen. There, floor-to-ceiling windows frame a sliding glass door. They provide a picture perfect view of the cove, Scarborough Train Station, and beyond them the Hudson River and the rolling hills and mountains of Rockland County.

Having moved here from Arthur Avenue when I was seven, the house holds most of my great childhood memories, including the earliest days of my friendship with one Kevin Kennedy. Today, as it has many times in the past, it serves as a serene sanctuary, a place to gather my strength and renew my spirit as I convalesce.

Over Porterhouses and beer, Dad, Kennedy, the kids and I smile and laugh. Dad winks at me. "Just a few more days till Jacobs has you cured for good." He raises his glass in salute, Kennedy and I mirroring him. "Thank God for that."

After getting the kids off to bed, we sit down in contented silence, watching the moonlight reflecting off the river. A few minutes pass, then Kennedy asks, "So what're you gonna do with yourself between now and the last treatment?"

I look out at the river and rub my stubble-filled chin, then decide it's time to bring Dad up to speed. "Kev's working an interesting case for the DMC. Could be a homicide or just an unexpected fatality from an experimental drug treatment." I turn to Kennedy. "Too early to tell, right?"

Kennedy nods affirmatively.

Dad sips his beer and also nods. "Sounds interesting, but what's it got to do with you?"

"The doctor who supplied the deceased woman the medication is the same doctor formulating my treatments for Jacobs."

Beer in hand, rising toward his lips, Dad freezes. "What? How long have you known this?"

"Since just before the second treatment."

Dad is flabbergasted. "And you're just telling me now? You could have been killed!"

I air pat my hands, trying to calm him down. "Dad, there's no evidence at this point that the other patient's death was a homicide."

"Homicide or not, you could've been killed. Christ, what were you thinking?"

"The treatment was my only chance at a cure."

Dad points toward upstairs. "You've got two kids who just lost their mother and who desperately need their dad right now. You can't go off half-cocked, risking your life like that."

"I know, but if I don't get better, I can't take care of them, and I've been pretty much useless of late." Then sheepishly, "Thankfully it all worked out okay."

Dad's eyes bulge. "Yeah, after you almost died—twice! Who's to say what the hell will happen next time?"

Kennedy's eyes dart back and forth between us, as if at a tennis match.

"Jacobs assures me, there's nothing to worry about with the third dose. Everyone who made it this far has done great with the last treatment."

"Jacobs know we may have a killer in play now?"

"Okay, okay, let's take a step back, not jump to any conclusions." I look at Kennedy, then back to Dad. "Right now I need to help Kev on this case."

Surprise fills both their faces as I explain.

"By looking through everything Kev has on the case, I may be able to help him sort out what's going on, which benefits me as much as anyone."

Dad shakes his head begrudgingly.

"Kev, can you get me the files to review?"

He looks at us. "Not exactly police protocol... aw, but who the hell am I kidding? I got stuff in the car I was gonna look over tonight. You can have it as long as you get it back to me tomorrow." His pointer finger jabs at me. "Nobody outside this room can know."

I motion as I say, "Cross my heart."

Dad: "So that's settled." Then sarcastically, "Any other bombshells to drop?"

Ill at ease, I look at Kennedy, then back to Dad. "There is one other thing. We met with Durand the other day and you're not going to believe what he said...."

# ⊳ Chapter 7 ⊲

The turmoil and tension with Dad behind me, I'm holed up in my old room, sifting through everything Kev has on the Malekoviec investigation. Questions dart through my mind. Anything I can point out that will help Kev solve the case? Or help me figure out if Hyslop's treatments are a danger to his patients? Anything here to support Durand's claims that Michelle is alive, or that he can help us solve this case?

I blow steam off a mug of hot chocolate, then take a sip as I look through the vic's medicals. Irina had a very aggressive, poorly controlled form of rheumatoid arthritis. Over the course of four years she went from a world class concert pianist with long, elegant fingers and magnificent dexterity, to a woman decimated by disease, with gnarled appendages reminiscent of a ninety-year-old. She had tried and failed all traditional therapy for RA, including non-steroidal anti-inflammatories, corticosteroids, and methotrexate. Hydroxy-chloroquine, the only med to give her any real relief, was discontinued after it caused her to lose two lines of vision in each eye. The ME, Doctor Audrey McGowan, had even found traces of gold in the joints of her fingers, which is rarely used anymore in treating RA patients. *Either some doctor didn't know what he was doing, or Irina was desperate to try anything.*

Doctor Jerome Gorelick, her latest rheumatologist, enrolled Irina in two drug trials, but results were poor with each. Enter Harold Hyslop. Irina's first treatment with his medication went smoothly but was ineffective. Her second treatment was more of the same when she left her doctor's office thirty minutes later, but the ME's report showed she died within four hours of that injection. *Consistent with what Jacobs said about one branch of the treatment failure group.*

I comb through the crime scene report. No signs of forced entry, a struggle, or a weapon of any kind. Malekoviec was not strangled or stabbed and didn't have any entrance or exit wounds at all. The only injection site noted was the one used hours before her death to give her the medication. Along with the tox screening that ruled out a poisoning. The only physical evidence at the crime scene were diffuse, blotchy hemorrhages covering most of Irina's body. I look through the half dozen gruesome pictures.

*Lesions look familiar but never seen them so wide-*

*spread before.* I sift through the papers and photos rapidly. *Come on, come on, it's got to be—ah, there it is.* I hold the close-up to the light, studying the pattern of the hemorrhages on her right upper arm as I nod slowly. This photo and years of work as a trauma surgeon confirm what I suspected.

None of the bleeding came from an *external* assault.

The pattern of blood is consistent with a widespread vasculitis, a damaging inflammation that affects blood vessels of all sizes. In her early fifties, with no other medical history save the RA, Irina should never have suffered such a fate. I look up from the photo and stare out the window at the barren oaks and maple trees that dot Dad's property. *What the hell happened to her to cause this?*

I think back to my discussions with Jacobs, to the analogies and explanations regarding my own treatment. Jacobs said all of Hyslops' treatments were immunologically based. His compounds were synthesized to control and suppress the immune system. In Irina's case the RA caused her own body to create antibodies that attacked the joints in her fingers. Hyslop's treatment must have been designed to turn off production of these harmful antibodies. I grab the photo and study it again, a smile spreading across my face as I realize what happened.

Irina's treatment didn't contain or suppress her immune system, it unleashed it!

I sift through the papers on the desk, tossing more photos and reports out of the way, until I find McGowan's report again. Cause of death: widespread organ failure, precipitated by glomerulonephritis. Hyslop's treatment worked differently than he intended. Instead of turning off production of her harmful antibodies, his medicine acted like an antigen, stimulating production. The medicine then did battle with these antibodies, attacking and destroying them.

In essence, Hyslop's medication created a widespread immunologic war throughout Irina's body!

Initially, this gave Irina great relief from her symptoms. But these antigen-antibody complexes were so immense and formed so quickly, Irina's body couldn't possibly get rid of them fast enough. So these massive structures came crashing out of her bloodstream, destroying the blood vessels in Irina's skin, kidneys, heart, and many other organs throughout her body. Hence, the blotchy bleeding in her skin, widespread organ failure, and glomerulonephritis found on her post-mortem examination.

*But how could this have happened so quickly?*

Tossing papers aside again, I search for Irina's labs from prior to both her treatments. Her BUN/Cr levels, markers for kidney function, were completely normal before treatment one. Just before the second treatment, they were still in the normal range but just barely.

It was basic immunology at work.

The immune system's initial response to unrecognized invaders is minimal as the body works hard to synthesize antibodies to attack the organisms. But, a second exposure to the same antigens a short time later produces an exponential increase in the production of these antibodies. This concept forms the basis for providing immunizations against the flu, for example.

But in Irina's case, the treatment backfired. The first dose produced little discernible effect because it neutralized only small amounts of her existing, harmful antibodies. This caused very mild damage to her kidneys when the antigen-antibody complexes deposited there, but it also primed her immune system. The second dose caused an explosive production of antibodies in just a few hours, and the resulting antigen-antibody complexes obliterated her kidneys and decimated blood vessels throughout her body. *Need to speak with McGowan, see the body and test results to be sure. Then visit Gorelick, Hyslop, figure out where it all went wrong.*

It feels good to be useful, contributing again, albeit in an unofficial capacity. A couple of weeks on the sidelines have shown me how much I miss it. But I temper my enthusiasm. Reviewing paperwork in the comfort of my old room is easy, with none of the stresses and risks of The Job. Risks to me and my health to be sure, but to my family as well.

Michelle knew those risks better than anyone. I shudder as my mind flashes back to the scene at the East River, to our first confrontation with Durand. Victory seemed at hand when Michelle lay Durand out by suddenly opening a car door in front of him. But a moment later, he sprang back up, grabbed her, and slit her throat, escaping into the water below. Tears flow down my cheeks as the pain takes hold. My hands ball up into fists, my anger flowing as freely today as the blood from her wound did then. I shake my head, trying to rid myself of the images. But it's no use. Something from that night calls out to me, haunts that part of my psyche that can't let go of Michelle, can't move on without her.

I grab the papers and photos and throw them against the wall. As they scatter in every direction my fists pound the desk, wishing it was Durand's skull, wishing there was some way to bring Michelle back.

# ⟩ Chapter 8 ⟨

Todd Zigler disembarks from the shuttle boat, another grueling but rewarding day in the lab done. He wraps his winter coat tightly around his neck, bracing himself from the strong, cold breeze coming off the East River as he trudges toward his car at the far end of the parking lot.

The figure lurks in the corner of the lot, dressed in darkness, observing Todd's every move. *The young man works incredibly hard, that much is certain.* The observer shifts position to improve his view and further his concealment behind another car. *But where do his allegiances lay? There's far too much at stake to leave that all-important question left unanswered.*

Zigler climbs into his black Mazda and turns over the engine. His teeth chatter while he waits for the car to warm enough so he can turn on the heater. He makes a mental note to get the remote starter he picked

Hyslop ran his lab, and they placed his program on probationary status for one year with regard to the lab's fast track status with the FDA. The three patients were all experiencing transplant rejections just after surgery with an unidentified surgeon from Washington General. Hyslop did intake on the patients with no documentation whatsoever, just a verbal history provided by the referring physician, whose identity he fiercely protected throughout the inquiry. Hyslop formulated medications for each victim with little help from his two technicians, carried out the quality testing himself, and hand delivered the compounds to the surgeon he worked with. The patients died within hours of their second doses, just like with Irina Malekoviec.

Hyslop kowtowed to the FDA's demands to hire a senior lab tech who would take sole responsibility for intaking patients; hiring and supervising technicians; overseeing quality control testing; sending the medications off to the treating physicians; and reporting serious patient side effects directly to the FDA. Todd Zigler was that technician, and single-handedly he restored the lab's reputation as he nursed it through its probationary period. Without his Herculean efforts, the lab could never have survived. Hyslop continued to be the brains of the operation and direct the lab's overall efforts while Todd shielded him from many of the day-to-day details of running the lab.

It was a system that worked beautifully and heralded a remarkable expansion in the lab's volume of patients and safety profile—until now.

Kennedy picks an unopened envelope out of Riley's personnel folder. *Returned to sender? Who lets their retirement check bounce back to the NYPD?* He grabs the phone and dials up human resources. "Detective Kevin Kennedy here. I'm trying to reach retired Detective Connor A. Riley as part of a homicide investigation. You have an up-to-date address, phone number on him?"

"One minute, Detective." Adele's 'Rolling in the Deep' takes over the line for the next few minutes as the worker follows up on the inquiry. "Deceased. Detective Riley died a month after retiring from the force."

"Ouch. Any details on his death, like if foul play was suspected?"

The worker scans the file. "I'm afraid not, Detective. That's all I have. Have a nice—"

"How 'bout his partner, Mitch Goldberg? Got a phone number on him?"

"Just his home. It's 718-555-1442."

"Thanks a lot." Kennedy returns the mouthpiece to the cradle, picking it right back up to dial the number.

"Hey, I can't get to the phone right now, but please leave a message and I'll get back to you as soon as I feel like it." Sounds of the ocean swirl in the background before the message shifts into recording mode.

"Hey Mitch, Kev Kennedy from your old stompin' grounds at the 1-7. Give me a call at the precinct when you get a minute. Wanted to ask you about a case you worked just before you retired. We've got another death to investigate from the same doc's lab and I could use your help."

## ⊳ Chapter 10 ⊲

Climbing the stairs two at a time at the 17th precinct, I do my best to crush the emotions welling up inside. I was Chief of the DMC for less than a year, but what a hellacious year it was, chasing after Durand as the bodies piled up throughout the city and across the country. But the story really began eight months before that. My mother's brutal attack, the vow I made to leave medicine behind and take up detective work in Ma's honor.

I glance at my watch: 12:52 p.m. I feel bad about dropping by later than expected, but Kev and I can grab a bite while I catch him up on things. Walking through the door on the third floor, I spot Kennedy at his desk pouring over documents, Detective Simmons seated across from him at my old desk.

"Hey, Chris, how's it going?" he yells as he pushes

the paperwork aside and grabs his coat. "Wanna grab lunch or something?"

I smile. An outsider now, but I still know a few things.

An avalanche of greetings, waves, and slaps on the back overtake me. "How ya doing, Chris?" "Not the same without you." "When you coming back?" Kennedy plows through the crowd, brings order to the chaos. "Geez, give the guy some air before we gotta do CPR!" He puts an arm around my shoulder and steers me through the crowd, toward the door I came through. "Who knew you were so popular? Most of these pricks couldn't stand working for you." He grins. "Now, you're like Elvis, the Pope, and Babe Ruth all rolled up in one."

It feels good to hear it, to be *here* where I'm wanted and did such valuable work. "Ay, what can I say? When you've got it, you've got it." I pull back a bit, slipping free of Kennedy's grasp. "Why don't we hang here a bit?"

Kennedy's eyes dart quickly back and forth. "Uh, sure." He does a one-eighty, motions to Simmons and a few others to clear out, and waves me to my old seat. I pull up, leaning on Kennedy's desk instead and wave him off. "Naw, I'm good here."

Kennedy talks just above a whisper. "Sure you want to do this here? You're not exactly on the NYPD payroll anymore, and lord knows we can't have anyone finding out Hyslop's treating you too."

Simmons circles back to his desk to grab his jacket. Kennedy's eyes bear down on him, sending him veering off instead.

I nod. "Got to confirm with McGowan, but it looks like Hyslop's treatment killed her. We just have to figure out how. Was it the formulation itself? Or did someone tamper with the medication by the time Gorelick injected Irina?"

Kennedy looks around nervously, his fingers drumming on the desk. "So how'd the med kill her?"

"Lesions are classic for vasculitis, a kind of inflammation of blood vessels." No need for more details; I can see I'm losing him already. "In this case caused by a bad reaction to the medication."

Kennedy shrugs his shoulders. "If you say so." Lowering his voice further, he says, "But where's that get us on the case?" Leaning forward, even softer, "and with your situation?"

"Narrows the focus a bit. The stuff Irina's husband and her brother were into, wouldn't waste much time on that. You're looking at someone with scientific expertise who laid hands on the medicine before she took it."

Kennedy wipes his brow. "So we're dealing with a homicide?"

"Not sure," I say with a shake of the head. "Have you spoken to Gorelick or his staff yet? Any of them could be suspects if it's a homicide."

I notice Kennedy's eyes dart again. *What the hell's up with him?*

"Made a quick pass with the doc, but I'll put someone on him, see what he's up to. Simmons'll have more background on Hyslop and company by tomorrow." Kennedy eyes me. "I'm starving, wanna head out?"

"Yeah, whatever." I jerk my head toward where I came in. Kennedy's eyes bulge as I continue, "Got all the stuff down in the car for you."

Somebody yells, "Hey Chief." Kennedy and I both turn. "You got a call."

I spin back around, face flushed, anxious to escape my embarrassment. "No worries, I'll meet you at the car, then off to McGowan's."

§

"What do mean, 'no go on McGowan's'? How can I help if I can't confirm my theory?"

Kennedy's face is contorted with discomfort as he holds his hands up in surrender. "You can't, Chris." He waves toward two boxes of files on my back seat. "Petersen would crucify me if he knew I let you look through that stuff. No way in hell we can go to McGowan's."

"Aw, c'mon. She's helped us on the sly before."

Kennedy's discomfort deepens. "Yeah, when we were both on the force...."

I'm such an idiot. As much as I want to help and Kev welcomes it, I can't put him in Petersen's crosshairs. A sinking feeling replaces all the warm, fuzzy feelings from a few minutes ago.

My back stiffens as I lean away from him. "I get it. Sorry."

Kev starts to speak, then searches for the words. "If it was up to me..."

"I know. Look, I'm gonna take a raincheck on lunch." I pat his shoulder. "Good luck with it. I gotta get going." Solemn and expressionless, Kennedy exits the car, reaching into the back seat for his files.

As he walks off, a box tucked under each arm, I swallow hard and shake my head, screeching the tires a bit as I pull out. Never enjoyed being on the outside looking in, and this time's no different.

# > Chapter 11 <

Kiki scans the document as she finishes typing. Like her, it is a complete mess, littered with errors throughout. Her fingers jab the keys, correcting each mistake one-by-one. If only she could straighten out her life this easily.

Where had she gone wrong? Hyslop and Limerock, two brilliant scientists. Either or both should have cured her by now. Instead, Hyslop's latest guinea pig is dead, his lab in disarray due to the ongoing police investigation. And the Limerock situation is no better. Intent on using him for her own benefit, Limerock turned the tables on her! And he is hell-bent on using her to steal secrets from the lab while he plots its demise. Kiki shakes her head. Since when did her beauty and guile fail her so miserably?

"Kiki, where is the Jamal Richards file?" Hyslop yells from behind her. "I need it for the reformulation."

"It's right here, Doctor. I'm just finishing up with it."

Hyslop stands before her, tapping his foot on the floor impatiently. "Hurry, please."

Pain jabbing at her fingers, she puts the finishing touches on the report and hits the print button. Hyslop snatches the papers from the printer and storms off. *Of all the overbearing, ungrateful, hot-tempered bosses.... Why can't he be dead instead of Irina?*

Back at Dad's, Christine and James jostle on his back as he chugs around the living room on all fours. I look on, vacillating between self-pity, self-loathing, and second guessing. Leaving the force means wracking my brain now for answers I can't possibly have.

"Sure you don't want to have a go of it?" Dad arches his eyebrows, his voice filled with sarcasm. "I feel bad hogging all the fun." Christine bucks her legs against the sides of his chest and urges him onward. "Faster, faster."

A sad smile fills my face. I should relieve him now but don't have the energy for it. "In a couple of minutes, okay?" The kids, filled with anticipation, smile back.

"Whoey!" Dad hangs his head with exhaustion as he pants like a dog and presses on.

Hands covering my eyes and forehead, I torture myself with ruminations. *Any truth to what Durand* said, that Michelle's alive, that he can help us solve the Malekoviec case? Or am I just desperate, the world's biggest idiot, for wishing it's true?

"Look Daddy, look!" James yells as he slides forward, wrapping his hands around Dad's nape. As he swings back and forth, Dad's face contorts in pain.

I snap out of my fog and lunge forward, pulling his hands apart as I ease him to the ground. "James, you need to be more careful before you break Grandpa's neck."

With downcast eyes, he says, "Sorry, Daddy."

I lift Christine off Dad's back as his hand goes to his beet-red, raw neck. Annoyed with myself for letting it get out of hand, I hold back my anger as Dad intervenes with a wink and a smile. "It's okay, slugger. No harm done." I pull back, taking a deep breath as I urge myself to keep calm. "You okay, Dad?"

"Yeah, fine." As he pulls his hand away, my eyes are drawn to his neck, absorbed by a close-up as time slows to a crawl. I shudder, jumbled flashbacks assaulting me.

A dagger, a slashing motion. I shake my head to drive the images away.

A trickle of blood forms on Dad's neck. It swells and stretches, straining to break free.

Oh God, Michelle! Her body crumbling to the ground as Durand gets away. The hospital, the operating room. No! Don't die.

The drop of blood on Dad's neck falls through

the air, splashes against the hardwood floor. My heart pounds in my chest.

"Chris, are you okay?"

I stare at Dad, his lips moving, the words not registering. Michelle's face now. The bandages wrapped around her neck as she lays in the recovery room. I blink once, twice, Dad's face reappearing before me.

Imploring me now. "Chris, Chris! Snap out of it."

I mumble, the words making sense only to me. "Holy shit, that's it! Gotta get back there now! No time to waste."

$

Back at the 17$^{th}$ Precinct, Kev stares at me dumbfounded as I wave my hands wildly. "...Need to see the tapes, the tapes from Durand's lab."

"Whoa, slow down big guy. What tapes, where?"

I catch my breath, try to slow the barrage of images racing through my mind. *Gotta make sense of it so he can help me.*

I put a hand on Kennedy's shoulder. "When I went undercover at Durand's lab in Westchester... paranoid, had cameras everywhere, taped everything." My eyes beseech Kennedy, please understand.

"Okay, yeah, I remember."

"I gotta see the tapes, gotta get the answer once and for all."

§

I fast forward, then stop, then fast forward again. "It's not here. This all you got?"

Kennedy looks at the DVD's strewn across the table, at the images whirling by on the monitor before us. "Yeah, that's it, buddy. You've seen all eight discs. What're you looking for?"

I pause the image, sift frantically through the discs before me. *It's got to be here... six, seven, eight discs. Shit! Where is it?* "Where's the evidence log? Gotta be more than this."

Kennedy shakes his head. "Down in the cage. But O'Rourke said this is all of it."

My eyes dart between Kennedy and the discs. I bolt out of the conference room toward the cage. "Gotta be at least one more."

Kennedy chasing behind me, I hear him say, "What the fuck?"

§

Standing in front of O'Rourke, I wait a second for Kennedy to catch up. "Need to see the full log of Durand's evidence."

Kennedy nods to O'Rourke.

"All right. But I already gave you all the recordings we have."

I grab the list from O'Rourke, scanning down the

first page, the second, third. "Says you've got four other discs! Where are those?"

O'Rourke grabs the list from me. "Those cover the twenty-four hours before we busted him. I thought you just wanted the stuff from a couple of days be—"

"Get me those discs," I growl.

"Okay, okay. Gimme a sec."

Kennedy stares at me, cautious and perplexed. O'Rourke re-emerges with the discs, hands them to me in a clear plastic bag.

§

I burn through the first three discs; nothing of use there.

The room I was in that night was small, dark. My interaction with Michelle was limited to seeing her through closed-circuit television. No wonder I hadn't picked up on it then.

I hold the last disc up in my latex-gloved hand, turning it from side to side as Kennedy looks on. *Gotta be here*, I think. I cue it up, fast forwarding it through useless crap after useless crap—*Wait, there it is!* I rewind a minute or so. There I am, walking down a long hallway, blindfolded, iPod to my ears, Durand's men guiding me. The view switches over as we enter a small, dark room. They remove the blindfold and iPod. There before me, on CCTV, a woman I believed was Michelle. My thoughts and emotions from those moments surge through me as I study the recording. She wore the dress I gave her from Mother's Day. She looked like Michelle, but her mannerisms, were they forced, rehearsed? It was hard to tell. Come on, come on turn just a little bit. Give me the view I need. I hit pause as Kennedy looks on.

"Got something?"

I rewind slowly.

Yes! There it is! I study the image. Need to be one-hundred percent sure. The CCTV feed is a bit grainy, but I see what I need to. Relief washes over me. My head tilts back, my closed eyes facing skyward. I catch my breath for the first time in weeks it seems, hope finally and completely back in play.

No fucking way that woman, the woman killed hours later by the FBI, was Michelle. It's just not possible.

$

I rise from the chair, a huge smile on my face. "Kev, call over to Rikers. We need another crack at Durand."

"You serious?" he says in disbelief. "What'd you see on the tape?" He shakes his head. "What the hell am I gonna tell them this time?"

"Dunno; you'll figure something out." I slide the disc out of the player, secure it in its case and a plastic baggy. "Come on, we'll take my car. You can call on the way."

# ▸ Chapter 13 ◂

Tires screeching to a halt, I jump out of the Firebird in front of the Otis Bantum Correctional Center. As we hustle toward the entrance I glance at Kev and feel bad. Tried to fill him in on the drive over, but got way too emotional to continue. I swing open the front door, slamming it into the brick façade as we march across the threshold.

Within minutes Kennedy and I traverse the same dark and dreary corridors and check points we did days earlier.

We nod to the guards poised in front of the small room where Durand is being held.

One of them addresses Kennedy with intensity and begrudging respect. "You got some kind of pull, Detective. Not every day we gotta jump to attention, haul an inmate out of circulation like this." He looks at me with disgust. "And for a civy, no less."

Kennedy nods to the guards. "Appreciate it. We owe you one."

The guard nods back, opens the door, and waves his partner, then us, through the opening.

Hands and arms shackled, anchored to the floor, Durand sits across a table, a smug, satisfied look on his face. "So nice to see you again, dear Christopher." A thin smile stretches across his face. "Finally come to your senses?"

I'm determined to play it cooler this time around, to not let him bait me. "Something like that." Kennedy and I pull out our chairs, settle in across from The City's most notorious serial killer. "Tell me more about the genetic marker you placed in all your clones, how we can use it to prove the woman I buried wasn't Michelle."

Durand's smile fills out, transforming into a sneer. "It's so simple even a surgeon can understand." Durand licks at his lips. "I attached a small, meaningless strand of DNA to an X chromosome on each of my clones. I'm happy to share the sequence with you, if you'd like."

Kennedy cuts in, "X chromosome? What if the clone was a guy?"

Durand rolls his eyes toward the ceiling and lets out a pronounced sigh. "Why must I endure such inane ramblings?"

I put my hand on Kennedy's forearm. "Everyone has an X chromosome. Women have two, guys, one X and one Y."

Looking surprised Kennedy makes a quick recovery, juts his thumb toward Durand as he laughs. "So, dickhead here has what, three X's and a Y?"

Durand says, in a mocking tone as he lightly claps his hands, "How very droll, Detective. Perhaps tomorrow we'll move on to finger painting and potty training." Then directed at me, as if Kennedy were not even there, "Shall we continue?"

I wave my arm. "By all means. You were saying?"

"Take a sample of your beloved's DNA from a hairbrush, toothbrush, wherever. Compare the dead woman's X chromosomes to hers and—Viola!— proof positive they are not from the same person."

"Easy enough with the hairbrush, but we'd need to exhume the body for that sample." I tap my fingers on the desk and speak deliberately. "That part's going to be... awkward... more sensitive. We'd need to keep it on a need to know basis so the press doesn't get wind of it."

Durand waves his hand dismissively. "Really, Christopher. Why even bother exhuming the body? You already know I'm right."

My eyes narrow. Kennedy's dart between us. "How can you be so sure?" I say, staring back with a perfect poker face.

Durand just smiles.

Kennedy, confused: "Yeah, how are we so sure?"

I pull two sets of latex gloves out of my pocket,

tossing one pair to Kennedy as I slip on the others, then fish the disc out of my coat. Nodding to the guard. "Permission to cue it up?" Then to Kennedy, "Could you?"

As Kennedy readies the disc in the player, I pull my phone from my pocket, bringing up the photo I will need, before slipping it back in my pants.

Kennedy hands me the remote. "All set. Fire away."

And so I do, bringing the recording to the moment of truth and freezing it. I rise from the table, head over to the monitor. "Michelle and I talking in Durand's lab via CCTV. I remember this moment like it was yesterday. So many emotions at play, so hard to keep them in check." I look down at the floor, then back to Kennedy. "I thought I had lost her once already, would have overlooked anything so I could believe she was still alive."

Durand smiles. "I was counting on it."

"She looked like Michelle, acted like Michelle. But something... hard to put my finger on it... something was off. With a small, dark room, seeing her through the TV, I just didn't figure out what it was until a couple of hours ago." I shake my head, annoyed at myself for not realizing sooner. I didn't want to share all this, but I needed Kennedy to understand my rationale, to know I wasn't just a desperate man grasping at something that wasn't really there. "A few days ago I had a dream about Michelle. Pristine, her body perfect, untouched by everything you," pointing angrily at Durand now, "had done to her. She called out to me as if she needed my help." I glance down at my feet. "I chalked it up to a bout of self-torture, a longing for the way things used to be." I turn to Kennedy. "But Kev, you made a comment the other day in the car, something about we've all got enough scars and time to move on."

He nods. "Yeah, I remember."

"It unsettled me just like the dream. I thought it was because I had so much work ahead in rebuilding my life, but I see now there was more to it."

A smug look overtakes Durand's face again. "At long last, dear Christopher."

"Then it all clicked a couple of hours ago when the kids were roughhousing with my dad and scratched up his neck. As blood flowed from his wound, it all fell into place."

I walk over to the table, pull out my phone, open to the photo of Michelle with the kids dressed up for Halloween. I point to my phone as I hand it to Kennedy and head back to the monitor. "Take a good look at Michelle. What do you see?"

Kennedy looks at the photo, shrugs. "I don't know. It's Michelle. What am I looking for?"

"Look at her face, her chin, then bring your eyes down lower."

Kennedy shifts in the chair. "Gotta say, this is creeping me out a bit, like I'm stalking her or something."

I shake my head and laugh. "All right, look at her neck. What do you see?"

"The scar that this fucker gave her when he slit her throat. She's not wearing make-up like she usually does, uh did, so it's real obvious."

I turn and tap on the monitor, pointing to the same area on Michelle's neck. "No make-up here either. What do you see?"

"Holy shit! It's different, the scar's different."

"Exactly, like someone knew a scar belonged here, but couldn't figure out how to replicate it." I turn to Durand.

Durand nods in deference then heartedly claps his shackled hands, the chains clanging against each other. "Bravo, Detective, bravo! Your wife's scar was over three months old at that point. No way to mimic it on my clone even if I slit her throat too. There just wasn't time for the scar to age properly, to settle in the way your dear wife's had." Durand waves his hand again. "So we faked it, hoping you wouldn't notice."

I smile. "And I didn't—until now." I consider what all this means. "For once, Durand, you've been truthful with us, at least about this woman," tapping hard on the monitor now, "not being Michelle." My face hardens. "But can we believe you hold the key to the Malekoviec case, to getting Michelle back alive, if she's alive? The FBI attack in which someone was killed happened less than twenty-four hours after this video. Plenty of time to switch out the clone for Michelle, though I'm at a loss for why you would want to do that."

Kennedy looks at Durand as it dawns on him. "Michelle was your insurance policy, in case you were caught."

Durand's eyes narrow as he ignores Kennedy. "What other choice do you have, dear doctor-detective, but to believe me about it all?" He licks his lips again. "But go ahead, exhume the body so your precious little heart and mind are put at ease. But move quickly. Michelle will not be safe much longer and you can be sure Malekoviec's killer will strike again soon." Durand's eyes blaze now. "Spring me or watch the bodies pile up again. Which will it be, Detective?"

My eyes fixate on Kennedy's. A madman's demanding release so he can free my wife and help us catch a killer. But I'm on the outside of this investigation looking in. How the hell can we make this work?

# ▷ Chapter 14 ◁

"**Y**ou want me to get a court order for her disinterment based on the ramblings of a sociopath and a picture on your phone? Are you guys out of your mind?" New York County Assistant District Attorney Kiernan Byrne shakes his fiery red head violently back and forth. "Right or wrong, the press will be on this like piranhas, and Jackman—holy shit!—Jackman'll be all over my ass too."

I speak up. "Which is why they can't know anything about it, at least not till we have this all figured out."

Byrne leans back in his chair, exhales as if he were smoking a cigar. "This is a hell of a tall order, Chris."

Kennedy chips in. "What's the alternative? We do nothing while the real Michelle is alive and in danger?" He looks at me. "Maybe gets killed? That story breaks you've got a hell of a lot more problems than with exhuming the body."

178

Byrne pulls a keepsake out of his pocket, a 1964 John F. Kennedy half dollar. He rubs it between his thumb and forefinger as he ponders Kevin Kennedy's words. I look on, helpless, knowing we've got no chance of moving forward, no chance of finding Michelle, without this.

Byrne is deep in thought as the coin rolls between his fingers. *This is nuts. He's buried her twice already.* The ADA avoids eye contact with me, staring at Kennedy instead. *Still, if there's a chance….* The coin stops rolling and Byrne leans forward. "There's a judge who owes me a favor. I'll get the order from him and lay pressure on Gate of Heaven to keep it quiet and move quickly." He slips the silver dollar back into his pocket. "I'll call McGowan myself, tell her to expect the body by later today and to work on it immediately." He shakes his head side to side now. "I sure hope you two know what the fuck you're doing. Now get out of here."

The last twenty-four hours have been a blur, my insides a wreck. Twice in the last two months I thought Michelle was dead and buried and tried to move on. Now there's hope, but deep wounds torn wide open are the price I pay for it. It's a frigid December day, a light frost gathered on the hard ground as Kennedy, Dad, and I stand at the grave, one worker poised behind the controls of a small backhoe while two others standby with shovels.

Kennedy nods toward the backhoe. "You really think you need that thing? This ain't a construction site."

The worker nods as chilled air escapes his lips. "The ground is frozen solid. Only way we can break through."

Kennedy waves him off. "Do what you got to do. Let's just make it quick, huh?"

Moments later the digging bucket tears into the earth, rending my heart as well.

Dad, Kennedy, and I stand by stone-faced, a stiff wind battering our faces as the ground gives way before us.

A few minutes later steel shovel strikes solid oak coffin. One of the workers with a shovel shouts to the other, "Careful. We're there now."

The two men spend the next five minutes clearing dirt all around the coffin, then bring another piece of heavy machinery in to lift it up and lay it on the ground next to us. At this point the workers pull back, knowing the next task is all mine. Poised by the casket I take a deep breath, saying a silent prayer as I lift the cover. I tell myself to be strong, that the body is not hers. But the tears well up as I stare at her face, thankful the weeks underground, embalmed and sealed in a sturdy casket, have not changed it much. I raise my hand to my mouth, ready to pull my thick black glove off with my teeth, but then decide no. The wind whistles through the trees now, scattering the last of the remaining leaves. I put one hand in front of my face, shielding it from the dirt and dust that swirls around me. With the other I reach out for the hair draped over her neck and tentatively push it off to the side.

A smile bursts across my face.

The scar is not Michelle's.

# FORBIDDEN CURE 4

## HESITANT HOPE

# ▷ Chapter 1 ◁

Perfunctory greetings behind us, McGowan stares through the oculars of her powerful electron microscope. My assessment of the dead woman's scar lifted my spirits, but we need *proof* to push the investigation forward. On the left side of the slide, both of Michelle's X chromosomes, painstakingly extracted from a sample I provided from her hairbrush. On the right, the same chromosomes taken from the corpse's hair.

I tread lightly. "What do you see, Doctor McGowan?"

Her head still, eyes darting between the samples. "Nothing definitive, I'm afraid."

Kennedy: "How could that be? Durand said the clone's X chromosome; it'd be longer than Michelle's, right?"

"By only about one hundred base pairs, I'm afraid," she replies. "An X chromosome is about one hundred fifty-five million base pairs long. Even at this resolution, that small a difference is hard to discern."

Kennedy shakes his head. "Shit."

McGowan, undeterred, lifts her head from the scope. "Not a problem. The high rate of crime in our city makes rapid sequencing of DNA a priority." She looks at the large clock on the wall. "And I started that processing almost an hour ago." McGowan offers the rarest of her facial expressions—a smile. "It should be done by now. Let's have a look at the reading."

I hold my breath as McGowan, her smile already gone, strides confidently across her lab and presses a series of buttons on the sequencer. "We won't need a complete printout of each sample, just a summary of base pairs per strand and the sequencing of any differences between the two."

Tension fills the space between us as she grabs the printout and looks it over, checking it against the sequence information Durand provided us for his clone.

The smile again. "The decreased is a clone, Chris, not your Michelle."

I fall forward, hands catching me on her lab bench. A sweet, intoxicating warmth spreads throughout my body, culminating in my face. Leaning back, Kennedy embraces me as I call out to McGowan, "Oh my God, thank you, Doctor! Thank you so much."

§

"*Twice* Durand's made us think he killed Michelle. This doesn't prove she's still alive, but at least we've got hope now," I say as I regain my composure and fill McGowan in on our conversation with Durand and his most unusual request. "We've got some heavy lifting ahead of us. DNA results are definitive to you and me, Doctor, but we need something else to support it, something tangible the DA's office will find irrefutable."

McGowan nods, the smile more subdued, controlled now. "I'll see what I can find with the autopsy."

I turn to Kennedy, ready to charge out the door toward the precinct, but McGowan's words halt us. "So, does this mean you're back with the NYPD, Doctor Ravello?"

A broad smile fills my face, then spreads to Kennedy's as well. I give a quick nod. "Damn straight, Doctor." Then I explode through the door.

# ▷ Chapter 2 ◁

Heading north on First Avenue, I make a quick left at 29th Street, then another to put us on Second Avenue heading south.

"What're you doing, bud? Precinct's the other way."

"I know. But I've got someone to see first about getting my old job back."

Kennedy smiles. "That you do, my friend. What are you waiting for? Step on it!"

§

Diana D's face fills with a sincere smile as I approach her desk. I respond in kind. "How are you, Diana? Is Commissioner Kelly in?"

She glances at Kennedy with a knowing smile, then offers me a wink. "Why yes, Chris, and he's expecting you."

I give Kennedy a look of feigned annoyance. "Oh really?"

He shrugs, then plants himself on the corner of her desk. While Kennedy and Diana flirt, I head through the door, entering the office of one of the most powerful men in The City.

John Kelly, a tough, crewcut man in his fifties, sits behind his desk, tapping his fingertips lightly against each other. Business-like, he says, "Have a seat, Chris. To what do I owe the pleasure?"

Sitting down, I get right to it. "I want my old job back, sir."

His eyes are like liquid steel, his jaw a block of concrete. "Really? I don't think we can accommodate your request. The position's already been filled."

I pull my head back and blink my eyes a few times, then point my thumb behind me. "Detective Kennedy's right outside. I'm sure he wouldn't mind."

"That may be, Chris, but it's not Chief Kennedy's call, it's mine." His steely eyes bear down on me as he leans forward. "And we can't have detectives going off the deep end, resigning one minute, only to come back a few weeks later, begging for their jobs back."

"Er, I'm not begging, sir, and I understand if this raises some issues for the department. I just thought..."

Kelly pulls his drawer open and in one motion grabs something and tosses it my way. *What the hell?*

He leans back, laughing deeply as my detective shield lands in front of me. "You need to sharpen your people-reading skills, *Chief* Ravello." He slides my gun and ID across the table as well.

"Knew you'd be back, Chris. That's why I never even filed your resignation papers." A faint smile appears on his face as he winks at me. "You've been on unpaid administrative leave these last few weeks."

I smile self-consciously as I reach for my gun. "Thank you very much, sir."

Kelly moves forward, blocking my hand. "Not so fast. There's one condition for reinstatement."

"Oh. What's that, sir?"

His eyes are piercing, the humor nowhere to be seen. "Your ass is mine, Chris. They'll be no more heartfelt speeches about how tough it is, no more resigning when the going gets rough, just damn fine police work and unwavering dedication." He extends a hand to me. "Agreed?"

A smile engulfs my face as I shake his hand heartily. "Agreed, sir."

Kelly releases his grip and nods his head. A beat goes by in silence, then two. "Well, what are you waiting for, Detective? The criminals don't catch themselves."

"Yes, sir. I'll get right on it."

# ⟩ Chapter 3 ⟨

I turn to Kennedy as I pull into a parking space at the 17th precinct. "This happened real fast. You okay with me taking my old job back?"

Kennedy's head arches back. "Hell yeah! Was never real comfortable as chief—too much medical crap to sort through." He punches my shoulder. "And now I can get the hell away from Simmons at last!"

I smile as we climb out of the car and head into the precinct.

Exiting the elevator on the third floor, I pause at the double doors ahead. The Job is as challenging as they come. Long hours filled with anxiety, stress, and frustration—and the deepest feeling of pride and satisfaction I've ever known when a case breaks right and we put a killer away for good. Kennedy pulls up. "We good?"

I nod with confidence. "Never better. Let's do this."

§

Kennedy holds his hands up high, yells over the racket that is the 17th precinct. "Listen up! We got an important announcement."

I step forward as the racket dies down and the men all turn their attention to me. "I'll keep it short and sweet everybody. Thank you for your understanding these last few weeks as I sorted things out in the wake of Michelle's death." I scan the crowd, making eye contact with many. "We've got the best damn group of law enforcement personnel anywhere. I'm very proud to be back as your chief."

Kennedy smiles broadly, slapping me on the back as my men erupt with applause and shouts of congratulations. I soak it all in for a few seconds, their energy reinvigorating me. I nod to Kennedy, then turn back to the crowd. "All right, let's get back to work. I know I've got a lot to get caught up on."

I make eye contact with Simmons as we approach my old desk. His face is a mixture of sadness and relief as he gathers his things up. "No hurry on that, Simmons."

"That's okay, Chief, I almost got it all. Good to have you back."

As Simmons slinks off, I settle in to my old chair as

Kennedy does the same. "All right, Kev, fill me in on every last detail of the investigation so far."

# ⊳ Chapter 4 ⊲

"No shit? When are these pictures from?" I say.

"Last night. Had the new guy, Miller, trail Gorelick and this is what he came up with."

I spread the photos across my desk as Kennedy pulls up a chair. "Walk me through it."

Kennedy points to a close-up of Gorelick's dinner companion. "Dmitri Korsakov. He's Irina Malekoviec's brother. Owns a bunch of dry-cleaning stores as a front. Real business is laundering money and taking action on sports teams for the Russian mob's high-net-worth clientele."

"So what's he doing at dinner with Gorelick? The doc owe him some money? Maybe he's pissed at what happened to Irina?"

"Or he's congratulating him."

"What?"

"Kerline St. James said Dmitri'd stop by the office a lot to chew Gorelick out. Jives with what Todd Zigler said, that the doc was heavily in debt to a Russian bookie."

"Okay."

"Miller poked around a bit. One of our snitches told him Dmitri might have tapped Gorelick to get rid of Irina in exchange for forgiving his gambling debts."

"That's one cold-hearted son-of-a-bitch, taking out his sister." I shake my head. "And the doc, he'd have to be all kinds of desperate to kill one of his own patients."

"According to the snitch, Dmitri didn't have a choice; mob offed her husband for having a big mouth. Between that and Irina having a fallout with Dmitri over the hit, the higher ups got nervous. They ordered her whacked, decided to test Dmitri's loyalty by having him arrange it." Kennedy nods. "And get this; Miller's snitch tells him Gorelick was close to six figures deep into the mob."

I whistle and shake my head. "Miller overhear anything at the dinner?"

"Naw, couldn't get close enough."

I smile at Kev. "Looks like we need to pay Dmitri and the dear doctor a visit, eh, Detective?"

Kev smiles broadly. "My thoughts exactly, partner."

# ⊳ Chapter 5 ⊲

"You make it a habit to dine with known mobsters, Doc?" Kennedy asks as I study Gorelick's expression.

"Last I checked, Mr. Korsakov is in the dry-cleaning business, detectives."

"So, what, you were discussing how you like your shirts cleaned?"

We had been at it ten minutes and were getting nowhere with this approach. Time for a different tack. "So Doctor Gorelick, you were one of the last people to see Dmitri's sister alive." I pull out photos of Dmitri and Gorelick laughing over drinks and lay them across his desk. "He doesn't seem too broken up about his sister's death. Why's that?"

"You would have to ask him, Detective. We all have our ways of grieving. Now, if you'll excuse—"

"Not so fast, Doctor. Why were you out with Dmitri?"

Gorelick sighs deeply. "Dmitri took a great interest in his sister's well-being, including paying for her care when the insurers rejected her treatments as experimental. I would meet with him from time to time to discuss her progress. Last night Dmitri expressed his gratitude to me for working so tirelessly on his sister's behalf."

Kennedy and I nod, unconvinced. I pull a copy of Irina's medicals out of my briefcase and place them on his near-barren desk. "Fair to say Irina's records accurately reflect the care you provided her?"

"Of course, Detective. Questions?"

I flip through pages on the left side of her chart. "Irina's medication was hand delivered to you on both occasions by Kiki Aloni from Doctor Hyslop's office?"

A bored look on his face, Gorelick nods as he points to the chart. "Yes. Sally in my office received the first treatment at 1:12 p.m. on Tuesday, December 8th. The treatment was administered to Ms. Malekoviec at 9:30 the following morning. The second dose was received Monday the 14th at 1:34 p.m. and the treatment given the following morning."

"Who handled the medication between when Sally received it and you administered it the following day? Where and how was it stored?"

"We have a refrigerator devoted exclusively to

storing medications. Sally, my nurse, Jane, and I are the only ones with access codes to it. The medication remained stored in the refrigerator until Jane brought it to me just before the treatment. Medicines are logged in and out, and there is a permanent electronic record of when each of us accesses the refrigerator. You see here? That's Jane's signature, five minutes before I administered the doses."

"Was Ms. Aloni always the one who delivered Hyslop's meds to you? Were the deliveries always early afternoon the day before a patient treatment?"

"As far as I recall. Sally can show you the records if you like. Now, if—"

Kennedy interjects, "Quite the gambler, aren't you, Doc?"

"Pardon me?"

"Word has it you like it all: football, basketball, baseball, even the ponies." Kennedy looks around Gorelick's swanky office, expensive artwork and sculptures accenting the space. "Amazing you can afford such a place. Must be a lot better doctor than you are a gambler."

Gorelick's face hardens as he folds his hands over his chest. "I have patients waiting for me, Detective. So I'll have to ask you to leave."

Kennedy places both hands on Gorelick's desk as he rises from his chair. He towers over Gorelick. "Looks like you're gonna be running behind, Doc, 'cause we got a lot of ground to cover."

Gorelick's face pales as he leans away from Kennedy. "Very, very well. Let's make this as quick as we can."

Kev smiles as he sits back down and flexes his hands. "We're waiting...."

Gorelick adjusts his shirt collar. "Well, yes, Mr. Korsakov does take wagers from me on various sporting events."

"How much you currently in to him for?"

"Nothing, actually. We reached a barter arrangement regarding his sister's care."

Kennedy stares back at Gorelick. "You sure it wasn't some other kind of bartering going on?"

Gorelick squeezes his hands together. "I'm afraid I don't follow."

Kennedy flips open his notepad, reads from it. "Sources tell me you owed Dmitri almost a hundred grand recently and that the Russian mob wanted his sister offed. Strange coincidence she's suddenly dead and your debt has been forgiven."

I watch sweat trickle down Gorelick's face. "That's absurd, Detective! I would never kill a patient, no matter what the situation."

Good, we're getting to him. "Tell me how Ms. Malekoviec was referred to you and about the care you provided for her."

"Ah, yes, well, she had been unsuccessfully treated by a rheumatologist near where she lives, er, lived.

NSAID's, steroids, even gold injections had proven fruitless." Gorelick taps his fingers on the desk. "The doctor, oh, what was his name? His treatments were outdated, and it wasn't he who referred Ms. Malekoviec."

"Who was it?" I ask.

"A former piano student of hers who now works at Doctor Hyslop's lab. He had kept in touch with her over the years and was kind enough to make the referral. Our lab works directly with Todd a lot."

Kennedy interjects, "Todd Zigler?" He looks at me, then back to Gorelick. "He took lessons from Malekoviec?"

"Yes, that's right. Ms. Malekoviec spoke very highly of Todd. Apparently, he was a very talented pianist prior to his scientific career." Gorelick adjusts his tie and swallows. "Todd is a very able technician and runs Doctor Hyslop's studies. Our offices share a great number of patients, so we've gotten to know Todd very well."

"No hard feelings when Todd pilfered one of your workers?" Kennedy asks.

"Ms. St. James? No. No hard feelings. She never really fit into the office culture. I was actually glad to see her accept a position elsewhere."

"I'll bet. One less employee to pursue sexual harassment and assault charges against you."

Gorelick's eyes shift away from us, running across

the chart on his desk, over to the phone poised in the corner. "Yes, that was quite unfortunate. Ms. St. James certainly has an active imagination. From what I understand, I'm not the first she's leveled such charges against."

"How would you know that?" I ask.

"My attorney. It came up when he checked into her background."

"So you deny harassing and attacking her?"

"Most definitely."

Kennedy takes the lead again. "What about her other charges?"

Confusion on Gorelick's face. "What other charges?"

Kennedy ticks off the accusations. "You have a drinking problem. Dmitri and you frequently meet behind closed doors here with a lot of yelling, and your staff can't stand you."

Gorelick's face reddens. "That's absurd!" Gorelick balls up his fists. "I'll sue her for slander."

Kennedy again: "Whoa, pipe down, Doc. She's not broadcasting any of this, just shared it with yours truly during an interview."

Gorelick stares back in silence.

I cut back in. "Any idea what killed Irina?"

"No, Detective. All of the treatments she received in our office seemed to have no discernible effect, including the last one. I was shocked to learn she died just hours after I treated her."

"Where do you keep the results of all the studies you're involved with?" I ask. "I don't see a computer anywhere."

"And you won't," Gorelick says with conceit. "Damn things just make life more difficult. My girls up front take care of all my data entry." He chuckles, "The hospital has been pressuring me for years to use electronic records but I like the feel and ease of a real chart in my hands. I'm happy to say I haven't even given them the satisfaction of learning how to type. Now, if there's nothing more?"

Kennedy taps his notepad on the desk as he looks at me. I reach for my card. "Thank you for your time, Doctor. Please give me a call if you think of anything else."

§

"What'd you think?" I ask as Kennedy and I crawl through mid-day, NYC traffic.

"Guy's got more skeletons in his closet than Party City at Halloween. We keep digging we're bound to find a smoking gun."

I nod my head in agreement. "Dmitri or McGowan?"

"Dmitri. Let's strike while the iron is hot."

"Dmitri it is. We got someone on Aloni and Limerock, right?"

"Yeah, Simmons and McCarthy. We're stretched

thin, but want me to put a tail on St. James and Gore-lick too?"

"Not yet." I stomp down on the accelerator. "Let's see what we find out with Dmitri first."

# ▷ Chapter 6 ◁

Kennedy holds out a crisp twenty-dollar bill. "This what yours looks like when you're done, Dmitri?" he says with a laugh.

Dmitri stares back at the detectives, unamused. "Why don't we discuss this outside, gentlemen?"

Kennedy looks at me. "Little chilly. Inside works better for us."

I nod my approval.

"As you wish. Follow me." The stout man with the block head turns toward the dry-cleaning racks behind him and trudges off, a tank trampling anything in its path.

Kennedy and I sidestep the counter and follow Dmitri through a rack of winter coats, down a narrow, dark hallway, to his office.

Korsakov waves us to seats across from an old, beat-up desk. "What brings you here today, detectives?"

Kennedy lays the photos of Gorelick and Dmitri at dinner across his desk. "You seem pretty chummy with the doc who might've killed your sister."

Dmitri's expression doesn't change as he turns his eyes to the photos, one-by-one. "Your point?"

Kennedy turns my way. "Somebody offs my sister, I'd be pretty broken up about it, not laughing it up with her killer."

"Me too," I say. "But to be fair, neither of us is Russian." I shrug. "Maybe it's a cultural thing."

"Doctor Gorelick did not kill my sister, gentlemen. In fact, we were celebrating her life and the exceptional care he provided her toward the end of it."

I pull out a photo of the deceased, her widespread hemorrhages on full display, and lay it on the desk. "This what you call great care? Looks like a pretty painful way to go."

Dmitri, reigning in his anger, picks up the photo and studies it, then puts it back down. "Anything else?"

I nod my head. "Yes, plenty. Fill us in on why almost a hundred thousand dollars in Doctor Gorelick's gambling debts were forgiven around the same time your sister bought it?"

Kev chimes in. "Family issues are one thing but bounty-hunting your sister... not cool."

Korsakov leans back, folding his hands across his stomach. "And why would I want my own sister dead, detectives?"

"Keep the peace with your associates. Seems they were concerned about what she knew about your operations," I offer.

Dmitri leans his head back and bellows. "Dry-cleaning business? What could be worth killing over? A lost blouse? Poorly pressed jacket?"

"You know what business we're talking about, Dmitri. The kind that launders money for the Russian mob and takes sports action for wealthy clients."

Dmitri's face turns cold as he leans forward, menacing, one hand poised on the desk. "No idea what you are talking about, detectives."

Kennedy leans forward, his size dwarfing Dmitri's. "We're not here on any of that, boss. Just fill us in about your relationship with Gorelick and your sister."

"Doctor Gorelick took over Irina's care after one of the neighborhood doctors could no longer help her." He rubs a meaty paw against his chin. "Unfortunately, Doctor Gorelick's treatments, despite their sophistication, seemed equally ineffective."

"And costly," I add. "Heard the insurance company wouldn't cover most of it."

"True. But business is good, so I helped pay the bills."

"Heard you and Irina had a falling out after husband Vlad turned up in a dumpster. How'd you keep up on her treatments?"

"Gorelick and I would meet from time to time, discuss her progress, take care of her expenses."

"And Irina didn't have a problem with that?"

"Irina was a practical woman." Dmitri nods. "She knew I paid for her care and would demand updates."

Kennedy cuts in, "What caused the rift with you and Irina?"

Dmitri taps his fingertips together. "She did not approve of my recent business dealings and thought my associates may have killed her husband."

"Did they?" I ask.

"Who is to say? Vlad and I were on different ends of the business. My brother-in-law was a good man, took great care of Irina after her career abruptly ended, but he had a big mouth." Dmitri shakes his head. "Not a good attribute for our kind of business."

"So your mobster buddies order the hit on Irina to keep her quiet too," Kennedy interjects.

Dmitri laughs. "You've been watching too many mob movies, Detective. Irina knew her place. She would never betray any of our interests and everyone knew that." He thrusts his hand toward the outside. "You should be out looking for her real killer." A confident sneer stretches across his face. "Not harassing an honest business man."

I laugh. "Tell us about how Irina was referred to Gorelick. Was that you, her previous doctor, or what?"

"Neither. Irina kept in touch with a few of her students. One worked for a lab, referred Irina to Gorelick, said he was doing great things." Sarcasm fills his voice as he pretends to play the piano effeminately. "Maybe he's your killer."

Kennedy smirks. "Yeah, we'll keep that in mind, boss. So what else can you tell us about Irina, her life, who might have wanted her dead?"

"Irina's world centered around her music. Performing, touring, recording." He shakes his head. "When that was taken away, she became a recluse. She had few friends outside of music and no enemies I know of."

Kennedy taps his notepad on his leg, looks at me. I nod. Kennedy says, "That'll do it for today, Mr. Korsakov. We'll be in touch if we have additional questions."

Dmitri nods to the detectives as they rise and head out of his office. He waits a minute to be sure they are gone, then pulls out his cell phone. "We may have a problem we need to deal with...."

§

Barreling out of Little Odessa, back toward The City, I turn to Kennedy. "What'd you make of Gorelick, Dmitri?"

"Stories fit together too well. Definitely worth taking a closer look at both of them."

"Yeah. Can't see Dmitri pulling off killing his sister without Gorelick's help, 'specially the way it went down." I weave the Firebird through heavy traffic on Ocean Parkway heading north toward the Brooklyn-Queens Expressway. "Gotta comb through everything again back at the station, see if anything pops out now that we know more." I smile, anticipating what we may learn at our next stop. "Meantime, off to McGowan's."

# ▷ Chapter 7 ◁

The killer swirls the red wine around in the glass, eyeing it with interest before taking a long sip and leaning back on the couch. The cabernet goes down smoothly at first, but a bitter aftertaste soon kicks in. Much like recent events. Irina's murder served its purpose and was carried out flawlessly. So why was there no great feeling of satisfaction and relief?

Because of the police.

These NYPD detectives were proving more formidable and troublesome than expected. A year and a half ago detectives investigated a trio of deaths linked to Hyslop's lab. The murderer expected the police would now reach the same conclusion in short order as they did then; Irina's death was accidental, due to the vagaries of a complex medication and its unpredictable interaction with the immune system. So why didn't they?

There was no evidence to spur the investigation on. No fingerprints, hair fibers, or bodily fluids. No clear motive for the killing. The deceased was a loner widow with few friends and no known enemies. No family members cried out for justice, and there was no political motivation to solve the crime. Hell, Irina's death didn't even appear to be a crime! So why were they making such a big deal of it? Why didn't they just move on to other, more pressing cases and leave this one alone?

With a shake of the head, the killer exhales in frustration and takes another swig of the dreadful drink. The wine's harshness overwhelms the murderer's taste buds as the bitter truth becomes evident—one murder won't be enough. No, not by a long shot. A new plan needs to be improvised, one that makes the police suspicious of someone else.

The killer slams the glass on the coffee table, breaking it. A glass shard pierces the killer's forefinger. Blood mixes with spilled red wine and drips from the killer's hand, pooling on the table.

Yes, the sooner the next victim dies, the better.

# ▷ Chapter 8 ◁

The early morning sun splashes through the windows at Doctor Hyslop's lab as his technicians work tirelessly at their craft.

"Todd, how is the Ravello reformulation coming along?" Hyslop asks.

"Great, boss. We're about halfway through," Todd says, his voice cracking. "Should be ready for quality testing in two days."

Hyslop folds his hands in front of him at the workbench, leaning his chin on them. "Excellent! That formulation is all that stands between Ravello and a cure. Let's do our best to assure the doctor-detective gets everything he deserves with that final treatment."

Hyslop turns to his left, toward a long work bench buzzing with activity.

"Kerline, where are we on Jamal Richards' compound? Gorelick needs that by later today."

"Just finish up wid de testin' on it. Ought to fix 'im real good."

Hyslop nods, a smile on his face. "Excellent work everyone. Another red-letter day for our lab." He starts clapping. "Give yourselves a big round of applause. All your hard work is making a huge difference in the world."

# ▷ Chapter 9 ◁

Jane smiles at the disheveled man-child before her, his underwear sticking out of his pants' tops, Yankees cap turned to the side. "All ready for your second treatment?"

Jamal flexes his biceps. "Hell yeah. Wanna be feeling stronger! Do me up good."

Shanteel rolls her eyes toward the ceiling. "Why you be getting all gangsta? Take it down a notch, brother."

Jane smiles again as she arranges the syringe and other supplies on the Mayo stand, then excuses herself. "I'll be back with Doctor Gorelick in a minute."

Jamal makes a hulk pose for Shanteel as she laughs. "So strong, baby. Gonna conquer the world!"

"Whatever. Just don't pass out again, baby."

The door swings open, Gorelick entering, chart in hand, with Jane right behind. Gorelick smiles at Jamal through his thick glasses as Jane attaches EKG leads to Jamal's arms and chest. "All ready, Jamal?"

"Never been better, Doc. Fire away."

Gorelick leans forward, cleaning Jamal's forearm with an alcohol pad, then betadine. Jamal winces. "Are you okay? Just cleaning the skin. No needle yet."

Jamal, his skin paler, squeezes Shanteel's hand hard. "I'm good. Let's get it done, man."

Gorelick pops the cap off the syringe. He taps it, releasing the air bubbles, then holds the needle just above the vein in Jamal's left forearm. An odd smile fills Gorelick's face as he pierces the skin. "Happy to oblige, Jamal. Always happy to oblige."

# ▷ Chapter 10 ◁

"Your theory was spot on, Doctor Ravello. Microscopic analysis and immunofluorescence testing confirm the skin lesions, widespread organ damage, and the glomerulonephritis were all caused by immune complex deposition."

The words are music to my ears. Kennedy's? Not so much.

"What the hell?" he grumbles as we stand over Malekoviec's body with Doctor McGowan.

I translate for Kennedy. "It's like I thought. The damage to Irina's blood vessels was due to a very intense response by her immune system, most likely due to the treatment she was receiving from Doctor Gorelick."

"So her body attacked itself?" he says in disbelief.

"Yes, which happens all the time, but not usually to this extent. Irina's RA was due to her immune system attacking her finger joints. The treatment she was receiving was an attempt to fix that."

"But instead of quieting down her immune system, it ramped it up and damaged blood vessels throughout her body?"

McGowan smiles, impressed. "Precisely, Detective Kennedy." She turns to me. "And you ascertained this from just a few photos Detective Kennedy provided you?"

Blushing a little, I say, "And Irina's labs from just before her treatments. I noticed her kidney function deteriorating between injections, which supported my theory that immune complex deposition killed her."

"What the hell is 'immune complex deposition' and how'd it kill our vic?" Kennedy asks with frustration.

I take a deep breath as I think about how to spell it out for him. "Irina's treatment was supposed to stop her body from producing the antibodies that attacked her finger joints."

"Okay..."

"But it didn't do that."

"So, what did it do?"

I rub my chin, choosing my words carefully. "The medicine stimulated Irina's body to make *more* antibodies. Then it bound to the antibodies, inactivating them. We call the medicine-antibody pairing, immune complexes. Follow?"

"Yeah. But I'm confused. If the medicine killed all

the harmful antibodies, that should be a good thing, right? So why'd Irina die?" Kennedy says with a shake of his head.

"Because these immune complexes were so big and so numerous they damaged the blood vessels throughout Irina's body before her body could get rid of them."

Kennedy nods as he excitedly jabs his index finger at me. "And those damaged blood vessels lead to all the bleeding in her skin?"

McGowan intercedes. "Yes, Detective. And the same process destroyed many of Irina's organs, including her kidneys, by cutting off their blood supply. When her kidneys stopped working, it caused her to have a massive, fatal heart attack."

"Got it. So why would the treatment do that?" Kennedy asks, puzzled.

I turn to McGowan, who shakes her head. "I'm afraid we may never know the answer. All the compound was used in treating Ms. Malekoviec, leaving none for analysis."

"We could have Hyslop's lab prepare another sample and study that," I offer. "But if Irina's medication was tainted to kill her, examining an unaltered sample will be pointless."

McGowan nods again. "Agreed."

Kennedy chimes in. "One thing's for sure. This isn't your run-of-the-mill case of poisoning. We're dealing with a knowledgeable, sophisticated killer."

"With an in-depth understanding of chemistry and immunology and access to the medication."

Kennedy scratches his chin. "But where's the motive? Our vic barely interacted with anyone day-to-day the last few months, except her students."

McGowan intercedes. "I'll leave the police work in your able hands. As for the other reason for your visit, follow me."

We walk over to another stainless-steel table. McGowan pulls the drape down, revealing Michelle's clone's face and neck. An involuntary shudder rips through me before I catch myself.

"I read through the OR records from Bellevue that described the wounds your wife suffered, Doctor Ravello, and how they were repaired." She holds up the records. "Durand's knife transected multiple muscles in the neck, including the..."

I put my hand up. "Can we skip the details, Doctor McGowan, and jump ahead to the conclusions?"

"Certainly. I'm sure Detective Kennedy would appreciate that," she says with a chuckle. "Where was I? Oh, yes. The knife cut through a number of muscles in the neck and transected various branches of the right jugular vein." McGowan puts down Michelle's medical records and picks up a small, metallic wand and points it at the scar on the corpse's right neck. "This scar extends through epidermis, dermis, and connective tissue only, never reaching the muscles and vasculature below." She lifts the corpse's hair and turns its head, revealing a patch of missing skin behind the ear. "In fact, the scar isn't a scar at all. A superficial wound was created on the neck. Skin was taken from behind the clone's ear, fashioned into the shape of a scar, and secured in place by a surgical adhesive."

"Like some kind of reverse skin graft?" I ask. "One used to create a scar, instead of eliminating it?"

"Precisely, Detective."

McGowan glances at Kennedy, his face awash in confusion.

"This scar isn't Michelle's, just a superficial likeness."

Relief washes over me as a smile fills my face. "Thank God!" I reach out and shake her hand. "And you too of course, Doctor."

§

A full minute goes by before I can even speak again, joy and hope overwhelming me. Finally, I gather myself. "The scar and DNA prove this isn't my Michelle." I turn to Kennedy. "You and I need to meet with Byrne again if we've got any chance of getting Michelle back."

<h1 style="text-align:center">› Chapter 11 ‹</h1>

Kiki Aloni looks both ways before entering the hotel. She smiles at the desk clerk as she receives the key to room 313, then trudges over to the elevator. *No choice but to act like nothing's happened. Can't afford to rouse Grayson's suspicions.*

Detective Simmons waits for the elevator doors to close, then enters the lobby and makes a beeline for the clerk, flashing his badge. "What room did you check Ms. Aloni into?"

"Uh, 313, Detective."

Simmons peppers the young woman with questions, then finds an inconspicuous seat with a view of the elevator.

Ten minutes pass before Limerock strides confidently into the hotel lobby, his flirtatious smile masking troubling thoughts as he checks into the room for his dalliance with Kiki. She's a good lay and an excellent conduit for information key to carrying out his plans, but she is far more resourceful than he bargained for. Drugging him and accessing his computer? He would have never guessed her capable of it. He chuckles. *Just adds to the intrigue and always up for that.* Grayson runs a hand through his slicked-back hair as he exits the elevator on the third floor and strolls toward the room. *Once I've destroyed Hyslop's lab, I'll deal with her.* He raps his knuckles on the door, Kiki greeting him a moment later wearing a snug teddy and a provocative smile.

"Well, don't you look ravishing?" he blurts out. Kiki bats her lashes at him, then in a sultry voice as she pulls him in, "Best way to put you under my spell."

Detective McCarthy, who tailed Limerock to the hotel, spots Simmons and settles in next to him, their faces shielded by newspapers they're pretending to read. Simmons puts his paper down, blows his nose, then returns the handkerchief to his pants, shielding himself again with the paper. "No telling how long or how short they'll be."

McCarthy masks his disgust. "Aye. We've got to be on our toes. I'll check with the front desk, see if this is a daily meet or what."

"All ready did that. Limerock and Aloni are a regular item here, at least a few times a week." Simmons peers over his paper at the elevator door before settling back in. Half, then a full hour passes, the detectives growing restless.

Simmons: "For a quickie, sure seem to be taking their time."

"Aye. Think they're exchanging more than bodily fluids?" McCarthy says with a wink.

Simmons nods. "All sorts of secrets given away during pillow talk, I'll bet." His eyes narrow as the elevator doors slide open. "And maybe other types of fluids being swapped as well." Out pops Kiki Aloni, donning Jackie-O-style sunglasses and a black, full-length coat. Simmons masks himself with the paper, then peels off a safe distance behind her as she exits the building.

Minutes later McCarthy repeats the exercise with a bright-eyed, confident Grayson. Eventually, he settles into a Starbucks in the lobby of Grayson's office building, in full view of the elevator banks.

# ▷ Chapter 12 ◁

"What time'd they go in?" I ask Simmons.

"'Bout ten-forty-five for her."

"Good ten minutes before I trailed Grayson there," McCarthy interjects.

"Same on the way out, her first, then him later." Simmons nods.

"Like a well-orchestrated plan," I say.

"Aye," McCarthy exclaims. "Clerk says they're there more than a wee bit, always room 313."

Simmons cuts in. "Always an hour, hour ten."

My hand reflexively rubs my chin. "Odd how ritualized they are. But it's a break for us."

Kennedy shifts at his desk, sending shockwaves across the floor as he turns to me. "We need eyes and ears there and a full accounting of what dates our lovebirds have been there."

I nod to him. "Make it happen, big guy. I'll meet you at Byrne's once I finish up here."

Simmons continues as Kennedy lumbers off. "Aloni dropped off another sample at Gorelick's, 'round 1:15, then back to North Brother Island. Left her at the dock on the shore to hustle back here."

More nodding on my end. "Okay. Get the delivery records from Hyslop's lab. Do Limerock and Aloni meet only when she's making a delivery? More? Less?" I tilt back in my chair and prop a foot on my desk. "How about you, McCarthy?"

McCarthy answers in his lilting, Irish tone as he holds up an empty Starbucks container. "Downed two of these then did double time back here. From what I seen, Grayson'll be there till eight, nine o'clock tonight, so I can catch up with him later, if you need."

"Where's he go after that?"

"Back home, a flat in the 80s between Madison and Park."

"So work, hotel, back to work, then home every day?"

"'Cept one day he met up in the mornin' with Todd Zigler at a donut shop Zigler frequents."

I swirl my own cup of tea. "Upper East Side too?" I ask.

"Nah, way down in Alphabet City."

My face registers surprise. "Helluva ways to go for donuts. Who's on Zigler?"

"Nobody right now, Chief. We're stretched too thin."

"All right. Cut Limerock loose tomorrow, start digging deep into Zigler instead."

"Smart move, Chief," Simmons says with a nervous twitch of his head.

"Yeah, thanks, Simmons. You turn up anything else of interest?"

Simmons scans his notes, reading from them, "Gorelick had threatened to call immigration on Kerline St. James, just before she jumped ship for Hyslop's lab." He flips the page.

"St. James has an adult daughter who's a US citizen, right? But she's illegal or just got a green card? What about the husband, her family?"

"Daughter's Shanteel St. James, age nineteen. Born here, so yeah, she's a citizen. Mother shuttled her back and forth to Jamaica first ten years of her life to see her father, grandma. Both died in a car accident 'bout ten years ago. Kerline's bounced from lab to lab, never had stable enough employment to get more than a green card. Applied for citizenship just last month."

"So, Kerline knew Malekoviec, is pissed at Gorelick over the harassment and assault, other shit with him. He threatens to have her deported." I shake my head. "Seems a bit shaky as a motive for murder, her killing a Gorelick patient just to get back at him. See if you can dig up anything more on her or Malekoviec and drop the tail on Aloni." I smack my hands together.

"Good work, detectives. Let me know when you turn up anything."

As I reach for my coat, Simmons snaps his fingers. "Way the murders went down, Chief, St. James wouldn't have been involved like this if things were on the up and up."

I give Simmons a perplexed look. *Another of his hair-brained theories, or is he really onto something?* "I got to get to Byrne's. Fill me in on the way to my car, Detective."

# ⊳ Chapter 13 ⊲

"**A**re you guys out of your friggin' minds?" Byrne says with intensity. "You want me to get Jackman to release Durand *and agree not to seek the death penalty against him* because he says he can help you catch Malekoviec's killer?"

"I know it seems crazy, Kiernan, but we've got no other choice. Durand says they'll be another murder soon if we don't catch the killer."

"Oh, well, if Durand says it's true, must be," Byrne says with sarcasm. "We don't even know if Malekoviec was killed. Could have just been an adverse drug reaction." Byrne shakes his head. "Why the hell would you come to me with such a hair-brained—" Recognition fills his face. "This is about Michelle." He nods his head. "McGowan filled me in on the dead clone. Durand's promising to deliver Michelle to you and help with the Malekoviec case if we spring him

226

for a couple of days and take capital punishment off the table."

I slump back in the chair. "Yeah. Didn't want to get into all of it, but that's it."

Kennedy jumps in. "You gotta make this happen, Kiernan. No telling how much longer Michelle will be alive."

"If she's alive," he says in a somber tone. "Look, I'd love to help but there's no way Jackman goes for this. He doesn't give a rat's ass about any of our personal lives. All he cares about is getting re-elected, and going soft on a serial killer's sentencing and releasing him, even temporarily, that ain't getting him re-elected."

My hands slide across the sides of my head. I know Byrne's right. This is a crazy request Jackman will never go for... but I *need* this to happen in the worst way possible. "Look, I'll be personally responsible for Durand while he's out. Anything happens to him, he escapes, whatever, my ass is yours."

Byrne stares at me. "That goes without saying, Chris, but it doesn't change anything."

Kennedy: "I'll be all over Durand. The guy won't take a piss without me being right there. Besides, it'll save us investigating another murder if we catch the killer now." Kennedy's words sound lame, even to me. I stare back at Byrne, his face set in opposition, my insides in free fall.

# ⊳ Chapter 14 ⊲

The green-tinged fluid flows into Jamal's forearm as he grimaces.

Gorelick smiles. "There, all done. You'll be good as new in no time, Jamal."

Shanteel kisses her man's head as he rubs his arm. "How you doing, baby?"

"Don't feel nothing yet. Sure you got it right this time, Doc?"

"Everything went as planned, Jamal. When you start feeling better in a few minutes, you can go, but don't stray too far. Sometimes the results can be unpredictable."

§

"You sure about this, baby? Doc said to stay close. So why you got to be pushing it?" Shanteel says as she and Jamal descend the stairs to the number six subway line.

Jamal waves her off. "Nothing gonna happen to me. I ain't felt this good in years, man. We got to get to the park, to our special place, and celebrate."

Shanteel wants to object but holds back. Jamal hasn't looked this good, this strong and hopeful, in forever. She smiles. "All right, baby. Central Park it is."

§

The sun peaks out from behind the clouds as Jamal and Shanteel come out of the 110th Street subway station and weave their way into the park, around Lasker Rink, to a secluded area of Harlem Meer that affords them privacy. Jamal wraps his arms around Shanteel as they both look over the lake, two swans the only other signs of life around them.

Jamal spins Shanteel around and takes her lips into his. He presses his body into hers, their down jackets collapsing under the strain. Shanteel's lips part, her tongue exploring his before she leans back and looks deep into his eyes. "I love you so much, baby." A lone tear slides down her cheek. "So happy you're finally feeling right."

Jamal smiles back, a mixture of hope, love, confidence. "Me too, baby. I—" But the words die in his throat as the color drains from his face and is replaced by fear. His pupils dilate as he starts shaking.

Sweat erupts across his face. In a moment he goes limp, collapsing in her arms.

Shanteel claws at his jacket. "Oh my God!" She tears the jacket open, desperate to give him some air. His eyes roll back in his head as Shanteel grabs at his pockets for his cell phone.

Dead.

She lays him on the ground as she fumbles for her own cell, his body now drenched in sweat despite the cool temperature.

No service.

She hits 9-1-1 anyway, hoping against hope. No use. Jamal lies still, not a muscle moving.

She tries shaking him, slapping his face, pleading with him to wake up.

Nothing works.

Tears stream down her own face as she leans in.

Not breathing.

Shanteel does her best, breathing for him, pounding on his chest as she clings to hope. Minutes fly by, his body limp, unresponsive. She keeps up the breathing, the pounding for over twenty minutes, until exhaustion and reality sets in, her spent body collapsing on his.

Jamal is dead.

# FORBIDDEN CURE 5

## TURMOIL

# ⊳ Chapter 1 ⊲

Kennedy and I head over to Central Park, dispatched there because a young man died shortly after receiving an injection in his doctor's office. We duck under the crime scene tape and approach the officer who called it in. "What do we know?" I ask.

"Young black girl and her boyfriend just got to the park, were kissing, then he collapsed. Girl tried to call 911, but no service. Tried CPR, but no use."

We sidestep a few barren tree branches, twigs crunching under my boots as we approach the body. Kennedy stands to the right of the body, notepad in hand, as I kneel on the left side and survey the deceased, head to toes. Blotchy hemorrhages cover the entirety of the vic's body, just like with Malekoviec. I point to one of the lesions. "Same as with Irina, and no signs of injury or a struggle." I nod my head as I flip him over and continue my exam. *Got to be the same killer.* Finishing up, I say, "We'll see what McGowan comes up with." I look over at the officer as I rise up. "Where's the girl?"

He jerks his head to the right where a distraught young African-American woman stands with two other officers.

I flash her my badge as Kennedy and I approach. "Detective Ravello. You are?"

"Shanteel St. James."

Recognition flashes across Kennedy's face. "Your mother works for a Doctor Hyslop?"

Surprise. "Uh, yeah, why?" she says with confusion.

Kev glances at me. "Detective Kennedy. I spoke with your mom the other day as part of another investigation." He points his thumb toward our vic. "Tell us what happened."

"Jamal and I was at his doctor's office. Jamal's got real bad diabetes." She shakes her head as tears fill her eyes. "Messed up his eyes and stuff. We was trying to get him better, using some experimental stuff Doc thought would help." She sniffles. "I knew we shouldn't a come up here. Doc said to stay close, just in case."

"Which doc?" I ask.

"Gorelick, that's his name."

My eyes dart to Kennedy's.

I pull out a packet of tissues, handing it to Shanteel. "Tell us about the treatment Jamal received with Doctor Gorelick."

She dabs her eyes, then her nose. "He got his second injection today. Didn't do much, but Jamal felt better. Doc let him go a little while later but told us to stay close by in case—"

"Shanny! Me baby!"

We all turn toward the voice, a solidly built black woman emerging through the tree limbs. The woman rushes over. "Mom!" Kennedy and I clear a path so they can embrace. The woman pulls back as she partially shields her daughter from us. She focuses on my partner. "Detective Kennedy?"

He nods. "Hello, Ms. St. James."

"Police call me 'bout Jamal, told me where you was." She shakes her head, then eyes her daughter. "Ya okay, baby?"

Shanteel holds back the tears, her mother speaking for her. "Can we do dis a bit later?" She side hugs her daughter. "Me girl is cold, tired, upset."

I nod at them, handing her my card. "Sure, meet us at the station in about an hour. We can take Shanteel's statement then."

"Dank you, Detective…"

"Ravello."

"We see you dere in a bit."

Mother and daughter depart as Kennedy and I fill in the timeline and details with the officers on the scene. "So Shanteel said one minute Jamal's fine, the next he's all sweaty and shaking and passes out?"

He snaps his fingers. "Yeah, fucking weird, happened just like that according to her."

Kennedy blows on his hands. "What do you make of it, Chris?"

I smile. "Diabetic, sweating on a day like today. Only one thing explains that..."

# ▷ Chapter 2 ◁

The New York 1 TV anchor's indignant voice continues on in the background. "...linked the murder of a Russian piano teacher from Little Odessa to that of a young African-American male who died just hours ago in Central Park. Reports have it the DA's office refused to cut a deal with an informant that could have averted the second murder."

New York City District Attorney Morgan Jackman snaps off the television with the clicker, slamming it on his desk as he barks at his senior assistant district attorney. "What the hell is this all about?"

"The informant is Durand. He wanted to be on a supervised release for forty-eight hours to help with this investigation, in exchange for taking the death sentence off the table."

"Christ, the baby-killer is looking for leniency? What the hell is the world coming to?"

Byrne shakes his head. "I figured Durand was bluffing. Holed up in Rikers, how could he possibly know about a murder that hadn't even happened yet? That's why I didn't even bring it to you."

Jackman nods. "Well, they've forced our hand now. Who brought this to you?"

"Ravello and Kennedy."

Jackman's right eyebrow arches. "Ravello? Couldn't stay away after all."

"Guess not."

Jackman's hand runs over the blotter on his desk as he deliberates. "We can use that to our advantage. Cut the best deal you can with Durand. Make it clear to Ravello and Kennedy, Durand is their problem while he's out. He causes any issues, anything at all, they're taking the fall, not my office." Jackman flips the TV back on. "In other news, incumbent DA, Morgan Jackman, trails his challenger, Cliff LeFevre, by six points in a recent Gallup poll."

The DA grumbles to Byrne. "Make it happen quickly, Kiernan. I've got more pressing concerns to deal with."

# ⊳ Chapter 3 ⊲

Kennedy and I sit across from Kerline and Shanteel St. James. Kennedy filled me in earlier on Kerline's antipathy toward Jamal Richards. That her role in Hyslop's lab, and her feelings about Gorelick make her a person of interest in both the Malekoviec and Richards deaths. But we'll take the soft approach, see what we can tease out without getting confrontational.

"My condolences for your loss, Ms. St. James. We understand you and Jamal were very close."

I study the young woman, who's much more composed than earlier. "Thank you, Detective. Yes, we were thinking about getting married as soon as Jamal was feeling better."

Kerline grimaces, then masks it.

"I see. What do you know about Jamal's condition, about how bad his diabetes was?"

Shanteel nods. "Was a real bad case." She gives a

glancing smile toward Kerline. "That's why my mom referred us to Doctor Gorelick. The diabetes was hurting Jamal's eyes, making it hard to focus. Was damaging his kidneys and messing with the feeling in his feet. He was gonna need dialysis soon if Doctor Gorelick didn't straighten him out."

"Who can get us a copy of Jamal's medicals? His mother? Father?"

"I can. Jamal gave me power of attorney. His folks are really messed up. Didn't want to leave them in charge in case anything happened, and he's got no brothers or sisters."

"That makes it easy. We'll have you sign some releases so we can get Gorelick's records and all of Jamal's other docs too." I turn to Kerline. "I understand you helped with the formulations for Jamal's treatments?"

"Ya, dat's right. I done work on dem bod times, for sure."

"Anything you can tell us about the compounds that would be helpful? Problems with the formulations, difficulties with quality testing, delivery? Anything at all?"

Kerline shakes her head. "Nodding unusual. First time round the med didn't work well so Doctor Hyslop done some tinkerin' wid it."

"That unusual?" Kennedy asks.

"Naw. Most times we gotta do it for de second dose, sometimes even de dird."

"Quality testing was good?"

"Ya. Done dat meself second time 'round." She holds up a thumb. "Turn out real good."

Kennedy asks, "I thought Todd Zigler always did some of the QT?"

Kerline nods. "With most a de techs 'e done dat. But wid me," she beams, "'e pretty much leave me alone on accounta 'e knows I real good."

"Okay," I say. "So he'd just take you on your word that the testing was fine?"

She shrugs. "'e take a peek at de testin', see it all good, den sign off on it."

"How about Hyslop? How closely would he look things over?"

"Sometimes 'e ask for more tests be done. Sometimes not. Den Todd tell Kiki where to deliver de med to."

Kennedy again: "Why'd Todd have the last look at the med, not Hyslop? Isn't that kind of weird since Hyslop's in charge?

"I don't pay it no mind. Todd told me dat's the way the FDA want it. Said Hyslop 'ad a few deaths before, dey wanna spread de power around, keep dings more on de up n up in de lab."

I nod. That jives with what Kennedy told me about the three deaths earlier. Still, I'll check with the FDA, confirm her story.

"Kiki always the one to deliver the meds?" Kennedy inquires.

"Long as I been dere."

"Jamal have any enemies either of you know about?" I ask.

Mother and daughter look at each other and shrug, then Shanteel answers, "No one I know. Jamal acted all tough, but he was a pussycat." Holding back the tears, she adds, "Never got on anyone's bad side."

Kennedy taps his notepad on the desk as I consider the information. "All right, thank you for your help." I smile as I reach across the desk. "We'll be in touch if we need anything else."

I look down at the number coming up on my phone as Kerline and her daughter disappear from view. *Shit, never got back to them.*

"Hello, this is Detective Ravello."

"Hi, Detective, this is Doctor Jacobs' office." I can picture the disapproving look on her face. "We need to set up an appointment for the last dose of your cure. I left a message yesterday."

"Yes, sorry about that. Things have been crazy lately."

"That's quite all right. Doctor Jacobs emphasized it's vital you be treated by Thursday—"

"—or risk losing my chance to be cured. Yes, I know." I look up at the ceiling. How the hell am I going to fit this in with everything else in play? This case has me going 24/7 as it is. "What's today, Tuesday?"

"Yes, Detective." Hearing concern in her voice, "Is everything okay?"

"Wait, Thursday's Christmas Eve. You have office hours?"

I hear her groan. "Yes, a full day, as a matter of fact."

"Wow, that's rough. What's the latest appointment I can get?"

"Uh, Doctor has a four-thirty open."

"Four-thirty it is. I'll see you then. Thank you."

§

"Well, Byrne and Jackman gotta take this more seriously now. It's all over the local news," Kennedy says as he runs a hand through his hair. "The old man must be shitting about the bad press."

"Yeah. Don't know how Durand's tapped into this, but he called it." I peer across my desk, over a mound of paperwork. "But if we spring him, is he going to come through with Michelle?" I rub my face with both hands, then shake my head. *Gotta focus on the here and now.* "What'd you think of the St. James connection to vic two?"

"Or the Gorelick link for that matter. He's in play on both as well, with Dmitri on the Malekoviec case. May be flying solo on Richards, unless the mob needed to get rid of him too." Kennedy breaks open the lid on a cup of joe, blows the steam away. "Really anyone in Hyslop's lab could've done it as well."

My head reeling, I press on. "Not to mention

Grayson Limerock. He's got the clearest motive: destroying his main competitor. And he's connected to the lab through Aloni and maybe Zigler. But something about it doesn't fit."

"Yeah. Why would a guy running a billion-dollar company with a swank office on the Upper East Side care about a competitor on some God-forsaken island that used to house Typhoid Mary?"

"Maybe, despite appearances, Hyslop's on to something Grayson isn't, and Grayson wants in on it before word gets out?"

"Could be."

"Gotta take a hard look at the science behind both companies. See if I can make heads or tails out of who's got what." I pull out my notepad and jot down tasks. "Also gotta talk to the FDA, corroborate Kerline's story about why the lab runs the way it does." I shake my pen, trying to draw down more ink, then toss it away in favor of another. "With any luck I'll uncover more than we bargained for."

"I'll stay on top of Simmons about Kerline. I can see why she would want to off Richards before he sucks Shanteel down the drain into the sewer he's living in. Can even see why she would want to ruin Gorelick in the process. But why kill Malekoviec first? She should've knocked off Richards first, then taken care of Malekoviec to smokescreen the Richards case and point it back to Gorelick." Kennedy reaches for his hours-old bagel and in between bites says, "She's got the order backwards."

"Maybe she just had to take it the way it came. Malekoviec's second dose came before Richards. The second dose is the one to do the deed with since it's the make or break treatment."

Kennedy nods, unconvinced. "So where's the secretary figure into all this? Plenty of opportunity with delivering the meds, but she couldn't have done it without some serious help, and what's her motivation to get all wrapped up in that kinda shit?"

I shoot from the hip. "What if Simmons is right? She's got bad RA. Desperate for a cure, she takes a job with Hyslop, and when she gets impatient, starts screwing Limerock to double down on getting her cure?"

"Guess even Simmons can be right once in a while, but why off Richards then? He's diabetic. It's got nothing to do with her RA cure."

"Could be Limerock's using her to get info to taint different kinds of treatments. If she knows, he keeps her quiet with promises of a cure for her."

"And if she doesn't, he's got the perfect cover cause she's the one carrying the meds, and he figures no one knows about their trysts."

I walk over to our suspect board and move around two photos. "That leaves us with Gorelick, Hyslop, Zigler, Limerock, and St. James and everyone else in Hyslop's lab and Gorelick's practice. Not sure why any of those workers would want to kill anyone, though. If Hyslop's or Gorelick's reputations are destroyed, they've got a lot to lose."

"Unless Zigler is Limerock's mole, helping to take down Hyslop's lab so he can then join forces with Limerock."

I laugh it off. "Might want to back off on binge watching *The Blacklist*, Detective. I think it's clouding your judgment."

Kennedy smirks. "Hey, stranger things have happened."

"'Cept we've got no evidence of a prior connection between Zigler and Limerock. First meet was just a couple of days ago." I tilt my head, "But who knows? We turn up something, you can go all Raymond Reddington on him," I say with a smile before my cell interrupts. I glance at it, then Kennedy. "Byrne. This oughtta be interesting."

# ⊳ Chapter 4 ⊲

Byrne spits the words at Kennedy and me. "Pretty convenient NY 1 breaks the story today about the informant, how the DA's office could have prevented the Richards' murder if we'd just played along."

I raise my hands. "Whoa, you're out of line, Byrne. Wasn't Kennedy or I who leaked it. We're on your side, remember?"

Kennedy looks pissed. "Durand's the one trying to get out, not us. He must've leaked it somehow."

Byrne stews in silence, fingers drumming the table before us as we wait at Rikers for Durand and his attorney. Byrne points an angry finger. "Whoever leaked it it's your asses if Durand pulls any shit while he's out. DA's office is washing our hands of it, putting it all on you two."

"What an inspiring example of teamwork," I say tersely. "Expected about as much."

Kennedy's hands ball up into fists. "We'll have eyes on him 24/7. He won't so much as take a shit without yours truly all over him."

We all turn toward the sound of the conference room door opening, toward Durand and his attorney's entrance. Byrne, softly: "Keep quiet you two. I've got this."

Durand shuffles over in shackles, a shit-eating grin on his face as his lawyer nods to us and shakes Byrne's hand. "Do you have the agreement, counselor?"

"First things first. What can your client tell us about the Richards case?"

Durand starts to speak, but his lawyer cuts him off. "My client has already made a good faith offering of information to these detectives, which they have followed up on and found to be true. That will suffice until we have a signed agreement."

Byrne scowls as he slides the paperwork across the desk. "We will only take the death penalty off the table if your client's actions and/or intel while he is released directly lead to the killer's or killers' capture and conviction." Byrne sneers at opposing counsel. "Such incarceration/conviction of the killer or killers in this case must occur prior to any further loss of life. In short, your client will have thirty-six hours to help us catch whoever is responsible for these deaths before they kill again."

"Thirty-six? The agreement was for forty-eight hours."

Byrne maintains his scowl. "Thirty-six is the best you're going to do." He grabs the agreement with both hands. "We can tear it up right now if that's a problem?"

Anger flashes across their faces. They whisper back and forth for a minute at which point Durand's attorney dons his glasses and studies the document, then passes it on to his client along with a pen. "It's all there, Jean Louis. You may sign it, here, here, and here." Durand, his attorney, and Byrne sign the document in rapid succession, a sinister smile engulfing Durand's face as Byrne slips the document into his briefcase. All of us rise as Byrne wraps up the meeting. "Your client will be released into Detective Ravello's and Detective Kennedy's custody as soon as we file the paperwork with the court and serve it upon the warden. Good day."

# ▷ Chapter 5 ◁

Simmons hands me the medicals on Jamal Richards. "Just came through on the fax, Chief."

"That was fast. Never got records this quick when I was in practice."

Simmons wipes his nose with the back of his hand and rubs it on his pants. "Nothing like a murder investigation to grease the wheels, huh?"

I nod, then settle in at my desk to study the packet, a mix of records from Gorelick, Richards' endocrinologist, primary care doc, and his eye doctor. The endo doc had tried multiple dosages and dosing schedules for insulin over the last year and a half, but nothing helped Jamal's body to process glucose properly. His elevated sugar levels, sometimes as high as 600, wreaked havoc on his body, causing bleeding and swelling in his eyes, loss of sensation in his feet, and severe damage to his kidneys. Shanteel was right;

despite being just twenty-three, dialysis was inevitable for Jamal.

But then he consulted with Gorelick, a rheumatologist with such extensive experience with Hyslop's treatments he often cared for patients with non-rheumatologic conditions, such as diabetes. Like with Irina Malekoviec, Jamal didn't feel any improvement from his first dose of Hyslop's med. But his labs tell a different story. His kidney function, still impaired, showed clear improvement, and his blood sugar came down about ten per cent.

I lean back, twist my head side to side, and mull things over as I stare at my partner, engrossed in his own paperwork. Everything I just read supports my theory on what killed Jamal, but I need confirmation. Time to bring Kennedy up to speed on this.

"Kev, give McGowan a call. I want to head over, see what she's got for us on Richards."

§

I peer through a direct ophthalmoscope into Jamal Richards' left eye, adjusting the settings to focus on his retina. "As I suspected, the bleeding and swelling in Jamal's eye is much, much worse than what his ophthalmologist described a month ago."

I lean back from the corpse and address McGowan as Kennedy stands by, notepad in hand. "If my theory is correct, Mr. Richards' autopsy and blood work revealed three things you'd never expect in a type one diabetic."

McGowan raises an eyebrow. "The floor is yours, Doctor Ravello."

"One, exceedingly high blood levels of insulin his own body produced."

McGowan's face morphs to a look of curious appreciation. "Correct."

"Two, his serum glucose levels were undetectable."

McGowan offers a knowing nod.

"And three, microscopic analysis of his pancreas showed a robust supply of Beta cells in the Islets of Langerhans."

Kennedy looks on in utter bewilderment.

McGowan breaks into a wide grin. "How did you know?"

"Simple, really. Richards' girlfriend, Shanteel St. James, described Jamal as suddenly nervous, sweating, and light-headed, despite the cool temperature in Central Park."

McGowan: "Classic signs of very low blood sugar brought on by insulin shock."

"Precisely. But Jamal didn't overdose on his prescription insulin, and he wasn't killed by an injection administered surreptitiously by someone else." I shake my head. "No, Jamal's cure killed him."

Kennedy's jaw goes slack. "Huh?"

I smile at my friend. "Beta cells in the Islets of

Langerhans are responsible for producing insulin, which breaks down blood glucose so the body can use it as energy. In type one diabetics the body's own immune system decimates these cells, causing a lack of insulin, which results in unsafe levels of glucose. That glucose damages blood vessels throughout the body, particularly in the eyes, the kidneys, and the feet."

Kennedy, tentatively: "Okay, but you just said Richards' blood sugar level was undetectable. So what caused the bleeding in his eye to get a lot worse?"

"Jamal's 'cure'."

Kennedy looks lost. "But how?"

"Remember about the immune complexes in Irina's case?"

"Yeah."

"Just like in Irina's case, Jamal's cure stimulated his body to make massive amounts of bad antibodies and the cure then rendered those antibodies harmless."

Kennedy puts his hands up, excitement in his voice. "Wait, I got it! The immune complexes then formed, and yada yada yada, BOOM! The bleeding in the skin, organ damage, etc." He smiles.

"Exactly!" I say.

Kennedy: "So that explains why Richards, a diabetic, and Malekoviec, who had RA, died exactly the same way from their cures?"

I snap my fingers. "You got it. There was literally a massive battle going on inside the blood vessels in both vics' bodies. The cure was binding to and destroying all the antibodies, which was a good thing. But the battle was too intense, too extensive. It damaged blood vessels throughout both vics' bodies, leading to the bleeding in the skin we saw and widespread organ damage, which is what killed them."

"Holy shit! What a way to go," Kennedy says.

"Yeah. The question is, why? Why did Hyslop's medication do this? Was it super-concentrated? Tainted? Did Gorelick intentionally or unintentionally overdose Jamal?" My hand goes to my chin as I consider the possibilities. "Have we analyzed the medication Gorelick gave Richards?"

McGowan shakes her head. "I'm afraid not. As with Malekoviec, all the medication was used in treating Mr. Richards."

"Shit, back to square one." I shake my head. "Have Gorelick's and Hyslop's offices confirmed that was the recommended dosing?"

"Yes."

My eyes narrow as I peer at my partner. "We gonna need a warrant for Hyslop's lab? I've got to see how they formulated the compounds for Malekoviec and Richards."

"Nay, they're cooperating fully. Just reach out to Zigler; he knows you're on the case now."

"Excellent. What about the warrant to look over Grayson's data on similar kinds of drugs?" I hold out my hand as I outline our reasoning. "We figure Grayson may be pirating Hyslop's work. Confirming that helps us build our case against him."

Kennedy shakes his head. "Judge squashed it, said all we got are theories and guess work."

"Grayson poisoning the compounds that Kiki was carrying, that's just guess work?" I say angrily.

Kennedy puts his hands up in surrender. "Hey, don't shoot the messenger. Judge said we've got no proof Limerock ever got his hands on those compounds."

I nod my head as I formulate a plan of attack. "All right, if proof is what he wants, then that's what we'll give him. Call Simmons, get him to grab a couple of our tech guys, set up a command center at the hotel in the room next to the one Aloni and Limerock meet at." I glance at my watch. "In the meantime you and I have to head over to Rikers, pick up Durand by ten."

"You're freeing him?" McGowan says in disbelief.

Kennedy: "Just for thirty-six hours, Doc."

She shakes her head.

"Desperate times. We need to use one killer to catch another before he strikes again," I say grimly. "And besides, Durand is the only one who knows where Michelle is."

She nods her head slowly. "I see. Well good luck, detectives."

As we turn to go, Kennedy mumbles under his breath, "I have a bad feeling we're gonna need all the luck we can get."

# ⟩ Chapter 6 ⟨

Kennedy throws the door open to room 315 at The Jameson Hotel and shoves Durand across the threshold. "Home sweet fucking home for the next day and a half."

Durand stumbles into the wall, catching himself with his face and shackled hands. I march past the two of them, toward Simmons and our techies. They're moving purposefully about the room, erecting a suspect board, organizing reports, medical records, and other paperwork.

Simmons jumps out of the way as Kennedy plows into the room and shoves Durand into a chair nearest to the window. "Look what the cat dragged in."

All turn to look at the serial killer we pursued in earnest earlier in the year, a man we have freed in a desperate attempt to stave off another murder—and to reunite me with Michelle.

Durand cranes his neck to look through the window at the masses scurrying on the street, wishing, I'm sure, he could disappear into the crowd below.

Time to read him the riot act and familiarize him with our plan of attack.

"Your ass is ours for the next thirty-six hours. You won't so much as wipe it without someone standing guard over you. Help us catch the killer before he strikes again, bring Michelle back, and you won't have to worry about the death penalty anymore."

Durand, strangely quiet, offers only a nod. "As you wish, Detective. Just tell me what you need of me."

I turn to my men. "All set up?"

Simmons speaks for the group. "Got the computer you asked for, Chief, and all the reports. Setting up the board now." He rubs his nose with the back of his hand, then holds up some papers. "Cross-referenced the days Aloni made deliveries for Hyslop and when she met Limerock here."

"And?"

"They met every single time she made a delivery as well as a few other times."

"Good work, Simmons. We got the go ahead yet on putting surveillance next door?"

He nods. "Came through an hour ago. Martinez bugged the room."

Martinez: "Ready to run an endoscopic camera through the wall. Just give the word."

"Where will it come out?"

"Next to the TV. Should be able to see everything."

"Perfect. Do it while we hash out our next moves. We've only got an hour or so before the lovebirds show up."

§

"Simmons, what d'you find out about Dmitri?" I ask.

Simmons' eyes dart nervously between Kennedy, Durand, and me. "Confirmed what Detective Kennedy found out earlier. Just after Malekoviec died, Dmitri wiped Gorelick's debt clean."

"Which tells us he was convinced Gorelick kept his end of the deal," I say. "Any ties between Dmitri and Richards?"

"Nothing. Phone records don't show any calls between Richards and Dmitri's cell, his places of business, or anyone known to us from the Russian mob. Most of Richards' calls were to Shanteel St. James, Richards' buddies, and his family."

"Could Richards have met with Dmitri face-to-face in lieu of phone calls?"

Simmons snorts and clears his throat, then jerks his head toward our techies. "Not too likely. Martinez and Kendricks analyzed the GPS from Richards's phone. Never placed him anywhere near Korsakov's residence or any of his business locations."

Kennedy: "What if he had the phone turned off?"

Durand rolls his eyes. "The GPS would still be active, Detective, unless he removed the battery as well."

"So Gorelick, Dmitri look good for the Malekoviec murder, but not Richards," I say, then thinking out loud, "even if Dmitri's got ties to Richards that we don't know about and wants him dead too, he's got to go through Gorelick to make it go down the way it did. But Gorelick's debt is wiped, so what motivation does he have for killing Richards too?"

"The thrill of it, of course," Durand says with a smile.

I glare at him. "Assuming we're not dealing with a sociopath, any other motive?"

Simmons and Kennedy stare back, then Kennedy speaks up, "Dmitri's got him by the balls for killing Malekoviec, tells him to off someone else that's got no relation to Dmitri or he'll tip off the cops."

Intrigued, I follow Kennedy's lead. "So Gorelick has no choice, has to kill again. But he's smart, realizes Richards is dating Kerline's daughter. And, of course, Hyslop's lab has made compounds to treat both Malekoviec and Richards. So he picks Richards to kill, figuring it may blow back on Hyslop's lab, maybe even Kerline herself instead of Gorelick."

Kennedy interjects, "Gorelick's hoping for that. Otherwise the second murder implicates him more while making Dmitri seem like less of a suspect 'cause

Dmitri doesn't even know the second vic." Kennedy whistles. "Hell of a chess match Gorelick and Dmitri have going."

Martinez' drill pierces the wall, momentarily breaking our concentration. Kendricks and Martinez look at us sheepishly. "Sorry."

Kennedy jumps in. "Gorelick'd have to tamper with the meds between the time his girl at the front signed for them from Aloni and when his nurse prepped the trays for treatment." Kennedy pulls out his notepad, flips through it. "On both Malekoviec's and Richards' samples Sally put the meds in the fridge within two minutes of signing for them. And Gorelick's schedule is packed both days. He's seeing patients the whole time, so no chance for him to duck out and grab the medicines before they go in the fridge."

"What if Sally puts something else in the fridge, not the medication she just signed for? Gives Gorelick plenty of time then to tamper with it since the treatments aren't until the next day," Simmons says with pride.

Kennedy shakes his head. "Except Sally'd have to be in on it too—"

"And the fridge has a scanner and camera as part of its security protocols. Everything going into the fridge is scanned in, photographed beforehand. When meds are taken out, the scanner and camera are used to confirm what was removed," I say.

Simmons snorts again and smiles. "That fridge is more secure than Fort Knox!"

We all stare back at him, unamused, then I continue, "Plus the fridge has an electronic lock, requiring a unique code each time to access it. Users go on the company's website, enter their information, and are emailed or texted the code to open it. It's foolproof."

Durand laughs heartily as he gazes at each of us in turn. "Nothing is foolproof. Allow me to demonstrate."

I read off the company website and office location to Durand, who types furiously at the computer. "Call over to Gorelick's office. Have someone other than Sally or Gorelick's nurse poised by the refrigerator."

I comply as Durand opens another browser. "What are Gorelick's and Detective Kennedy's cell numbers?" Durand asks. Kennedy reads them off to him. Durand tells Kennedy to give him the code when it's texted to him. "I've disabled the camera/scanning features on the refrigerator and am porting Gorelick's phone number to Detective Kennedy's. Do you have Gorelick's office on the line?" he asks me.

I nod. "They've got eyes on the fridge."

Kennedy reads off the code. "523-974," which Durand types in. He turns to me as he hits ENTER on the keyboard. "Viola."

I nearly drop my cell. "Fridge door just popped open."

"With the camera/scanner disabled, they can take

out or put in whatever they wish," Durand says with a smile.

I nod as I instruct the office to close the fridge and thank them for their help before hanging up.

Kennedy: "What the fuck?"

Durand holds his hands up. "Just think what I could do unshackled."

I nod to Kennedy to release him.

"Impressive, Durand. It's clear *you* could have helped Gorelick from prison if you had access to a computer, but Gorelick's inept with technology. The guy's still using paper charts and doesn't even use a computer in his office." I turn to Kennedy and Simmons. "Hyslop's lab confirmed Gorelick used the right doses. Without access to the meds to tamper with them, I don't see how Gorelick's our killer."

Simmons: "What about Dmitri wiping the debt clean?"

"All that tells us is that Dmitri *expected* Gorelick to kill Malekoviec for him."

Kennedy jumps in. "If you're Gorelick and somebody else does you a favor and kills Malekoviec, you gonna tell Korsakov you didn't do the deed?" Simmons shakes his head as Kennedy continues, "Didn't think so."

Martinez yells over as Kendricks secures the camera line to the wall. "All set, Chief. The camera's in place, and we've got visualization of the room."

I cross over to him. "Good work." Turning to Simmons, I say, "Have the front desk call up as soon as Aloni or Limerock checks in." I smile. "Time to nail this bastard in the act."

§

Simmons nods in my direction as he finishes his conversation and hangs up the hotel phone. "Go time. Kiki Aloni is on her way up."

"All right, Martinez, Kendricks, pull up the camera feed. I want eyes all over that room. Kev, cuff Durand to the desk and gag him. We can't take any chances." My men move quickly into position. Moments later, we see Kiki Aloni walk through the front door of room 313. She passes right by the camera, heading toward the desk, in the fringes of our view.

I whisper to Martinez, "Can we adjust the mag, our field of view?" He nods and rotates it toward Aloni as she drops her purse on the desk and doubles back to the bathroom.

"Go in tight on the handbag. Show me what's in there."

Martinez twists and angles the small joystick, then looks at me, helpless.

"Zipped shut, no good."

"All right, pull back. Give me the rest of the room, low mag."

We fall into silence as Kiki emerges from the bathroom wearing a sexy red bra with matching panties. She removes her earrings, placing them on the nightstand closest to the bathroom, and pulls her hair off her face.

The phone starts ringing in our room! All eyes turn toward it as Simmons lunges forward and grabs it. "Okay, great, thanks," then returns it to its cradle. "Grayson just came in." I let out a breath as I refocus on Aloni, who's folding the sheets back and sliding her legs under them. The door opens up, Limerock walking in with a shit-eating grin on his face. "Not wasting any time today, I see." Much to our disgust he quickly disrobes and joins her, nearly devouring her face with his lips. Fortunately, most of the next ten minutes are shielded by the sheets. After a few minutes of obligatory post-coital caressing and hugs, the lovers separate, Kiki heading to the shower while Grayson makes a beeline for her bag.

Moment of truth.

Eyes fixed on the bathroom door, he unzips the bag and searches its contents, grumbling as he shifts the contents to and fro, "C'mon, c'mon. Where the hell is it?" More pushing and clawing. "Gotta be here, wait.... Fuck!" he says with a scowl as his hands emerge from the bag, empty. Grayson stares at the bathroom door in disbelief, then sets about restoring the purse's contents to their original position. The shower goes off as Grayson slides back to the bed and slips his pale ass under the covers. Moments later, Aloni emerges while Grayson pretends to busy himself on his phone. "Quick one today, baby?

She nods. "Hyslop didn't have the delivery ready in time. Told him I'd grab a quick lunch and head right back, so I'll be gone before you're out of the shower." She pecks him on the cheek. "Until tomorrow." Grayson grabs her face and gives her a suffocating kiss, then throws her onto the bed as he marches to the shower, winking at her. "Until then."

As Aloni begins dressing, I turn to Kennedy in a panic. "We need to grab her."

"What for?" he says.

"No way we get the warrant like this. We need to interrogate her, get her to spill something we can use."

Kennedy nods. "Where you want to grab her?"

"Lobby, then double back up here."

"What about Limerock? Can't risk bumping into him."

I turn to Simmons, then Martinez. "Don't take your eyes off Durand. Keep yours on Limerock. Once we've got Aloni, we'll take the stairs or the elevator, depending on what you tell us." Both men nod as I glance at the screen. She's almost ready, time to move. Kennedy and I take the stairs to the lobby and settle into chairs that offer an unfettered view of the elevators. Martinez texts me: "Out the door."

I nod to Kennedy as we slide behind two columns separated by about ten feet that delineate the edge of the seating area from the lobby proper. I take the column closer to the elevator and watch its doors open. Aloni strides quickly toward the exit, oblivious to me. I imagine her strides as she disappears from view, then spring out from behind the column just as she passes by. Kennedy appears in front of her. "Detective? I, I don't understand."

Kennedy holds his index finger to his lips to quiet her as I place one hand on her shoulder and turn her to me. "You will. Detective Ravello. Come this way, quickly." My phone vibrates in the other hand. I glance down. "Elevator," it says. "Shit. Behind here. Not a word." We duck behind the column. Kennedy scrambles for cover as Limerock emerges from the elevator and glides toward the exit. Kiki and I rotate away from Grayson's line of sight as he approaches, then passes us. Kennedy does the same a moment later as Grayson disappears onto the street.

Kiki looks at me, incredulous. "Mind telling me what's going on, Detective?"

§

Back in the suite Kennedy and I close ourselves into the far room with Kiki.

"Doctor Hyslop expects me back by now," she says.

I stare right through her. Grabbing a chair, I plant it in front of her and motion her to it. "Detective Kennedy will offer your boss our apologies. You're not going anywhere until you tell us what we need to know."

Visibly shaken, Aloni slips onto the chair. "I don't know what you're talking—"

Kennedy presses his face close to hers. "We know about your escapades with Limerock." Leaning back, he nods as I hold up the list of delivery dates and days she met Limerock. "Every time you had a delivery to make for Dr. Hyslop, you met Grayson Limerock here." I smile. "Two people have died as a result of medications you transported. Start talking or you'll find yourself at the center of a double murder investigation."

Aloni, face bright red, recoils. "S-so what do you want to know?"

Ten minutes later a rush of emotions, including lust, yearning for a cure, and betrayal, leave Kiki spent, distraught.

"Quite a story, Ms. Aloni. We know your lover is our killer," I say sternly. "Only way you come out of this in one piece is by cooperating with us."

Her eyes are red-rimmed, fear written across her face. "I don't understand. I just told you everything I know."

Kennedy and I leave Kiki to stew on her fear, moving far enough away so she can't hear us. "Her suspicions Grayson switched the meds or tampered with them are good, but they won't get us the warrant." I glance back at Kiki, nervously fidgeting as her eyes dart around the room. "Pretty clear she's not involved in the murders—doesn't have the stomach for it."

Kennedy nods. "Yeah, and the stuff she found on his computer, it's not much help, just corporate espionage crap. No smoking gun there." Kennedy runs his hand along his face, no doubt tired and frustrated. "What d'you wanna do with her? We cut her loose now, she may warn Grayson we're on to him."

A smile breaks across my face. "Follow my lead. I know just how to get that warrant."

We amble over to Kiki. I grab a seat across from her while Kennedy stands, arms folded, menacing. "We appreciate how hard this has been on you, Ms. Aloni. But I've got to be honest with you." Index finger and thumb held an inch apart. "We're this close to nailing Grayson for the murders of Irina Malekoviec and Jamal Richards. And when that happens, we can't protect you. The full force of the DA's office will come down on you and Grayson."

Her hands go to her lips. "Oh my God, I can't go to prison! I didn't do anything wrong!"

I glance at Kennedy, then lean forward, peering into her timid eyes. "You help us to nail him red-handed, we'll protect you."

She nods quickly.

My smile resurfaces. "Great. So here's what we'll do...."

# ⊳ Chapter 7 ⊲

Kennedy and I sit across from Harold Hyslop in his office as I outline our needs. "We have every reason to believe Grayson Limerock has engaged in corporate espionage aimed at eliminating your lab."

"I can't say that I'm surprised. He's always felt threatened by my work." Anger flashes across Hyslop's face. "He may be better financed, but our science beats his, hands down. What do you need from me?"

"A compound that appears to be one of your cures but is chemically altered so we can trace its whereabouts."

"Easy enough," he says smugly.

"We also need you to fabricate data showing this compound is breakthrough technology." I nod. "And you'll be delivering a dose to a referring doctor tomorrow. That combination should prove irresistible to Limerock."

"Not a problem. But how will Limerock have the opportunity to steal it? Kiki delivers all the medicines for—oh no!" Worry is etched on Hyslop's face. "I can't in good conscience allow you to endanger her."

Kennedy and my eyes meet for the briefest of moments. "No one is more interested in bringing Grayson Limerock to justice than Ms. Aloni. She's already agreed to help us. Rest assured, we will keep Kiki out of harm's way."

Hyslop's face registers confusion. He starts to speak, but pulls back, raising his eyes to the ceiling, his brow knit in concentration. Kennedy and I wait in silence.

A full two minutes pass before Hyslop's gaze meets mine, his face unreadable. "All right, detectives, you have my assistance." He reaches for his intercom. "I'll have Todd begin formulating the compound right now."

I reach out for Hyslop's hand to stop it. "Actually, we need you to handle that. No one else in the lab can know."

Shockwaves roll across Hyslop's face. "You think Todd... or one of my other technicians is involved in this maleficence?"

I lie, hoping Hyslop won't connect the dots. "We're sure Grayson's found a way into your lab, we're just not sure how. We need to keep it between you, Ms. Aloni, Detective Kennedy, and myself."

"Fair enough. I'll upload the fake information and

get started on the compound. It will be ready by day's end. Anything else?"

I glance at Kennedy before replying. "We don't want any delays after the exchange in analyzing the compound and moving on Limerock. So I'll need a small, portable kit to analyze the compound at the hotel."

Hyslop nods. "Not a problem. I have just what you'll need. Is that all?"

I blink twice, then add, "I'd like to look over all your records on the formulations for Malekoviec and Richards."

Hyslop nods. "I'll have Todd provide you access to everything you need."

I reach out and shake Hyslop's hand. "Excellent, Doctor. By this time tomorrow we'll have the goods on Grayson Limerock."

# ▷ Chapter 8 ◁

S how time.

I huddle around Martinez, Kendricks, and Simmons, eyes glued to the camera's monitor. Kennedy stands guard over Durand, handcuffed and gagged like yesterday. We haven't made as much use of Durand as I would have liked, but that will change as soon as we finish with Grayson and can focus on getting Michelle back.

Kiki is already in place, her open bag on the desk next door, the medication peeking through. She looks nervous, and why not? Carrying out an undercover sting against a lover who doubles as a murderer is a tough task. Not to mention having sex with him while our camera rolls. I offered her assurances we would look elsewhere during the escapades, but it did little to settle her.

Grayson enters with a kiss and disrobes in no

time, laying his suit next to her bag. So much for the art of foreplay.

After the lovemaking ends, Kiki kisses our mark and embarks for the shower, relieved, I'm sure, that the heavy lifting is over for her. Limerock waits a minute, then slides over to the bag. Shit no! His naked ass stands between us and the medication. So much for direct visual evidence. But that's why the compound is traceable. If he makes a switch, we can track our med right to his lab. If he taints the treatment, we'll know too. Grayson reaches into his suit pocket for something, his butt again impairing our view. He glances to his left at the bathroom door then moves quickly. A minute later he's redeposited a test tube of medication into Kiki's bag and put something back into his jacket pocket. I'd love to bust him right now, find out what's in his jacket as well, but chide myself to be patient. Soon enough we'll have our warrant, and shortly thereafter the proof we need.

Shit, not that! Full frontal nudity as Grayson does a one-eighty. Hope his bank account is fuller than what we just saw. Wishing I could unsee it, I motion Simmons to head down to the lobby, where he'll make himself inconspicuous until he confirms Grayson has left the building.

The next twenty minutes fly by, the lovers both showering, changing, and bidding each other adieu. Simmons gives us the thumbs up downstairs, then collects Kiki and our precious medication from next door.

"Great work, Ms. Aloni. I know that had to be very difficult for you."

She smiles self-consciously and hands me her bag so I can retrieve the medication. I don latex gloves, handling the compound with care.

"Kev, you got the instrument and stuff from Hyslop's lab?"

Durand draws our attention as he strains to speak through the gag, his face red with effort. Kennedy pulls the gag out and drops it on the desk, slapping Durand lightly on his cheek. "Aw, can our little serial-killing scumbag breathe better now?"

Durand glares at him. "And the cuffs?"

"Let's wait on those, and just get him away from the desk," I say as I motion to Kennedy, who hands me a black bag of supplies and equipment and pulls Durand away. "Let's see what Grayson, and his naked ass, was up to."

Kiki looks at me oddly. I wave her off. "Uh, never mind."

I lay the bag on the desk and unzip it. Emptying out its contents, I set up a test tube holder, pull out supplies for a slide and a dropper. I place the tube of medication in the holder and use the dropper to extract a tiny amount of it, which I put on the slide. I watch the liquid spread under the cover slip. Excitement builds as I slip the slide into a hand-held device that will search for the amount of tracer on the compound and identify the compound's molecular structure. I expect there to be no tracer and the mixture to be different than what was in Kiki's bag, meaning Grayson switched the drugs.

Lights flash on the device as it makes a humming sound and runs the chemical through a battery of tests. I stare intently at it, confident. Ten seconds go by, then twenty, my fingers drumming on the desk. "C'mon already." The flashing lights finally stop, a green one coming on in their place. I smile as I push a red button on the side of the device to get the reading.

"What the hell?"

My men gather round, leaning over me to get a look.

Kennedy: "What's wrong?"

"It's the exact same compound Hyslop gave Ms. Aloni earlier," I say with disbelief.

"How's that even possible?" snorts Simmons. "We saw him making a switch."

"No, we saw his hands moving between his jacket pocket and the compound, but his friggin' ass shielded our view."

Kennedy: "So what the hell was he doing if he wasn't switching the meds?" He points to the device. "Can that thing tell if he slipped a poison or something in it?"

Crestfallen, I mumble my reply, "It's got the exact same chemical composition as Hyslop's compound.

Not so much as a nanoliter of anything else in it. Shit. We're never gonna get a warrant at this rate."

Kiki: "I don't understand. I thought you had all the proof you needed already?"

"Simmons, Martinez, Kendricks, escort Ms. Aloni next door. I need to think this through."

§

"So he didn't switch the meds, and he didn't tamper with this one? So what'd he do? Think he was on to us, just putting on a show to make it look like he did something?" Kennedy asks.

"Complete with full frontal nudity? Naw, I don't think so." I turn to Durand. "Not looking good for you. We've got just over twelve hours till you go back to Rikers and we're no closer to catching our killer."

"That can change in an instant, dear doctor-detective," Durand says with a sneer.

"I don't follow."

"You need a warrant to peruse Limerock's records in order to nail him. I suffer no such constraints."

Kennedy: "What, you're gonna hack in...?"

"That's exactly what I'll do, Detective."

Kennedy: "That's not gonna fly in court."

I chime in, "Of course, we don't even get to court without more evidence." I exhale forcefully. "Tough call. Is there some other way?"

Durand says with a scowl, his voice dripping with sarcasm, "Sure, you could just ask. I'm sure Limerock'd be happy to incriminate himself if you're nice about it."

I stare at Kennedy, unsure what to do. Desperate men do desperate things, but shit, this isn't in our playbook. Meanwhile, Durand powers up the laptop and starts typing.

"What the hell are you doing?" Kennedy yells. "We didn't give you the go ahead."

"Which means you have plausible deniability, detectives," Durand says with a sick laugh, his fingers moving at breakneck speed.

I shrug my shoulders at Kennedy then switch gears. "What was Grayson up to? Was he going to switch the med or taint it but got cold feet instead?"

Kennedy shakes his head. "I'm not buying that. Guy's killed two people like this, what's a third?"

"Maybe he thought it through, figured there was nothing to gain from offing someone else while the heat's on? Figured we must be taking a hard look at someone else for the murders so he should lay low." I shake my head. "But it doesn't explain his hands moving between Aloni's purse and his sports jacket. If he was gonna bail on it, we wouldn't have seen any movement. He would've just walked away."

"Maybe he made the switch, then switched them back?"

I study the mini-lab set up before me. "Naw. Got to

be something else... but what?" I pick up the test tube, turn it around in my hands, considering its appearance, the testing we just performed on it.

"Shit, that's it!" I say. "Grayson didn't want to switch the meds to kill anyone. We had Hyslop act like it was a groundbreaking compound...."

Kennedy looks at me, the realization hitting. "Grayson needed a sample to analyze." He points to the instrument in front of me. "Look what you figured out with just a drop. Bet he wouldn't need much more than that to figure out all sorts of shit."

"That's got to be it. Only problem is, we've got no way to prove it. Damn thing looks as full as when Hyslop gave it to Kiki earlier. We're back to square one."

Durand slumps forward and pounds his fists on his lap. "Make that square zero." Durand grabs the laptop and tosses it next to him on the bed. "There's no way in hell I'm hacking into Immunogenetics Offerings with this piece of shit. Their firewalls are too sophisticated."

"And without that we've got no shot at a warrant. Fuck!"

"Not only that," Kennedy offers, "but once Limerock realizes we gave him glorified sugar water, he's gonna know Kiki helped in trying to set him up." He shakes his head. "No telling what's gonna happen then."

Durand jumps in. "You need to face reality, detectives. None of this adds up to Grayson Limerock being the killer." His beady eyes jump between Kennedy and me. "I suggest we move on to other suspects before someone else loses their life."

"And before we need to ship your ass back," Kennedy says. "So who's next on our list, and how is dickhead here gonna help us nail him?"

§

Having dispatched Kiki to Hyslop's lab with the medication and supplies, and Martinez and Kendricks back to the precinct, Simmons, Kennedy, Durand and I gather around the suspect board at the hotel. I tap on the photo of a beautiful African-American woman.

"Kerline St. James. Next on our list. Kev, summarize what we've got on her."

"Jamaican, late thirties, works at Hyslop's lab as one of their more senior techs. Worked at Gorelick's while Malekoviec was a patient there. Referred vic two, who dated her daughter, Shanteel, to Gorelick's for treatment. A real firecracker. Definitely some anger management issues there," Kennedy says with enthusiasm.

"Just like you," Simmons snorts as I roll my eyes.

Kennedy glares at Simmons. "Like I was saying, St. James couldn't stand Jamal Richards. Would she go so far as offing him? Not sure." He grabs a sip of water. "Gorelick angle is interesting. St. James couldn't stand him, and the feeling was mutual. He threatened

smile off his face. "Okay. The investigation was real hush-hush. Press never got wind of it, and no one but Hyslop ever knew the details, but Goldberg filled me in. All three vics were transplant patients, supposedly from Washington General."

"Your old stomping grounds, dear Christopher. Perhaps you worked on some of them?" Durand says with a glint in his eye and his trademark twisted laugh.

I ignore him and plow ahead. "I say supposedly because they all came to Hyslop with no records whatsoever, just a verbal account from their anonymous surgeon."

Simmons: "No records, no idea who the surgeon was? What the hell was Hyslop thinking?" For once Simmons makes a good point.

"Not sure. Goldberg was certain Hyslop knew who the surgeon was and was protecting him, which makes you wonder why? Did Hyslop know something underhanded was going on with the transplants? Or was he just happy to have the business, afraid to burn his referring doc?"

Blank stares all around.

"Either way, all three patients were experiencing transplant rejection despite heavy-duty immunosuppressives. The surgeon needed Hyslop's wizardry to pull them through."

Durand: "Clearly that didn't work out."

"Exactly. Hyslop tries his best over a four-month

period of time last year, but one-by-one the patients die."

Kennedy cuts in, "Kinda weird he was treating all transplant patients back-to-back-to-back like that." He points toward the treatment list we obtained from Hyslop that's tacked to the suspect board. "I combed through that list. Not one transplant patient since then, just patients with arthritis, diabetes, thyroid problems, that kinda stuff."

Simmons: "Could be he got gun-shy with the transplants. Wants to try his hand on stuff he's more comfortable with for a while."

I nod. "Kev, didn't Hyslop tell you eliminating transplant rejection was his endgame, that all these other diseases were easier for him to treat?"

"Yeah, like the other patients were stepping stones for him. Each one of them helped him figure out a piece of the puzzle to solving the whole transplant rejection thing."

"And didn't Zigler say that Hyslop talked a lot about the need to find a cure for his brother before it was too late?"

Kennedy, excitedly: "Yeah, his brother, Phil. Got a bad ticker, been on the transplant list for years, but they don't think he's gonna get one in time."

I study our serial killer's face: not a flicker of surprise or fascination. "Nothing to add, Durand?"

"Only that the premise is scientifically sound.

Success with this myriad of other types of patients would give him the answers he needs for the transplant patients."

"I agree. Crazy as it sounds, Hyslop's work with suppressing and controlling the immune system would make it possible for transplants to be carried out without the need to match donors and recipients anymore. And that would save his brother's life if he figures it out in time." Deep in thought, I stare straight through everyone as I feel things click into place in my brain.

"Chris? So Hyslop's been using these patients as guinea pigs so he can cure his brother? Why kill Malekoviec and Richards then?" Kev asks.

"I don't think the deaths were intentional after all, just reckless."

Simmons, his voice squealing with delight, "Like involuntary manslaughter?"

"Exactly. Hyslop was pushing the envelope, taking chances he shouldn't have as he got increasingly desperate to cure his brother before it was too late."

Kennedy: "Makes sense. But shit, we just met with the killer, got his help so we could nail Limerock. So how we now gonna get the goods on Hyslop instead?"

"Hyslop figures we're going to charge Grayson for the murders. We'll use that misdirection against him." I smile. "He won't know what hits him until it's too late."

I turn to our convict. "Time to step front and center, Durand. You up for it?"

Subdued, he responds, "I must warn you, time is of the essence."

"What the hell are you talking about?" Kennedy says with agitation.

I put up my hand to quiet my friend. "Go on, Durand."

"My deal with the DA's office is void unless you catch the killer before he strikes again."

Kennedy: "Yeah, so?"

Durand shakes his head. "Within hours the killer will claim another life. Figure out who the next victim is and you'll know for sure who the killer is."

"How could you possibly know that, and why should we believe you?" I ask skeptically.

"I have my sources, dear Christopher, and the best motivation—saving myself from a lethal injection."

"So why not just tell us who the next vic is?" I ask.

Durand laughs heartily. "Has the last year taught you nothing, Detective? I enjoy the game of cat and mouse too much to be transparent," he says with a sneer.

"So you're willing to risk your own neck hoping we solve this in time?" Kennedy asks, incredulous.

Durand replies in a derogatory tone, "*Detective Ravello* is more than capable of connecting the dots." He turns to me. "But will you figure it out in time?" He laughs again. "Come, Detective Kennedy, lets you and I go fetch his beloved for him."

Kennedy's fists ball up as Durand continues, that

sick smile on his face now, "It's simple really. Save the victim, catch the killer, and Michelle will be your reward."

"And if I fail?" I ask.

"Then all hope is lost for saving my life, and no happy reunion for you."

The veins in my neck bulge as I grab Durand by the shirt. "You do anything to her, anything at all..."

"And what, Detective, you'll kill me?" He laughs.

As if I need any more pressure to save the day.

I stare at the mountain of a man who is my partner. "All right, Kev, go with Durand and get Michelle." I shake my head in frustration. "I'll figure out how to save the next vic, then meet up with you after."

My eyes bore a hole in Durand's skull. "Play it straight with Michelle and you'll have no more worries about the death penalty."

Durand nods confidently and gives me a mocking salute, his handcuffs clanging together as Kev drags him away.

"Simmons, we need to keep the commiss in the loop."

His face lights up. Never before has Simmons been entrusted with such a vital role in an investigation. "What do you want me to tell him, Chief?" And that's not going to change today.

I scribble a note, place it in a sealed envelope, and hand it to him. "It's all in here. Don't open the letter or give it to anyone but Kelly himself. Not even his secretary, you understand?"

His face sags. "Yeah, I hear you."

"Good, hurry, we don't have much time."

Simmons hesitates. "Something I got to ask you, Chief."

Impatiently I say, "Can't it wait? Really under the gun now."

He walks over to the suspect board, taps on the patient list from Hyslop's office. "How come you're on this?"

The color drains from my face. "Huh, where?"

He taps on the list insistently. "Right here, Chief, see?"

I lean in, then look at Simmons gravely. "Anybody else see this list?"

"Just you, me, and Kennedy."

"Not McCarthy, or Martinez, or Kendricks?"

Looking right at me. "No sir. Those guys are too busy with other stuff. What's going on?"

I stare at him, then blink twice. Word of this gets out, I'm screwed. The administration will realize I faked my medical records to get into the police academy, and they'll kick me off the force for good. I put a hand on Simmons' shoulder and peer into his eyes. "This needs to stay between us. You understand? Pretty soon I'll have my own cure and be in the clear, but no one can ever know about this. I've got two young kids, Simmons. My livelihood depends on you keeping this quiet."

He swallows hard, then wipes his nose on the back of his hand before extending it toward me. "You can count on me, Chief. I done a lot of shit I ain't proud of, wouldn't want anybody knowing about." He snorts. "You're just trying to do right by your family and you're a kickass chief."

I smile and shake his hand. "Thank you. All right, off you go. I've got work to do."

As the door closes behind Simmons, I grab the list off the board, then a stack of reports from the FDA and set them and my phone in front of me on the desk. The reports cover the last two years of activity at Hyslop's labs. Far enough back to cover all three transplant patient deaths. Just got to confirm a few things before kicking my plan into high gear.

Poring through the reports, it's clear the FDA had no issues with the science in Hyslop's lab. The compounds themselves, testing, administration, etc. were all good. It was the *protocols* Hyslop had in place a year and a half ago that landed him in hot water. The FDA didn't want one person, namely Hyslop, in charge of the entire process from patient intake all the way through to delivery of the medications. The flaw in that approach was evident with the three transplant deaths and Hyslop's decision to treat those patients with no physical records, just a verbal account by an unnamed surgeon. The FDA forced Hyslop to accept their recommendations to split up responsibilities, ushering in Todd Zigler's employment. Under Todd's careful guidance, the lab's efficiency and volume of patients grew to the point where there are now waiting lists for patients seeking treatment for certain kinds of disorders.

Reviewing the FDA reports, Kennedy's and my notes on the investigation and our interviews, and something Simmons said earlier, it's clear I'm finally on the right track about our killer. I just have to prove it.

I lean back in the chair and stretch my arms and neck. I've been going almost non-stop for the last two days, but there's just one part of me aching now: my heart. With any luck, in just a few more hours I'll finally see my baby again.

I wipe a tear from my eye as I sift through the other info we have and decide to double check the patient list. *Our next vic has to be on that list.* The list is categorized in several ways, including alphabetically by patient name and indicates their diagnosis, demographics, treating physician, and dates of treatment. I scan the list, line-by-line, but halfway down the first page, I give into a growing sense of anxiety about Simmons' delivery. *Better give Kelly a quick call to make sure he got the letter.*

As I dial Kelly, the alarm on my phone goes off. Four p.m. Appointment with Jacobs in half an hour. I continue dialing. Gotta make this quick if I'm going to get to Jacobs, then stop vic three from being killed.

Kelly answers on the first ring. "Got your note, Chris. Everything going okay with Durand?"

I lie my ass off. "Yes, fine Commissioner. Sometimes I almost forget what a serial-killing bastard he is—almost," I say with a laugh.

"Good, glad to hear it."

The next words stick in my throat as my eyes freeze on the list. Holy shit! It's got to be him! I glance at my watch. *Might make it if I leave right now.*

"Chris, you still there?"

"Yes sir, but gotta run."

"All right then, Chris, I'll—" I hang up before he even finishes. An instant later I'm a blur as I bolt out of the room.

# ⤳ Chapter 9 ⤳

Only in New York City could I face such an avalanche of obstacles.

The streets are packed with holiday shoppers and tourists, their bags and bodies scurrying about. My destination is a mere five blocks away but my task is Herculean.

I barrel down the street, a blur racing through the crowd. Arms and legs pumping as fast as they can.

Can't be late—too much at stake.

Weaving between pedestrians, I knock bags loose, send children running for cover. I dodge oncoming traffic at crosswalks as cars blare their horns at me. One driver curses me out for sliding across the hood of his car as a 'DON'T WALK' sign flashes angrily.

Three blocks down, just two more to go.

Heart pounding. Gasping for breath. But no time to rest. Gotta get there before they do the unthinkable.

Before they kill him.

A homeless woman with a laundry cart of possessions lunges in front of me. I try to avoid her, careen-
ing off the metal cart instead, landing hard on my right
shoulder as her goods scatter in the air. Shaking off
the pain, I lunge forward toward the next intersection,
clearing it just as a yellow taxicab hurtles by.

One more block. Not sure I'll make it in time.

In the distance I see a line of large oak doors with
wrought iron handles and impressive signs, the status
symbols of Manhattan's well-heeled, Upper East Side
doctors' offices. One of those could have been my
office if it wasn't for mom's attack.

Out of nowhere, they slam into me, knocking me to
the ground. My head smashes into the pavement. Disoriented, I stumble to my feet and ready myself to fight.

But they're already gone.

Head is throbbing and bloody. Legs wobbly, vision
doubled. I press on, hoping I get there in time to save
him.

I see it now, third door on the right.

I storm through the large, oak door like a running
back breaking through a defensive line. Still woozy,
blood dripping from my head as I traverse the small
waiting room, I hold my badge ahead of me, yelling
to the receptionist just ahead, "Police! Buzz me in or
someone dies!" The stunned receptionist does just
that as I slam into the door separating waiting room

from a long hallway ahead. My eyes dart left, then right. Five exam rooms on each side. No time to try them one-by-one.

I thrust my badge at the flabbergasted receptionist to my left. "Detective Ravello. Chief of the Division of Medical Crimes. Which room is Aaron Lefkowitz in?" She stares at the badge for a long moment, frozen, then points. "Third door on your right." Her voice trails behind me as I power forward. "But you can't go in there. Doctor's doing a procedure." My hand reaches the doorknob an instant before my shoulder slams into the door. I half open it, half knock it off its hinges, splinters flying. I hear a scream as the scene unfolds in slow motion. A man in a white lab coat pushes a needle into the IV line. His thumb readies to push the plunger as I yell, "Nooo, don't do it!" The doctor, stunned, falls back, the syringe hanging by its needle from the IV. He gathers his wits as he stares at me. "What is the meaning of this?"

I yank the syringe from the IV before he reconsiders. "Shit, that was close," I say breathlessly. A stunned and speechless patient stares back at me.

Over the next five minutes I explain myself to doctor, nurse, and patient. "The medicine is tainted. It would've killed him."

"Are you sure?" Doctor Johnson says. "His first dose barely had any effect."

"Positive. Second dose is the deadly one." I gather

myself, straightening my hair, taking a gauze pad from the nurse to stop the bleeding from my forehead. "Mr. Lefkowitz would not only have continued to reject his heart transplant, the rejection would have accelerated, killing him in a few hours."

Lefkowitz and the nurse look at each other, their jaws hanging open.

I hold up the syringe of green-tinged fluid and cap the needle. "Mind if I take this?"

The doctor shakes his head no. "Thanks. You've been a big help." I offer a quick nod, then hurry out of the office. Hustling back toward the hotel, I give Kennedy a call. "Hey, what's up partner? Disaster averted on this end. Have you got Michelle?"

# FORBIDDEN
# CURE 6

## THE RECKONING

# ⇥ Chapter 1 ⇤

"Here's the burner you asked for," Kennedy grumbles as he tosses it into the back seat. "Now set up that damn meet." Durand, handcuffed to the inside of the door of Kennedy's Civic, punches the phone number in as he leans against the door. "Ready her. Detective Kennedy and I will meet you in a half hour. Yes, the field by the abandoned warehouse, near the dock that goes to North Brother Island." Durand flips the phone shut. "All set, Detective."

Kennedy peers at Durand through the rearview mirror. "You better not try any shit, Durand. I'm in no mood for games." The detective enters the FDR Drive near the Queensboro Bridge and heads north, wishing they were in a police cruiser so he could cut through the heavy traffic. The next twenty minutes pass by in silence, Kennedy taking the RFK Bridge through Randall's Island, then going north on the Bruckner to the Port Morris area of the Bronx. At exit 48 he makes a hard right turn, traveling due south on East 149th Street. A seedy, industrial area, they pass by a moving company and a beer distributor. Kennedy slows the car as they approach the massive, old, warehouse building. Broken windows and graffiti litter the worn brick structure. Adjacent to it a small field with patches of grass, garbage strewn about. Just beyond that a parking lot, fenced in with barbed wire, leading to a makeshift pier housing a few boats to provide transport to North Brother Island, located about six hundred feet off shore.

Kennedy eyes the area with suspicion. Alone, no backup nearby, he realizes how vulnerable and exposed he is, knowing the warehouse provides the perfect shield for an ambush. He punches in the access code and pulls into the parking area's tiny entrance, driving to the far end of the lot. He leaves the car idling close to the pier, facing toward the warehouse and vacant lot, as the gate rumbles shut. *Best view in case they try anything,* he muses.

Fifteen minutes go by, the only activity a stiff breeze swirling trash in the air on the lot ahead. Kennedy turns to Durand. "Looks like your men got cold feet. We're outta here in five if—" Just then a black Town Car materializes in the distance beyond the warehouse. Durand smiles as the car stops at the field and the driver gets out.

Kennedy cuts the engine, then slips out the passenger side and back in next to Durand. He recuffs him, freeing him from the door, and pulls out his Glock. Holding it up, he pushes the serial killer out of the car, gun pressed against his head.

Kennedy yells through the fence to the man standing next to the car. "Where the hell is Michelle Ravello?" He releases the safety. "No time to be fucking around, unless you want your boss to suffer the consequences."

The man, dressed in a dark winter coat, approaches the gate as Kennedy again enters the code. The man slips through the gate as it grinds open, his dark hair flapping in the breeze. "There's been a holdup. We can have her here soon."

"Stop right there," Kennedy yells. "Throw any piece you have on the ground and kick it toward me."

Durand: "Do it, Tony."

The man complies, placing a handgun on the ground and pushing it away.

"I need to speak to Durand alone for a minute," Tony says.

"No chance of that, douche-bag," Kennedy yells back. "Whatever you need to say, say it."

The thug looks at Durand, unsure of himself.

Durand nods. "It's fine." Then to Kennedy: "The delay is my doing, Detective. As I said earlier, stop the next killing, catch the killer, then and only then will you get your dear Michelle Ravello."

Kennedy protests, but his phone kills the words in his throat. "Hey Chris. At the meet now, but no Michelle. Durand's insisting we prove you saved the vic, then catch the killer, before he'll release her to us."

Ravello: "Tell him Aaron Lefkowitz is safe and sound at Doctor Johnson's office and I'm on my way to North Brother Island. Where are you guys?"

"At the pier that takes us there. Hold on, lemme relay the message. Hear that Durand? Aaron Lefkowitz is safe at Doctor Johnson's office and Ravello is on his way here."

Durand smiles, then nods at Tony. "Excellent. Go get the girl and meet us on the island."

Tony moves toward the gun.

Kennedy: "Leave it right there unless you want your hand shot off." Defiant, Tony continues forward. Kennedy rips off a shot, the criminal jumping back as it hits the ground just in front of him. "Next one's between your eyes if you try it again."

Tony backs away toward the gate, Kennedy yelling the access code to him. The thug looks at Durand. "Be back in an hour, boss."

Kennedy yells to Tony, "Make sure it's just you and Michelle Ravello. Anyone else and your boss pays the price." Back to his phone call, Kennedy asks, "When you getting here, buddy?"

"About ten minutes."

"Good. We'll be in my car at the lot near the pier.

Be on the lookout for Durand's men. One's leaving now to get Michelle."

"Will do, Kev. Ready for the big showdown?" Ravello asks.

"Ready as I'll ever be," Kennedy quips as he licks his parched lips.

§

As I hang up with Kennedy another call comes in. Shit, Jacobs' office! "Hello, sorry I missed my appointment. I'm in the midst of—"

"Chris, what the hell is going on?" It's Jacobs himself. "You can't wait on this treatment. Every hour that goes by your chances of being cured dwindle."

"I know, I know. Shit's hitting the fan on this end and we're about to catch our killer." No time to explain further. I've still got another call to make before I meet Kennedy. "I'll call back to reschedule. Bye."

I hang up and dial Hyslop's lab. Pressing the phone to my ear as I drive through Randall's Island, I spend the next few minutes in intense conversation. "It's going to be difficult for you, I realize. But everything is riding on you doing exactly as I say."

§

Detective Kennedy cuffs Durand to the car door

and shuts it, then moves with caution toward the gun Tony left on the ground. His own firearm drawn, he scans his surroundings, squinting to see through the swirling debris and dust ahead as the sun sets off in the distance. Wind batters the coast, crashing waves onto the shore behind his car. His muscles tense and ready as he creeps forward. Suddenly, movement off to his right. He turns, ready to fire.

A stray cat, scurrying off in search of its next meal. Kennedy shakes his head and exhales as he reaches the gun and pockets it. He twists side to side, his gun poised, backing slowly toward the car. Ten feet... five... one. The detective takes one last look around then enters the car, still on guard, but glad to have cover.

Minutes roll by. Darkness blankets the area. Far off a car winds forward, its headlights lighting the way. Kennedy strains his eyes, trying to identify the car, but its high-beams make that impossible. His face set in grim determination, Kennedy raises his gun as the vehicle approaches. A smile breaks across his face.

Chris' Firebird.

Ravello enters the lot and swings the car around as the gate closes, angling the Firebird so it blocks off the parking lot's entrance/exit. *Smart move,* Kennedy thinks. *We can't get out, but a bunch of them can't come barreling in either.*

Ravello hustles over to the Civic as Kennedy emerges from the car with a cuffed Durand. Smiling, he shakes hands with Kennedy, then studies their surroundings. "The Firebird ought to slow them down, but we'll still be safer on the Island than here." Ravello nods toward the two small rowboats. "With oars, gasoline, and oil cans taking up space, each one can only hold three, four people tops so no worries a bunch of them attack us over there."

$

*Everyone's on dinner break, so now's my chance.* Kiki Aloni slips into the lab undetected. *Where does he keep it?* She slowly opens and closes two drawers, her eyes surveilling the area. Pulling open the next drawer, she smiles as she looks down at the shiny handgun before her. *Third time's the charm.*

$

We grab a boat, Kennedy and Durand up front as I man the outboard motor, my foot resting on the gasoline canister. I steer the rowboat through a stiff wind and choppy waves, a full moon our only light for the short trip to North Brother Island.

My phone jiggles in my pocket. I grab it and peer at the text message from McCarthy, smiling as I run through the plan again in my head. *Gonna be a full house. Gotta keep everyone safe.* We tie up at the pier, next to three other boats, and head toward Hyslop's grand, dilapidated lab. The full moon, overgrowth, and a web of tree limbs above us make it look like a scene out of a horror film. The door creaks as I open it, a strong wind ushering us in as Kiki greets us. "Nice to see you again, Detectives." She extends a hand toward Durand, but I wave her off. "This is Jean Louis Durand, of serial-killing fame, you may recall."

She pulls back, one hand going to her chest. "Oh my..." Gathering herself, she says, "Were you here to see Doctor Hyslop, Todd, or some—"

I cut her off. "Yes, that would be great."

Her eyes dart between Kennedy, Durand, and me. "Right this way."

# ⤇ Chapter 2 ⤆

The lab is abuzz with activity as I greet Hyslop. "Full steam ahead, I see, Doctor."

"Yes, Detective. We have a number of new formulations in the works I'm proud to say." He looks at Durand, confused. "Isn't that... ?"

"Yes it is," my voice, tinged with accusation. "We planned to keep Doctor Durand out of this, but even the best-laid plans can go awry. Isn't that right, Doctor?"

Hyslop shrugs. "So what can I assist you with? And how did your final treatment go? You look well."

I frown at the mention of my treatment, my eyes going wide. Whatever happened to patient confidentiality? I look at the bevy of technicians tending to their tasks as they sneak furtive looks at us. Todd Zigler stands apart from them, typing at a computer a few feet behind Hyslop, unfazed by it all.

"Had to miss it. More pressing matters to tend to."

Hyslop senses tension, something important and unspoken between us. He turns to his workers. "It's been a long day, everyone, and it's Christmas Eve, why don't we pick things back up after the holiday?"

The technicians glance at each other, ready to abandon their posts.

"We won't be long, Doctor Hyslop. Perhaps everyone could retreat to the breakroom for a few minutes instead?" I say.

"Fine, Detective." He nods to them. "Be back in twenty minutes."

The technicians groan. Kerline St. James, stationed closest to the door, leads the egress, the other six trailing behind her in silence. Todd continues his typing for a moment then looks up. "Okay if I stay?"

"Fine with me."

Hyslop nods in agreement. "So were you able to apprehend Grayson Limerock?"

I shake my head. "'Fraid not, Doctor. The investigation has gone in a completely different direction." I glance at Kennedy and Durand, then back to Hyslop, his face registering surprise at what I say. "Would you excuse me for a few minutes? I promise to fill you in as soon as I come back."

§

Ten minutes later I return from the breakroom, startling Hyslop as I re-enter the lab. "Where did we leave off? Oh yes, Grayson Limerock." I stare with intensity at Hyslop. "Turns out he wasn't our man after all."

"Are you sure?" Hyslop says incredulously. "You said he's committing corporate espionage, stealing my secrets."

"And he is," I say flatly. "But there's no evidence he's committing murder." I run my hand along the lab's wooden countertops as I approach Hyslop, dodging a few gas-lit burners along the way. Todd finishes typing and makes his way to his work area. Kennedy and Durand look on in silence. I stab my index finger at Hyslop. "But the same cannot be said of you."

"What? This is absurd. Why would I kill my own patients? What could I possibly gain from it?" Hyslop says with a huff.

"For yourself? Nothing. But for your brother Phil? A chance to save his life, restore him to good health."

Hyslop looks quizzically at me. "I don't follow."

I offer a solicitous smile. "Allow me to explain. The three deaths that occurred in your lab beginning a year and a half ago were all patients experiencing transplant rejection. They were your test runs for finding a cure for Phil. But unfortunately that cure proved elusive."

"I didn't murder those patients," Hyslop says, his voice starting to crack. "The police and the FDA investigated and ruled the deaths accidental." He looks to Kennedy, Durand, hoping to find support.

"Yes, I know. I've read the reports and spoken to the detective on the case." I lean back against the lab counter. "You never intended to kill those patients, but your recklessness, your desperation to find a cure for your brother clouded your judgment. You cut corners, took chances you shouldn't have, hoping to accelerate your efforts. But your eagerness to save your brother's life cost three patients theirs."

Hyslop, flustered, defensive: "You have no proof of any of this."

"Ah, but I do. I just re-interviewed your entire staff. They all confirm you spoke often about your brother's plight and the intense pressure you felt to save him."

"Nonsense, I did no—"

"Phil desperately needs a cure. But you couldn't keep killing transplant patients." I shake my head. "That would be too obvious. So you devised a scheme. You used other types of patients: diabetics, arthritic patients, and the like as 'stepping stones' to find your cure." I look over to Kennedy. "In fact, you admitted as much to Detective Kennedy a few days ago."

Kennedy reads from his notepad: "'Curing patients with endocrine and auto-immune disorders... helps unlock the secrets that will lead to my greatest accomplishment, eradicating the need for transplant patients to be matched with donors.'" Kennedy closes the pad. "It goes on, Doc, but we all get the idea."

"A brilliant plan, but just a couple of flaws. You

didn't have enough patients to perfect your cure, and you didn't want any more patient complications or deaths to blow back on you." I smile. "So you pressured your staff to recruit patients for you. More patients, more testing, faster cure for Phil, right, Doctor? That solved problem one."

Hyslop's face reddens. "You have no idea what you're talking about."

"But what about problem two? When the three transplant patients died, it was just you and a skeleton crew. No one else to blame then. But the last year and a half, under Todd Zigler's careful tutelage, the lab has grown tremendously and you now employee seven other technicians." Todd sifts through a drawer, his face bright with embarrassment as I pretend to be thinking. "You still needed to propel your work forward to save your brother. And to do that you'd have to take big risks with some of your patients." I snap my fingers. "So why not take those risks with patients closely connected to others, including your new technicians, and not to you?"

"You have quite an active imagination, Detective Ravello." Hyslop groans. "And after all I've done for you."

"Irina Malekoviec, a patient of Doctor Gorelick's. Gorelick has enough issues to make him a suspect in her murder. But Kerline St. James, who knew Irina, also worked at Gorelick's lab, and she has a well-documented hatred of the man. Kerline also has quite the temper." I shake my head. "The police might believe Kerline killed Irina to frame Gorelick or that Gorelick did it himself. Either way, St. James or Gorelick, the police wouldn't look to you as a suspect in Irina's death."

Hyslop's eyes roll up as he shakes his head.

"Irina dies and you still don't have your cure." Now, I add with sarcasm, "So why not really send the dogs after Kerline and Gorelick? You take your chances with Jamal Richards' cure and when it doesn't work out, all roads again lead to Kerline and Gorelick. My eyes dart to Kennedy and Durand, then back to Hyslop. "Except they don't."

I extend a hand toward Kennedy. "Great detective work rules out Gorelick—never had a chance to tamper with the meds before injecting them." I rub my hands together. "And St. James never felt right as our killer. Hot headed, impulsive? Absolutely. But not a calculating killer, especially with her new lease on life at your lab."

I twist my face into a befuddled gaze. "At this point Detective Kennedy and I are stumped, frustrated as all our good suspects are cleared." I snap my fingers again. "Ah, but what about Grayson Limerock? He's having an affair with Kiki Aloni—oops, cat's out of the bag on that one—he could have tampered with the meds. But when we gave him the perfect opportunity to do just that, he didn't. Which brings us right back to you, Doctor Hyslop."

Hyslop's confidence returns. "It's all just wild speculation, Detective. There's no proof of any of this."

I put up the stop sign. "I'll get to that in a minute. But first, any idea where I was earlier today?"

Hyslop shakes his head and shrugs his shoulders.

I pull the patient list out of my coat and slap it onto the countertop. "I was wracking my brains with this list, trying to figure out who potential victim three was and how knowing that would reveal the identity of our killer." I tap on the list repeatedly. "Then I saw it. A heart transplant patient having a tough time, rejecting his new heart. He was perfect for you to take your chances on, Doctor. He'd die soon if your cure didn't work out, so why not use him to try out a new version of a cure that has killed five people since last year? Cure him and brother Phil, who is clinging to life by a thread, can be saved too. Kill him and who could blame you for trying?"

"That's preposterous! For all you know my medicine would have saved, not killed, the last patient."

"True enough." I wave my hand toward the door to the lab. In walks Kerline St. James as I reach into my jacket and pull out Lefkowitz's medication. "Which is why Ms. St. James is going to test the sample for me, see if it matches up to the quality tests done yesterday before you signed off on it."

The air is thick with tension the next few minutes as Kerline runs a series of tests on the medication. I look to her with my eyebrows arched. "And?"

She shakes her head. "Don't pass any a de quality testin'."

I shake my head as well. "Such a shame."

"Wait! There has to be a mistake," Hyslop pleads. "You filled her in on your whole crazy theory. She thinks I tried to frame her. Let me take a look at those results." Hyslop storms forward.

My hand meets his chest. "That's far enough, Doctor."

Hyslop pulls back. "Get your hands off of me." He adjusts his tie. "I want that sample independently tested."

"And it will be. But it proves my point." I turn to Kerline. "One last thing, Ms. St. James. How often do you do QT work?"

"Me an de oder techs take turns; ev'ry seven weeks we do a full week straight."

"Switch weeks with anyone lately?"

"No man. Just follow de schedule dat was made."

"Thank you, Ms. St. James. You're free to go now." Kerline gives Hyslop a dirty look before departing.

I turn my attention back to Hyslop. "It's not easy to fake quality testing or alter samples after they've been tested, Doctor, but then again, your testing isn't really very helpful to begin with, is it?

Hyslop looks bewildered. "What are you talking about?"

"Your compounds have gotten more sophisticated

than your ability to test them. Quality testing is a sham, a way to make it seem like the compound is what it should be when it really isn't."

Hyslop's face turns a dark shade of red. "My lawyers will have a field day with this witch hunt you call an investigation."

I turn to Todd, hands still immersed in the drawer before him. "I can only imagine how you must feel, Todd. You come into a ramshackle operation, pour your heart and soul into it. Streamlining operations, improving efficiency. Hiring and supervising new staff, you turn the lab completely around." I look at Hyslop with disdain. "Only to have the lab's reputation destroyed by the very man who should be safeguarding it."

Todd smiles awkwardly. "Well, uh, wow. Not sure what to say."

I wave him off. "I'd be speechless too." Pointing to Hyslop. "If this man hadn't screwed it all up, in no time you'd be one of the most celebrated people in the industry. The man who single-handedly turned Hyslop's lab around." I smile. "It would all be yours: big salary, fancy car, all sorts of perks." I shake my head in sorrow. "All gone because of what Harold Hyslop did."

My face twists into a hardened stare. My eyes are like steel beads. "Except that's not the way things really went down, right Todd?"

Zigler looks at me, confused and scared. "What're you saying, Detective?"

"I'm saying you almost pulled it off, Todd. Almost." I shake my head. "With Hyslop set up beautifully, all you had to do was watch us stick a fork in him and you'd get off scot-free."

"I, I'm just not following you, Detective. Sorry."

I sneer at him. "I'll lay it out for you then. A few lies on your part, none of them earthshaking on their own. But taken together they got me thinking, digging until it all fell into place."

"Kev, remember when Todd told you Hyslop's QT wasn't worth shit, that his compounds had become too sophisticated to be properly tested?"

"Sure. Had me thinking Hyslop could pull a fast one whenever he wanted and nobody'd be the wiser," he says.

"Except the FDA reports show all the testing in the lab was being done *exactly* as it needed to be. There were no inadequacies with QT."

Kennedy nods.

"And for all the issues of record-keeping and separating intaking patients from formulation, from QT and so forth, did the FDA mention, *even once*, in any of their reports that they had a problem with the science being carried out in the lab?"

Kennedy smiles. "No they did not."

Todd's face grows pale as I stare at him. "Guess what else I found out in the breakroom, Toddy?"

He shrugs weakly.

"None of the other techs even knew Doctor Hyslop has a brother." I look over at him. "Apparently, he never discusses his personal life with them. But you, the office psychologist, everyone's best buddy, you know everyone's secrets. You knew about Hyslop's brother and tried to kill Mr. Lefkowitz so you could frame Dr. Hyslop for it. You knew about Kerline's issues with Gorelick, with Jamal Richards too." I laugh. "It was child's play for you to set up Hyslop and Ms. St. James."

Todd shakes his head. "First you blame poor Doctor Hyslop, now me. Which is it, Detective?" he mumbles.

"Oh, it's definitely you, Toddy." I rub my hands together. "You're the only one who does patient intake so you're the only one who knows where each patient comes from and when the lab will be working on their formulation. You hired most of the technicians, including Kerline St. James, and you make-up the technicians' schedules, including when they work on QT. You're even the last one in the lab to handle the medications before Kiki delivers them." I stare intently at Zigler. "Must be nice to control the whole process? Makes it easier to taint medications and frame others for it."

Zigler: "What are you talking about?"

I nod. "You referred Irina Malekoviec to Gorelick's office for treatment, figuring she'd ultimately need Dr. Hyslop's wizardry to help her."

Todd shakes his head vigorously.

"You brought Kerline St. James over to this lab because of her intense hatred of Gorelick, and you used that hatred against her." I lick my lips. "You wanted us to believe Kerline killed Irina to trash Gorelick's reputation by framing him for the murder."

"I don't know what you're talking about, Detective. Kerline's my friend."

"No, along with Hyslop, she's one of your patsies. One death suggesting Kerline is the killer is kind of shaky. So you killed someone else Kerline couldn't stand: Jamal Richards." I pause. "Whoever killed Malekoviec and Richards and tried to kill Lefkowitz did so by tainting the medicines and faking the QT or by tainting the medicines after QT was done." I turn to Kennedy. "When was QT done on our vics and who did it?"

"Monday, December 14th, Tuesday, December 22nd, and yesterday, Kerline St. James all three times," Kennedy says with a smile.

"Each tech rotates through QT for a week every seven weeks. But you scheduled Kerline to do QT on Malekoviec, Richards, and Lefkowitz in back-to-back weeks, knowing that would put her in our crosshairs."

I smile at Zigler. "How am I doing so far, Toddy?"

His face is expressionless.

"So, you've got the best access for tampering with meds since you oversee QT and are the last one to handle the medications before Ms. Aloni delivers them. You could taint the medications and fake the QT because, let's be honest, Doctor Hyslop trusts you completely and never checks if the compounds really passed QT or not. He just glances at the results and signs off on them."

I crack my knuckles.

"But if someone took a closer look at the QT on the killer compounds, that approach would make you a suspect since you oversee everyone's QT work - everyone except Kerline St. James. She's your most experienced tech and everyone knows you never look over her shoulder." I slap the countertop. "And low and behold, she did QT on both murders and the attempted murder. So it will look like Kerline tampered with the medications and faked the QT when in fact you tampered with the meds *after* the QT was done. Or it will look like Hyslop is guilty due to your lie about the testing being inadequate." I nod my head. "Impressive planning, pointing the suspicion everywhere but you, Toddy."

Todd shakes his head. "Elaborate plan, but why would I want to kill anyone? Makes the lab and me look bad, so there goes all the goodies you said I'd get from turning the lab around single-handedly."

"Revenge. Against the one person who, years ago, destroyed your hope of becoming rich and famous."

Zigler's face takes on a skeptical look. "And who would that be, Detective?"

"Irina Malekoviec."

Hyslop gasps. "What? Why?"

I turn to the dear doctor. "When Detective Kennedy and I interviewed Doctor Gorelick, he mentioned in passing that Todd had taken lessons with Irina. Well, I did a little digging. Turns out Irina strung poor Toddy along for years, telling him he would enjoy a wonderful career as a concert pianist. Until one day when Irina, perhaps bitter her own career was failing due to her rheumatoid arthritis, changed her mind. She told Todd he didn't quite have what was needed to succeed in that world."

I turn back to Todd. "How am I doing so far?"

Todd's face is hard like stone.

"Devastated, Toddy decides he'll have his revenge. What's that saying, Todd? 'Keep your friends close and your enemies closer'? So he stays in touch with Ms. Malekoviec as he pursues his backup plan of being a lab technician, eventually coming to work with Doctor Hyslop. When Irina's arthritis worsens to the point of hopelessness, Todd sees his opportunity."

Zigler shakes his head in denial as his face reddens. "That's not how it was."

"He refers her to Doctor Gorelick, one of Hyslop's biggest customers, knowing eventually Irina will need one of Hyslop's treatments. But Toddy can't be exposed. He'll need someone to take the fall for him when the time is right. So he hires a beautiful, young, talented woman from Gorelick's office. She's grateful to Todd for helping her escape the abusive environment at Gorelick's lab. She'll never suspect Todd would use that abusive environment and their friendship to set her up."

Todd's anger swells. "Lies, all lies!"

I study Todd's face. "You hoped Irina's investigation would be perfunctory, reaching the same conclusion as a year and a half earlier with the transplant patients; the death was accidental." I shake my head. "You didn't count on Kennedy or me, on us sinking our teeth into this investigation. You were desperate, in need of another plan to save yourself from scrutiny. So you concocted a few lies to implicate Hyslop and you let slip about Kerline's problems with Gorelick and Jamal Richards." I pause, my eyes honing in on Zigler. "Then your big break came along: Grayson Limerock saw you as key to taking down Hyslop's lab. He tracked you down, offering you a tremendous raise and a high profile job with his esteemed company. Now you could implicate St. James and Hyslop, destroy his company, and come out squeaky clean with a fat bank account and the notoriety you so desperately craved."

Todd screams, "Enough, enough already!" as he brandishes a gun. "You're so very clever, Detective Ravello. Setting up Kerline and Doctor Hyslop, I should have been in the clear. The Lefkowitz murder would have been my icing on the cake." He points the .38 at Hyslop. "Sealing this fool's fate once and for all."

I walk toward Todd as he levels the gun at my chest. "It's over, Todd. We've got your confession. Don't make this any more difficult than it needs to be."

Zigler laughs as he looks at the gun and then me. "You seem to have overlooked one small but lethal detail, Detective."

I shake my head. "It's not loaded, Todd. Ms. Aloni took care of that earlier. Just left it there so you'd confess."

Zigler pulls the trigger repeatedly to no avail, then throws the gun at me before grabbing a filled test tube. Holding it toward me, he says, "Recognize the name?"

I stop in my tracks. "My treatment. So what?"

"The last of your perfected cure, Detective. It's all that stands between you and a lifetime of suffering and disability."

I smile. "You're forgetting the dose at Doctor Jacobs' office."

"A dose that would have killed you too, Detective," he says sarcastically, "if you hadn't been so damn noble, missing your appointment to save Lefkowitz and to catch the killer."

"Adding attempted murder of a police officer to your charges, Todd. My, you've been busy." I inch closer to him. "Doctor Hyslop can just formulate more of the compound for me."

"'Fraid not, Detective. My busy work on the computer earlier? I scrubbed all information regarding your compound from our computers in case you were on to me and I needed a bargaining chip. Not even Hyslop can recreate the formulation from memory." He jiggles the cure. "This is your last hope, Detective. Let me go and it's yours."

"I'm afraid that's not going to happen, Todd. Hand it over or smash it to pieces, the result will be the same: jail for you." I stretch out my hand to receive the medicine. Zigler looks at it, uncertain what to do. Moments pass in strained silence, then Zigler's hand creeps toward mine. Just another second or two and the cure will be mine.

Suddenly the lab door swings open behind Durand. Zigler pulls back, clutching the cure to his chest as my eyes hone in on the source of the noise.

In walks a sight I never thought I'd see again.

§

After months of anguish, heartache, and hope-lessness, a tidal wave of euphoria and relief crashes through me. "Michelle!" I cry out with an all-encompassing smile as tears run down my face. "Thank God you're alive!" Overwhelmed by utter, blissful disbelief, I'm transfixed by her beauty.

Tears well in Michelle's eyes. Her heart bursts with joy and relief, but something is amiss. "Chris! Watch it. It's a trap," she yells. Aching to hold her, I start toward her anyway, then see Durand's goon, his gun jammed into her back.

"Stop right there, Ravello, or she gets it." He pushes Michelle forward. "Time to disarm, detectives. Ravello, you first. Slide your gun away on the counter." As I comply, he adds, "Thatta boy. Now Kennedy, turn your gun backwards and hand it to my boss along with the keys to them cuffs."

Kennedy angrily passes his Glock and the keys to Durand. The sociopath undoes the cuffs, making a show of dropping them to the floor, then slides behind Kennedy and jabs the gun into his back.

Durand: "Now, that's more like it." He nudges Kennedy toward Zigler. "I'm going to need that test tube now, Mr. Zigler."

Todd's eyes dart between Durand and his henchman as Todd clutches the glass tube and backs away.

Durand pushes Kennedy off to the side, opening up a clear path to Zigler. He creeps forward. "Nothing to worry about, Todd. I'm not going to hurt you. All I want is the detective's cure, and then you'll be free to go." Durand smiles and extends his hand. "Just give it to me and off you go. Honor among criminals, and all that good stuff, right Toddy?"

"The second you give it to him, you're a dead man," I yell.

Todd mumbles, "I never even met him before." He stops backpedaling, then reaches out to Durand with the compound. "How could he want me dead?"

Durand steps forward. "How indeed?" He shakes his head. "Ravello just doesn't want me to have his precious medication." He motions to Todd to hand it over. Todd steps forward, placing the tube in his hand. Durand looks Todd in the eyes. "There, that wasn't so hard, was it?" The sociopath secures the medication and starts to turn away, then twists back and fires on Todd, the bullet tearing through his right eye. Todd falls to the ground, dead.

Durand slips my cure into his coat pocket. "Shame on you, dear doctor-detective." He shakes his head. "Trying to warn Zigler like that."

"Why would you kill him, Durand? He didn't even know you, for God's sake."

Durand shakes his head. "It's what I do, Detective. I'm one of the bad guys, remember?" His face turns icy cold. "And bad guys kill people."

I glance at Kennedy, see his hand edging toward his jacket pocket. Could he have another gun?

Durand's eyes trace my line of sight, setting off a whirlwind of motion. "He's got a gun, stop him!"

Michelle jabs her elbow into her captor's solar plexus, hitting him over the head as he doubles over in pain, the gun flying out of his hand. Kennedy fumbles in his jacket for the gun as the gangster straightens up and lunges at him, slamming into Kennedy just as he frees the pistol from his pocket. The two men roll around on the ground, struggling for control of the firearm.

I take a quick step toward Durand, then duck for cover as he fires wildly on me. Three shots ring out. Glass shatters and flies all around me. I stay low as caustic chemicals and powders cover the countertops, dripping onto the floor. A burner topples over, igniting the chemicals. Flames race across the wood countertop in every direction. Kennedy rolls on top as his adversay, in control of the gun, takes aim. Kev strikes his hands just as he's firing, sending another bullet past me. A loud thud reverberates to my left as Durand takes aim at Kennedy. Michelle yells "Duck!" just as Durand pulls his own trigger. Kennedy gets clear just in time, as Durand's bullet strikes his man dead. Flames rise up from the ground, overtaking the countertops, running up the walls as Durand eludes Kennedy's flailing hands and jumps over the dead man's body. The door to the lab opens, the rush of oxygen into the room fanning the flames as Durand escapes. Off to my left I see Hyslop on the ground, injured but moving.

I yell out, "Kev, grab Michelle and get the hell out of here! I gotta get Hyslop." I hear Michelle's cries. "No, Chris! Leave him!" I half hear, half see Kennedy fight his way over to Michelle and subdue her as she struggles to break free to save me.

"Get out now, Michelle, before it's too late! I'll find my own way." Flames lick the air in front of her, illuminating her face and the beautiful scar on her neck that brought her back to me. As Kennedy drags her away from me, I hear his voice. "No way out. Too many fucking flames... Hold on, what if I..." Kennedy's primordial scream rings out as he grabs the thug's dead body, jerking it off the ground with one hand as he holds Michelle with the other. Using the body as a shield, Kennedy guides Michelle and himself out of the lab. I hear their footsteps receding as I crawl over to Hyslop, hoping, praying there's still time to save us both.

# ▸ Chapter 3 ◂

Kennedy explodes through the front door of the burning building, flames shooting after him, the smell of burned flesh in his grasp. Gasping for air, the body slips from his grip as he and Michelle stagger to safety, then collapse to the ground. A full minute passes before either stirs.

Kennedy looks up first, pushing Tony's charred body away. Michelle lies face down, motionless. Kennedy swallows hard and tentatively reaches out for her. His hand touches her arm.

"Michelle, are you okay?"

Silence.

Tears gather in Kennedy's eyes as he turns her over and leans into her chest to listen for breathing.

Nothing.

Suddenly coughing, sweet merciful coughing, as Michelle lurches forward!

"Oh God... passed out." Michelle's eyes search the area. She sees the dead body, smoke rising off its charred flesh. "Chris! No!"

Kennedy intercepts her, shakes his head. "Not him." He points. "He's still in there. I'm gonna get 'im."

Michelle nods, emotion choking the words in her throat as tears stream down her face.

Kennedy stumbles to his feet, staggering forward as the front of the building, engulfed in flames, collapses before their horrified eyes. Wood and brick crash to the ground in a series of loud thuds. Sparks and embers fly everywhere, leaving no way into—or out of—the building.

# ❯ Chapter 4 ❮

Isling Hyslop's still body across my shoulders and plow through the flames, hoping against hope to find a path out. Smoke stings my eyes as the pungent order and taste of ashes assault my senses. Coughing, eyes tearing, lungs on fire, I stagger forward, through the lab door. *Just gotta stay conscious, keep moving.* Flames jump out and recede in front of me. No use trying to dodge their unpredictable paths. Searing pain fills my body as the fire scalds me with each step. Hyslop's weight bears down on me, threatening to stop us dead in our tracks.

Up ahead I glimpse it—the rotunda. Only ten, fifteen feet to go after that. I yell as I trudge forward into the circular space. Flames rush up the walls, engulfing the ceiling. Smoke obliterates my view. Front door is to the right, a few steps away. Just have to push through the fumes. I take two steps, then it happens. A blinding light ahead, fire everywhere, eating the building alive. Beams crash down in front of me. Not going to make it.

# ⟩ Chapter 5 ⟨

Kennedy stops dead in his tracks as the front of the building collapses to the ground. Michelle runs toward it. "No! Chris!" The detective intercepts her, Michelle's fists pounding his chest to let her go. She shrieks, her words unintelligible as Kennedy drags her back to safety.

"Stay here." Kennedy rushes toward the left side of the building, toward the lab itself. He frantically searches for a way in, but the jutting flames hold him back. Smoke billows before him as the ground trembles. Suddenly, an ear-shattering, concussive blow sends Kennedy flying backward as the lab explodes, hurling debris and equipment through the air. Glass, wood, brick, and metal rain down around Kennedy as Michelle shrieks louder.

Moments later a smaller explosion, then another, rock the lab. Kennedy struggles to his feet, hoping against hope for a way to save Chris. He pulls back from the building and scans the area for a way in. There isn't any.

Michelle, a few feet away, falls to her knees, her hands clawing at the dirt, tears pouring over her ash-covered face. *No way Chris survived this.* Her screams die in her throat, her voice overwhelmed by a piercing anguish. She crumbles to the ground face first, sobbing, spent, and defeated, her will to live all but gone.

Thirty seconds goes by, then thirty more. Kennedy leans over, speaking softly to Michelle. Slowly, she lifts her head and stares into the abyss of the raging fire, her spirit destroyed.

Kennedy tries to console Michelle as he helps her to her feet, but it's futile.

On the right side of the building glass shatters. Motion. An animal? Michelle blinks, refocuses, straining to see. "Oh my God! Chris?" She sprints toward his beleaguered body as it crawls away from the wreckage. Kennedy races over, spotting Hyslop's still body several feet behind Chris. He grabs the scientist and hauls him away from the fire as Michelle wraps her arms around Chris. "Thank God! Thank God you're all right. I thought you were dead." Michelle smothers him with tear-drenched kisses as Chris smiles feebly and mouths "My baby" as he collapses in her arms.

§

"This is Detective Kevin Kennedy of the 1-7. We have an officer and scientist down on North Brother Island. Repeat, officer and scientist down on North Brother Island. Send EMS and the FDNY. Building is burning to the ground, injuries may be life-threatening." Kennedy catches his breath as he looks at the dock, the remaining boat doused in flames. "Also need an APB on Jean Louis Durand, aka "The Giver," presumed to have fled the island via boat about twenty minutes ago."

Kennedy hobbles over to Ravello, a concerned look on his face as he sees Chris buried in Michelle's arms. "How is he?"

Michelle smiles back, her arms holding Chris tight. "Exhausted but alive."

"Just called for EMS, FDNY. Not sure how long it'll take them to get—What the fuck?" Kennedy's head snaps to attention as several boats approach the shore. They bypass the dock with its burning boat. As they run aground, Commissioner John Kelly disembarks, walking purposefully toward Kennedy. Medics stream out of the other boats, racing toward Ravello and Hyslop. "Cavalry is here, Detective. How are you holding up?"

"Hanging in there, sir. How d'you get here so quickly? I just called it in," Kennedy says.

Kelly points toward Ravello, EMT's caring for him and Hyslop as they ready them for transport. "Chris sent word earlier about his plan, asked us to stake out Port Morris for when Durand tried to escape."

Kennedy smiles. "You got him?"

Kelly's face fills with satisfaction. "We did." The commissioner uses his right hand to crack the knuckles in his left. "Fucker thought he'd outwitted us when he got off the boat and tried to grab his car and go." A broad smile on his face now. "Till we converged on him like feeding time at the zoo." Kelly laughs. "Two officers are running him back to Rikers as we speak." Kelly juts his chin toward the burning building. "What happened here?"

"Durand killed our perp on the Malekoviec and Richards murders, then lit up the place on the way out." Kennedy's face registers fear as the realization hits him. "Shit, the lab workers and secretary never got out."

Kelly places a hand on Kennedy's shoulder. "Relax, Detective. We found them a few minutes ago. Chris sent them out before the fireworks started, telling them to hover off shore in the boats until we arrived." Medics hustle by, loading Chris and the doctor for transport. Moments later everyone sets off for the mainland, the fire raging on like an ominous beacon in the eerie, dark night.

§

Kev, Michelle, and I commiserate on shore as EMT's speed off into the night with Hyslop, siren and lights blaring. A few officers mill about, overseeing the impounding of Durand's car. Kelly waves to us as he slips into his Town Car and leaves the scene.

Kev turns to me. "Clear something up for me."

"What's that?"

"Zigler's plan, setting up St. James to make it look like she was setting up Gorelick while also making Hyslop look suspicious." He shakes his head. "Pretty involved. How d'you know for sure you were reading things right?"

"McCarthy."

"McCarthy?" Kennedy says with surprise.

"Sent me a text while we were taking the boat out to the island."

"What'd it say?"

"Found it just like you said."

Kennedy shakes his head. Michelle and he look at me.

"I was pretty sure Zigler was our man but not a hundred percent. So I had McCarthy go to Zigler's apartment to find the proof."

"And?" they say in unison.

"No way Zigler could taint the medicines, kill his vics without a lot of trial and error. And he sure as hell couldn't test out his theories at Hyslop's lab."

Kennedy: "So you told McCarthy he'd find a small lab there, and that would cinch it?"

"Bingo. And that's just what he found, right down

to the notebooks Zigler kept on his experiments with some unlucky rodents," I say with a laugh.

"Nice," Kennedy says with appreciation.

The next minute drifts by in silence before Michelle, looking out toward the island, cuts in, "Can't believe how fast it burned to the ground." She shakes her head and says in a somber tone, "All the good work being done there, destroyed in a few minutes." Brightening, she hugs me. "Thank God we made it out alive."

Kennedy chimes in, "Your cure, too." He smiles. "Durand left with a vial of it. 'Bout time that fucker did something right."

Michelle, excited: "That's right! You're overdue for your last dose. Should we get the medicine tonight?"

I wave her off. "Nah. They'll confiscate it at Rikers. We can get it in the morning. No way Jacobs would be giving it to me before then anyway."

Michelle: "Tomorrow's Christmas, Chris."

"Aw shit, I forgot!" I shake my head in frustration, then do my best to try and laugh it off. "Fortunately, Jacobs is Jewish. Maybe he'll do me a favor and shoot me up after Mass."

Michelle offers a disapproving smile and shakes her head. "We can only hope."

A minute passes in silence, then Kennedy asks, "Why do you think Durand offed Zigler? The guy didn't even know him."

"Not sure, but my gut tells me we're dealing with

something much bigger than meets the eye," I say, "and knowing Durand, he's at the center of it."

A medic approaches, handing us each towels to clean up. "Need anything else?"

I glance at Kennedy then side hug Michelle. "No, I've got all I'll ever need." Reaching out a hand, I add, "Thank you for all your help."

The medic nods and trudges off. Finally a moment to ourselves! I take Michelle's hand in mine, slowly caressing then kissing it before I envelope her in a soulful hug neither of us wants to end. When at last it does, I lose myself in her beautiful blue eyes, feeling eternally grateful that she somehow cheated death, not once but twice. I take a slow, deep breath, cupping her chin in my hands, then our lips intertwine as we enjoy a passionate kiss that takes her breath away. At the sound of Kev's coughing we come up for air, both embarrassed by our public display of affection. Hoping to ease my buddy's self-consciousness, I play it casual. "Hell of a night, huh?"

"Hell of a few months," Michelle chimes in as she rolls her eyes. Then smiling, she says, "Let's get home, baby."

I nod. "Best idea I've heard in weeks." I turn to Kennedy and shake his hand as I pat his shoulder. "Great job, partner." He breaks out in a knowing smile as he eyes both of us. "Merry Christmas, guys. Now get outta here before you two get arrested for public indecency."

# ⟩ Chapter 6 ⟨

I place a quick call to Dad as Michelle and I climb into the Firebird and we drive through the gate. "...We'll be there soon. But Dad, it's very important you talk to the kids about their big surprise. Christine and James are so young. I don't want them to be frightened or confused so here's what you should tell them...."

The next forty-five minutes speeds by as we wind our way north of The City to Peekskill. Michelle and I hold hands, her dozing off intermittently as we enjoy the first moments of peace for either of us since raiding Durand's lab months ago. I smile at her as we exit Route 9 at South Street, then a few minutes later pull into our driveway.

Climbing the stairs to the porch, I feel a vibration in my pocket. I free my phone and look at the number with annoyance. *Just going to have to wait.* At the front door I pause and kiss Michelle softly. Then I step in, hiding Michelle behind me as I place my keys and phone on a small table next to the door. Dad's sitting in a chair in the living room, the kids on each side of him, reading "The Little Engine That Could."

I smile from ear to ear. "God's given us the most wonderful, beautiful Christmas present ever." I step aside and see their faces light up as Michelle comes forward and drops down to her knees. "Mommy!" they scream as they rush toward her. Tears of joy stream down our faces as the kids hug Michelle for dear life. She kisses them all over. "My babies, mommy loves you so, so much." I wrap my arms around Michelle, Christine, and James, then lean back and wave Dad over. "What's a family hug without Grandpa?" I say with a broad smile.

Arms interlocked in the tightest of group hugs, I can hardly breathe but have never felt better, freer, or happier.

In the midst of our revelry, I hear the phone dancing on the stand next to us, its incessant vibrations impossible to ignore. I curse under my breath as I break from our family hug. *What disaster is so bad it can't wait till the frigging morning?* My jaw falls open as I read Kev's text.

**THE END**

Never Miss A Sale, Preorder, Or New Release!
Follow Me On Bookbub:

https://www.bookbub.com/authors/william-rubin

§

Want To Find Out How Michelle Survived The Most
Horrific, Terrifying Experience Of Her Life?

Read On For A Sneak Peak At *Michelle's Captivity*,
available now at all major retailers!

# MICHELLE'S CAPTIVITY

# PROLOGUE

Michelle's heart pounds with fear as she tears down the stairwell. Rick's boots hammer ever closer, each reverberation amplifying her anxiety as she dodges gaps in the rotted wood. Lunging onto the next landing, she stumbles and slams into the floor. Panic overtakes her as she scrambles to her feet with Rick bearing down on her. *One more set of stairs, then I can outrun him on the street!* But Michelle's heart sinks as the front door flies open. Tony comes crashing in, gun drawn. His beady eyes lock in on Michelle, unaware Rick is close behind her.

Only one chance to get out of this alive. Michelle pauses a split second, waiting till Rick is almost on top of her but still out of Tony's line of sight. It's now or never. Here goes...

# ABOUT THE AUTHOR

William Rubin is a practicing physician who enjoys weaving tales of medical/scientific intrigue. Writing for him is equal parts catharsis, creativity, and escape from the rigors of a busy medical practice and the joys and challenges of raising a family.

The works of James Patterson, Robin Cook, Michael Palmer, and Patricia Cornwell inspired Dr. Rubin to create the Chris Ravello Medical Thriller Series. Each book in the series has regularly enjoyed a place on the Amazon Best Sellers lists for Medical Thrillers and Medical Fiction since their releases.

Challenges and tragedies in Dr. Rubin's life, particularly the untimely death of his mother, provided some of the underlying drama, conflict, and turmoil for the series' lead character.

When he isn't busy practicing medicine or crafting his next medical thriller, Dr. Rubin enjoys time with his family and friends, running, playing piano, and traveling.

To find out more about William and what is coming next for Chris Ravello, visit the author on Facebook (william.erubin), Twitter (https://twitter.com/werubin671), or follow him on Goodreads, Amazon, or Bookbub. You can also email him (werubin67@gmail.com) to receive a link to sign-up for his newsletter

William values your thoughts, insights, and feelings on *Forbidden Cure*, so please post a review on your favorite websites/blogs.

# ACKNOWLEDGMENT

Many thanks to my insightful and supportive team. Your efforts are invaluable and much appreciated:

Tristan: Beta Reading

Christine Keleny: formatting and editorial work

Anne Pottinger: proofreading

Carl Graves, Extended Imagery: cover design

Thank you to all the devoted men and women in the fields of medical/scientific research and healthcare. Your tireless efforts and dedication make the world a better place for all of us.

To Eilene, Diane, and James: know that little in life would be meaningful without you.

# DISCUSSION GUIDE

1) What are the main themes in *Forbidden Cure?*

2) Did you enjoy the balance between medical thriller and family saga in the story?

3) What parts of the story did you enjoy most and why?

4) If you were Chris Ravello, would you have done anything differently in this tale?

5) What parts of Chris' journey resonated the most with you and why?

6) How did you feel about Michelle Ravello's return and how it was handled?

7) Before reading *Forbidden Cure* had you ever heard of biologics and how they are used to treat a host of illnesses and disorders? Has reading this book

inspired you to learn more about this area of biomedical research?

8) What do you think Chris learned in the closing moments of this book that has him so shaken?